A SCARLET DEATH

Also by Elaine Viets

Angela Richman, Death Investigator

BRAIN STORM
FIRE AND ASHES
A STAR IS DEAD *
DEATH GRIP *
LIFE WITHOUT PAROLE *
LATE FOR HIS OWN FUNERAL *
THE DEAD OF NIGHT *

Dead-End Job

FINAL SAIL
BOARD STIFF
CATNAPPED!
CHECKED OUT
THE ART OF MURDER

Josie Marcus, Mystery Shopper

DYING IN STYLE
HIGH HEELS ARE MURDER
ACCESSORY TO MURDER
MURDER WITH ALL THE TRIMMINGS
THE FASHION HOUND MURDERS
AN UPLIFTING MURDER
DEATH ON A PLATTER
MURDER IS A PIECE OF CAKE
FIXING TO DIE
A DOG GONE MURDER

* *available from Severn House*

A SCARLET DEATH

Elaine Viets

SEVERN
HOUSE

First world edition published in Great Britain and the USA in 2024
by Severn House, an imprint of Canongate Books Ltd,
14 High Street, Edinburgh EH1 1TE.

severnhouse.com

Copyright © Elaine Viets, 2024

All rights reserved including the right of
reproduction in whole or in part in any form.
The right of Elaine Viets to be identified
as the author of this work has been asserted
in accordance with the Copyright,
Designs & Patents Act 1988.

British Library Cataloguing-in-Publication Data
A CIP catalogue record for this title is available from the British Library.

ISBN-13: 978-1-4483-1144-6 (cased)
ISBN-13: 978-1-4483-1355-6 (e-book)

This is a work of fiction. Names, characters, places and incidents are either the product of the author's imagination or are used fictitiously. Except where actual historical events and characters are being described for the storyline of this novel, all situations in this publication are fictitious and any resemblance to actual persons, living or dead, business establishments, events or locales is purely coincidental.

All Severn House titles are printed on acid-free paper.

Typeset by Palimpsest Book Production Ltd.,
Falkirk, Stirlingshire, Scotland.
Printed and bound in Great Britain by
TJ Books, Padstow, Cornwall.

For Sue Schlueter, with thanks

Acknowledgments

Writing a novel is a team effort, and I'm blessed with the best. Special thanks to
 Detective R.C. White, Fort Lauderdale Police Department (retired) and licensed private eye. And Harold R. Messler, retired manager-criminalistics, St. Louis Police Laboratory. Gregg.E. Brickman, author of *Imperfect Protest*, helped kill off my characters.
 Love and thanks to my husband, Don Crinklaw, my first reader and best critiquer.
 Thanks also to my agent, Joshua Bilmes, president of JABberwocky Literary Agency, and the entire JABberwocky team.
 Thanks to the Severn House staff, especially Editor Sara Porter for her deft editing, as well as eagle-eyed copyeditor Anna Harrison and cover artist Piers.
 I'm grateful to Alan Portman, Jinny Gender, Alison McMahan, and Marcia Talley, author of Disco Dead. Sarah E.C. Byrne made a generous donation to charity to appear as Nitpicker Byrne in this novel. She's a lawyer from Canberra, Australia, and a crime fiction aficionada.
 Special thanks to the many librarians, including those at the Broward County, St. Louis and St. Louis County libraries, who answered my questions. I could not write without your help and encouragement. Many more people helped, but I'm running out of room.
 And thank you, readers, for your support. Please enjoy Angela Richman's latest adventure. Remember, all mistakes are mine.

eviets@aol.com

Praise for the Angela Richman novels

"Enjoyable . . . Plenty to like"
Publishers Weekly on *The Dead of Night*

"Will appeal to fans of Patricia Cornwell and Kathy Reichs"
Booklist on *Late for His Own Funeral*

"Angela's usual snark and fondness for wine help propel the twisty plot"
Publishers Weekly on *Late for His Own Funeral*

"A fascinating exploration of sex workers, high society, and the ways in which they feed off of one another"
Kings River Life on *Late for His Own Funeral*

"Viets consistently entertains"
Publishers Weekly on *Life Without Parole*

About the author

Elaine Viets returned to her hardboiled roots with her Angela Richman, Death Investigator series. *A Scarlet Death* is the latest, following on from *The Dead of Night*, *Late for His Own Funeral*, *Life Without Parole*, *Death Grip*, *A Star Is Dead*, *Fire and Ashes*, and *Brain Storm*, as well as the novella *Ice Blonde*. Elaine has thirty-six bestselling mysteries in four series. A St. Louis native, Elaine took the Medicolegal Death Investigator Training Course for forensic professionals at St. Louis University, and has won the Agatha, Anthony and Lefty Awards. Elaine lives in Hollywood, Florida with her husband, writer Don Crinklaw.

www.elaineviets.com

ONE

Selwyn Skipton's murder scene was one of the strangest, and I've seen a lot of them in my job.

The seventy-year-old CEO was buck-naked on a bed with black satin sheets. A silk tie, in a muted shade of blue, was knotted around his neck. There was nothing muted about the large, red letter 'A' stapled to his gray-haired chest.

Yep, stapled.

I thought Skipton would be the last man to die on black satin sheets. He was a devoted husband who made big donations to charities – unfashionable causes that helped the illiterate read, the hungry eat, and the homeless find shelter. In short, a good man.

Selwyn was strangled in an apartment above the Chouteau Forest Chocolate Shoppe. My town is so rich, we don't have shops. We have prissy shoppes.

I'm Angela Richman, a death investigator for Chouteau County, a fat cat community forty miles west of St. Louis, Missouri. Chouteau Forest is the largest town in the county.

Selwyn's murder was discovered by Maya Richards, the chocolate shop owner. When she opened the store that morning, Maya smelled something that definitely wasn't chocolate. She followed her nose up the back stairs to the apartment, where the door was unlocked, and poked her head in. One look at the strangled Selwyn, and she sprinted downstairs. When Maya recovered her breath, she wailed like an air raid siren, then called 911.

That's how Detective Jace Budewitz and I wound up at the scene at eleven o'clock on a freezing December morning, an hour after the place usually opened. The chocolate shop was chaos. The front doors were locked, with the three responding uniformed officers inside. Mike Harrigan, an old pro, was guarding the back door. Scott Grafton was drooling over a rack of chocolate Christmas candy, and Pete Clayton, the new hire, was at the front door. Crazed chocolate lovers stormed the place, oblivious to the falling snow. Jace shooed them away, and had Pete string up yellow crime scene tape.

Maya Richards unlocked the door with shaking fingers, and let us in. I was familiar with the interior, thanks to my craving for sea-salt truffles. The decor hadn't changed since 1890. Curlicued dark wood framed mirrors behind mahogany counters. The chocolates were displayed like jewels in beveled glass cases. The cases were empty today. Maya knew her shop wasn't going to open for a while.

Maya was about forty, wearing a chocolate-brown suit, the same color as her hair. Her face was pale as paper and her red lipstick looked like a bloody slash. Maya was shaking so badly, I was afraid she'd collapse. She was clearly in shock, and could barely talk.

Jace was worried about her. He made sure Maya sat in a chair and called 911. I went back to find her a cup of coffee. I couldn't find any, but there was plenty of the shop's double-dark hot chocolate. I heated a mug in the microwave, and brought it to her. Maya wrapped her hands around the mug, and nodded. After a few sips, she recovered enough to talk. There were long pauses between her words, but she forced them out. Then the words tumbled out in a rush.

'I . . . get . . . here . . . about seven . . . to set up the shop,' she said. 'I have a very keen nose, and something didn't smell right. I thought a squirrel might have gotten into the store and died. I checked everywhere, and finally decided the smell must be coming from upstairs.

'Mr Selwyn Skipton has the entire apartment upstairs. I thought he kept it as a second office, or a pied-à-terre for when he worked late downtown. He owns the building, you see, and he's a regular customer. He loves our bear claws.'

'Me, too,' I said. Jace frowned at me for interrupting.

Maya took another sip of hot chocolate and kept talking. 'I've never been upstairs in the apartment. Mr Skipton's kept it for years, and he likes – I mean, liked – his privacy. I was afraid he might have had some kind of accident. He has his own entrance in the back of the building, and I need a special key to open it. I also need a key to open the door at the top. The upstairs door was left unlocked.

'I ran upstairs and knocked on the door. No one answered. I jiggled the handle and the door swung open. All I saw was this giant bed, covered in black satin, and Mr Skipton in the middle of it. Dead. And naked. With bugs crawling on him!'

Now Maya's teeth were chattering. Her breathing was rapid and shallow and her skin was clammy. She set her mug on the floor.

'Are you OK, Ms Richards?' Jace asked.

'I'm fine,' she said, and fainted.

'See if she has any family, Angela,' Jace said. 'I'll call nine-one-one.'

I found her cell phone and ran back. It needed the owner's fingerprint to unlock it. I grabbed Maya's limp hand, used her index finger to unlock the phone, scrolled down to an entry that said 'Sis,' and called the number. Her sister Anita answered, and once I calmed her down, Anita said she'd leave her office and meet Maya at the hospital.

'That's the ambulance,' I told her, as the siren died with a squawk. Doors slammed. Pete opened the shop door, and four paramedics rushed in, bringing a blast of cold. Jace explained what happened. They checked Maya's pulse. 'Do you know if this has happened to her before?' the biggest paramedic asked. He looked like he bench-pressed Buicks.

'No idea.' Jace shrugged.

'It could be a panic attack,' the paramedic said, 'but we'll take her to the ER to make sure.'

Jace asked Pete to stay with Maya at the hospital until her sister showed up. The young crew-cut mountain gave Jace a sour look and stomped out the door.

I raised an eyebrow in surprise.

'Pete's got a bad attitude,' Jace said. 'He tried to get hired by a big force, and wound up here. Thinks he's too good to do scut work.'

I nodded, and let it go. Some detectives wouldn't have bothered taking care of Maya at a murder scene, but Jace had a kind heart.

Meanwhile Mike, one of the responding officers, had set up the crime scene log. Jace and I gloved up, put on booties and trudged up the dark, narrow private staircase. I dragged my death investigator's suitcase behind me.

The apartment door was open from when Maya fled downstairs.

Jace looked in and said, 'Good lord.'

TWO

The stink of decomposition slapped us in the face, and the heat was unbearable, even on a cold, snowy day. I opened my death investigator suitcase, and used my point-and-shoot camera to photograph the thermostat.

'Someone jacked the temperature up to eighty-nine degrees, Jace.' I was glad we'd left our winter coats and wool scarves downstairs.

Once we got past the extreme heat, we tried to take in our surreal surroundings.

'This place looks like a New Orleans bordello,' Jace said.

'When was the last time you were in one?' I asked.

Jake turned a deep shade of red. 'Uh, I meant, from what I've seen on TV.'

I was teasing him, but he was so embarrassed, I felt a little ashamed.

'I've never seen anything like this in the Forest,' I said. 'That's for sure.'

I wasn't talking about the decedent. We'd get to him in a moment. Right now, we were trying to comprehend the strange, vast room.

'That bed is enormous,' I said, 'way bigger than king size.'

'I think it's an Alaskan king size,' Jace said. 'That mattress is nine feet square. My wife and I have been shopping for a new bed. I'd love an Alaskan king, but our bedroom isn't big enough.'

We were both babbling about the satin-covered bed to avoid another uncomfortable subject: the nude women. Yes, I know Jace and I were adults and professionals, but you weren't looking at those larger-than-life naked ladies like we were. Jace was uncomfortable with this in mixed company. He's old-fashioned, but I liked him for it.

The painting behind the bed was almost as big as the mattress. There was no headboard to obstruct the view. The artwork was framed in gold and suspended from the ceiling. The huge, pale nude with the tangled black hair had a parrot flapping its wings above her hand.

'That painting's too classy to be from a girlie magazine,' Jace said.

'It's not a pin-up,' I said. 'It's a reproduction of *Woman with a Parrot* by Gustave Courbet.'

I pointed to a whopping female on the right wall, her bare body surrounded by dull red fabric like gathering storm clouds. 'And that woman is another Courbet, *Nude Reclining Woman*.'

'Right.' The tips of Jace's ears were red.

Might as well get this over with. I pointed to the huge painting on the left wall of a woman's private parts. No face or limbs, just the gynecological close-up. 'That's a third Courbet, *The Origin of the World*.'

'Of course.' Jace tugged on his collar, as if it was too tight.

'And on the wall behind the bed is Edouard Manet's *Olympia*.'

Olympia was nude on a white bed, staring boldly out of the canvas, as if daring you to look at her. Behind her was a black woman servant, offering her a bouquet of flowers. Olympia ignored them both.

'All these were pretty scandalous in the nineteenth century,' I said.

'Some still are.' Jace was trying hard not to stare at *The Origin of the World*. 'You sure know a lot about them, Angela.'

'Read an art article on the internet.' I didn't mention that Olympia was a prostitute. Instead, I pointed to a safe subject, the painting's bouquet. 'See these brush marks, Jace? I'm no art expert, but I think these oil paintings are so-called museum-grade copies. You can buy them on the internet, frames and all.'

My art tour was over. Jace and I examined the rest of the place in a kind of stunned silence. The apartment was the same size as the store on the first floor. The door opened on the enormous black satin bed and the huge Courbet. The polished hardwood floor was covered with an enormous ruby-red oriental rug.

To the right was a living room grouping with a gold velvet couch, two club chairs, and a coffee table. The furniture looked like it was from a high-priced hotel.

Under the monstrous *The Origin of the World* was an ornately carved mahogany desk, though how Selwyn could work with that painting overhead was beyond me. But the desk was piled with papers, pens, and other office paraphernalia.

'No computer?' Jace asked.

'Not that I can see.'

Behind the bed, a large area was walled off. The door was partly open, revealing a marble bathroom. Jace checked to make sure it was empty.

The rest of the space was a galley kitchen with a microwave, a full-sized fridge, sink and cabinets. The cabinets were stocked with every variety of chocolate from the shop downstairs, including truffles, bear claws, and caramels, in milk and dark chocolate.

Jace opened the fridge carefully, so he wouldn't disturb any fingerprints. The inside was crammed with expensive champagne.

'Champagne and chocolate,' I said. 'I could live on that.'

'When you get tired of champagne, the bar is stocked with top-shelf Scotch and fancy gin and vodka,' Jace said. 'The kind you see in TV ads.'

'Wow, that heat is getting to me,' I said. 'Can we open a window?'

'As soon as Nitpicker gets here and prints a window, we can open it.'

I was relieved to hear footsteps coming up the stairs, and my favorite tech, Sarah 'Nitpicker' Byrne, burst through the door and stopped dead.

'Jeez Louise,' she said. 'What the hell is this place?' Nitpicker whistled and shook her head, framed by magenta hair. She was short, curvy, and funny, and changed her hair color as often as most people changed their socks.

'It's Selwyn Skipton's love nest.' I deliberately used that outdated term. We sounded prissy, but we did it out of deference for Jace, who was trying to clean up his speech to be a good example to his son.

'And that has to be old Selwyn on the bed,' Nitpicker said. 'I used to see him on Sunday mornings with the missus, going into church. The two of them looked all starched and starchy. Who'd guess the old boy was getting some on the side? And in style, too. What have you two done so far?'

I felt a stab of shame. I'd broken one of my cardinal rules: respect for the victim. I'd wandered around the decedent's apartment, mocking the dead man and making inappropriate jokes.

Jace looked as hangdog as I felt. 'We were orienting ourselves,' he said. 'Could you start with those windows, Nitpicker, so we can open them?'

'You bet,' she said. 'The heat is killing me. I guess if Selwyn and his friends were running around nekkid, they'd want it warm in here.'

'The heat probably speeded up decomp,' Jace said.

While Nitpicker worked on the two front windows, which were shrouded in heavy red velvet curtains, I returned to my DI suitcase, slipped on a fresh pair of nitrile gloves, and stashed more in my pocket. I'd change them as I conducted the investigation. Then I opened my iPad to the Body Inspection form, and photographed the body with my camera, taking wide shots, medium and close-ups.

A cloud of flies surrounded Selwyn's head. After death, blowflies and common houseflies were the first to arrive at a body, even in closed rooms in the dead of winter. The body was infested with maggots. I hated this part of my job, but these disgusting critters would tell us how long Selwyn had been dead and if he'd been poisoned. I took samples of the eggs and larvae, and labeled the specimens. I was relieved that part was over. Bugs creeped me out.

I started at the victim's head, and gently brushed the nasty creatures away. They were concentrated in a spot on the frontal bone. Something had hit the victim on his receding forehead, and tenderized that area. I wondered if the blow was enough to kill Selwyn, or just stun him. I photographed the area and noted it in the section 'specific marks of violence on body.' Selwyn's gray hair was retreating quickly, but there was no other damage to his face.

On to the neck, where he'd been strangled, apparently with a blue Zegna tie. I left the tie's knot the way it was, but photographed the knot from several angles. The medical examiner would remove it. The type of knot might tell us about the killer's occupation.

'I'm finished here. It's OK to open a window,' Nitpicker said. The sturdy tech and Jace struggled to lift the heavy casement window. Refreshing cold air rushed in, and we stood by the window to cool down before we went back to work.

Nitpicker examined the fatal tie's label. 'This tie is silk. We might be able to get fingerprints off this fabric back at the lab. Do you think he was strangled to death?'

'That's my guess,' I said. 'I don't see any scratches around the neck. I hope that means Selwyn was unconscious, and unable to fight for his life.'

Nitpicker shook her head. 'What a cruel death. Ligature strangling is slow torture. After about a minute, the victim's head feels like it's exploding. I didn't see any signs that he lost bladder and bowel control. You think the killer changed the sheets and the mattress cover after he killed the guy?'

'He must have.' Jace came over to check Selwyn. 'Unless the victim was drugged or unconscious, he would have thrashed around. The killer would have to be fairly strong to move the dead body. Also, the decedent has no broken nails or other injuries on his hands and feet.'

He did, however, have that giant red 'A' stapled to his chest, over his right breast. It appeared to be made of wool. Both legs of the 'A' measured ten inches and the line across the 'A' was four inches. Twenty staples held the 'A' to Selwyn's chest. There was very little blood, and I guessed that Selwyn was dead when the 'A' was stapled to him.

'What do you think the "A" stands for?' I asked.

'Abs?' Jace asked. 'A red-letter day?'

'He doesn't have much muscle tone,' I said. 'Abnormal?'

'Abuser?' Jace had resumed guessing.

My turn. 'Ass and its many variations?'

'Jeez, you guys,' Nitpicker said. 'Were you asleep in English class? What about *The Scarlet Letter*? Hester Prynne, a young woman in colonial Boston, gave birth to a baby and refused to name the father. She was convicted of adultery and forced to wear a scarlet letter.'

'Oh, right. The novel by Nathaniel Hawthorne. That makes sense.'

Nitpicker moved closer and examined the 'A.' 'The three red pieces of the "A" appear to have been cut out of some kind of knit garment, like a wool sweater,' she said.

'And hey, lookie here, I've found a brown hair.' Nitpicker used tweezers to pull out the hair and bagged it. 'Maybe we'll get lucky and have the killer's DNA. I'll see if I can find any sweater scraps when I check things out.'

My DI form asked me to describe the victim's clothing. Other than the scarlet letter on his chest, and the knotted silk tie around his neck, Selwyn was as nude as his painted ladies. I completed as much of his death investigation as I could.

Half an hour later, I said, 'Hey, Nitpicker. Have you found any men's clothes?'

'Not a stitch so far.'

I checked for a clothes closet, but didn't find one. There was a linen closet in the massive marble bath, stuffed with sets of black satin sheets. On the bottom shelves were a box of men's dress shirts from the Forest Dry Cleaner still in their wrapping, six pairs of men's black executive-length socks, and six black silk boxer shorts. But no suit, shoes or anything Selwyn could have worn on his final day.

'This whole apartment is oddly clean.' Nitpicker brushed a stray hank of magenta hair out of her face. 'I haven't found any fingerprints, not even in the places where I always find them – the chrome toilet flusher and doorknobs.'

'There's no dust on the tables,' I said.

'Someone has cleaned this apartment, polished the furniture, scrubbed the bathroom fixtures, and vacuumed the carpet,' she said. 'Even the vacuum cleaner bag has been emptied. I wish I could hire the killer to clean my apartment.'

Nitpicker was triumphant when she found a blond hair stuck in the corner of Selwyn's metal bed frame.

That was it. Two hairs – one blond and one brown – were our only clues.

THREE

Selwyn Skipton's Victorian mansion was as grim as a rainy day funeral. Even the snow didn't soften its graveyard gray stone.
   The snow was starting to seriously pile up, and as I parked my black Dodge Charger, the car slid on the cobblestones in the Skipton courtyard. I pumped the brakes to avoid smacking Jace's car.
   As we walked toward the black front door, Jace asked, 'Do you know Mrs Skipton?'
   'Estelle? Only by reputation. She's one of the ladies who lunch, and volunteers for charities that help the "deserving poor."'
   'Who are the undeserving poor?' Jace asked.
   I bit my lip to keep from laughing. As he rang the doorbell, I pasted on my serious face.
   A stocky, fifty-something housekeeper with white nurse's shoes, a starched white uniform, and steel-gray hair opened the door and frowned at us.
   'We'd like to see Mrs Skipton.' Jace gave her a somber smile.
   'She's not available.' The housekeeper's voice was flat.
   Jace flashed his badge. 'We need to see Mrs Skipton. Now.' The charm had evaporated.
   'She's taking a nap.'
   'Then wake her,' Jace said. 'Or I will.'
   'Wait here,' the housekeeper said, and stomped up the staircase, abandoning us in a vast, chilly hall. We sat in two tall carved chairs that belonged in a cathedral. Stern bearded men glared at us from dark oil paintings. They looked like versions of Selwyn in outdated clothes.
   'I wonder what Selwyn's ancestors would think of his art collection?' I said. 'All those naked nudes.'
   Jace glared at me, but he wasn't as good at it as the old guys in the portraits.
   His effort not to grin made his face go pink.
   We sat for fifteen minutes in the hard chairs before we heard light footsteps on the stairs.

Estelle Skipton wore a dark blue Chanel suit, the uniform for the Forest's lunching ladies, but the bow on her blouse was askew and her eye make-up was smeared. Delicate red veins crisscrossed her aristocratic nose. She wasn't fashionably thin – Mrs Skipton was downright scrawny. I wondered if she drank her lunches.

'What do you mean showing up at my home?' Her shrill demand wafted booze our way.

'Mrs Skipton, when was the last time you saw your husband?' Jace asked.

'What business is that of yours?' Now she was belligerent.

'It's important. Did he come home last night?' Jace asked.

'No. He spent the night in town at his pied-à-terre.'

'When was the last time you saw him?'

'Four days ago. We had dinner at the country club. Then we went home. He left for his office in the morning, about six o'clock. I was still asleep.'

'You may want to sit down.' Jace's voice was soft. 'I have bad news.'

'Don't tell me what to do in my own home.' Her voice was imperious. 'If you have something to say, out with it.'

'Your husband was found dead in his downtown apartment this morning.'

Estelle's toothpick legs couldn't hold her. She swayed and tottered backward. 'That's not possible.' Her face was bone white.

Jace grabbed her arm and guided her into a small, stuffy parlor that looked like it had been furnished in 1890. He settled her on a red velvet love seat framed in mahogany loops and whirls.

'Angela, would you get Mrs Skipton something to drink?' he asked. 'Maybe she needs some lunch.'

'I've had lunch,' Estelle said, blasting me with booze.

I heard the housekeeper banging around in the back of the house and found her unloading the dishwasher in the kitchen. She had a fistful of silverware. 'Mrs Skipton has had a bad shock,' I told her. 'She needs coffee or brandy.'

The housekeeper waited until she'd put away the silverware, then said, 'Brandy. The missus will want brandy.' She armed herself with a bottle of Remy and a water glass.

As we approached the parlor, I heard Estelle ask, 'Did my husband have a heart attack? The doctor told him to watch his cholesterol, but he insisted on eating all that chocolate.'

'No, we believe he may have been murdered,' Jace said.

'That's absurd,' Estelle said. 'My husband doesn't associate with those kinds of people.'

'Anyone can be murdered,' Jace said. 'What business was your husband in?'

'He manages our family finances.' That translated as: 'We're so rich he doesn't have to work.'

The housekeeper steamed in, carrying the brandy and the glass, and set them on the elaborately carved table next to Estelle. The new widow poured herself a hefty slug – I couldn't have drunk that much and stayed upright.

'Anything else, ma'am?' the housekeeper asked.

'No, Lucille. You may return to your duties.' The housekeeper left. Estelle didn't thank her or mention that Selwyn was dead and she didn't offer us anything to drink. Estelle chugged the brandy like it was lemonade, and poured herself a second tall glass.

Finally, her color improved. She acted as if I were invisible and addressed her questions to Jace. 'How did my husband die, Detective?'

'He was strangled.'

In my experience, this was about when a wife would show shock or horror and ask if her husband had suffered. Estelle stayed stoic. Instead she asked, 'I assume I shall have to identify the remains.' Not 'my husband,' or 'Selwyn,' or even 'my husband's body.' He'd been demoted to remains.

'No, ma'am, the manager of the chocolate shop has identified him.'

'Why was she interfering in our private business?'

'She found your husband's body, ma'am,' Jace said.

'How?'

She smelled his decomposing body, I wanted to say, but I knew that was mean. Instead, Jace said, 'He didn't come down at his usual time this morning.'

'Humph.'

Estelle sat stoically silent while Jace opened his cell phone and found a photo of the fatal tie, a part that wasn't wrapped around Selwyn's neck or covered with maggots. 'Do you recognize this tie?'

'Yes, that's the tie my son Jasper and my daughter-in-law gave him for his birthday. It was one of Selwyn's favorites.' Her voice softened when she said her son's name. She didn't mention her daughter-in-law's name.

'Does the letter "A" mean anything to you?' Jace asked.

'It's the first letter of the alphabet. Why?'

'We found a red letter "A" on your husband's body.'

'That means nothing to me.' Estelle dismissed the idea with a flick of her hand.

'Does your husband have any enemies?' Jace asked.

'Certainly not.' Estelle sounded offended. 'Everyone liked my husband.'

'Not everyone,' Jace said. 'Or he wouldn't be dead. Who do you think would want to kill him?'

'No one.' She took another long drink of brandy, and finally said, 'Unless it was one of his . . . charities.' She spit out that last word as if it was something unpleasant. 'My husband did not support the same established charities I do. He helped the homeless, illiterates and immigrants. I warned him to stick with his own kind, but he didn't. Now look where it got him.'

Estelle may have gone to church on Sunday, but the lessons didn't stay with her.

'Yes, well.' Jace cleared his throat and kept asking questions. 'Have you ever been to your husband's apartment over the chocolate shop?'

'No.'

'Do you know who he invited there?'

She shrugged her skinny shoulders. 'Business associates, I assume. He never talked about his work with me.'

Jace had trouble hiding his surprise. Estelle finished the glass of brandy and poured herself a third. By now, she'd downed most of the bottle. I estimated her weight at about ninety-five pounds. How could such a small woman hold so much booze?

'I am very old-fashioned, Detective. Mother told me the aim of a woman was to be united in marriage to a deserving man and bear his children. Selwyn was that man. We have been married for fifty years.'

Wow, I thought. She really does belong in this Victorian museum.

'I never wanted a career like the young women of today. I run my household and work on committees in aid of a number of charities. I give dinner parties and entertain for my husband.

'I knew nothing about Selwyn's business affairs, and I didn't want to. He took care of all money matters and gave me a generous allowance. If I wanted more money, I simply had to ask.'

'So you wouldn't know who decorated his apartment?'

'Decorated?' She sounded outraged. 'Why would he need a decorator to arrange a desk, a bed and a sofa? I assume that's what he had there, isn't it?'

'Uh, more or less,' Jace said. 'Does your husband like champagne?'

'No. He drank Scotch.'

'Does your husband have any interest in art?'

'Art? Are you implying that my husband was homosexual?'

'No, ma'am.'

Why was Jace acting like a student intimidated by a difficult teacher?

'Then where are you getting these ideas that my husband was a champagne-drinking art lover who used a decorator?'

'I'm not implying that your husband was gay, Mrs Skipton.'

Estelle's voice was ice cold. 'I don't use that word to mean a moral degenerate, Detective, the way people do now. Sodomites, among their other sins, have perverted a perfectly good word. I can assure you, my husband was a normal man. In every way. In fact, we have two sons.'

That wasn't proof of anything. I knew gay men who'd fathered children.

Jace ignored her and kept talking.

'Does your husband have a computer at home?'

'He has a laptop in his home office.'

'We'd like to take it, and search your bedroom.'

'You can search my bedroom, and you can also search his. We have had separate rooms since our children graduated from school. My husband was past all that, and has been for some time.' She made it sound like sleeping with your spouse was a nasty habit.

'The housekeeper will show you to our rooms.' She rang the bell for Lucille.

While we waited, I said, 'I have some questions for you, Mrs Skipton. I need to fill in the demographic information for the report.'

Finally, Estelle swiveled her head and looked at me. 'Are you the detective's girl?'

'No, I am a Chouteau County death investigator.'

'And your family lets you do that?'

'My parents are deceased.' I launched into my demographic questions. 'What was your husband's age?'

'Selwyn just turned seventy. His birthday is March sixth.'

Estelle knew her husband's height, weight, Social Security number, office phone number, and his cell phone carrier. She knew everything.

Except Selwyn Skipton.

FOUR

After we left the Skipton house, Jace and I wound up in a corner table at Supreme Bean to discuss the case. We were both a bit dazed after talking to Estelle, and needed strong black coffee to clear our heads. The shop felt cozy on this cold day, and smelled of cinnamon and fresh-ground coffee.

While I was at the coffee counter, ordering the house blend, Jace checked his cell phone. I carefully brought two mugs back to the table. While Jace talked, I sipped my fragrant coffee.

'I had two messages,' Jace said. 'First, Maya Richards, the chocolate shop owner, has been released from the hospital. She's home and OK. It was a panic attack, like the paramedics figured.'

'That's good news,' I said.

'There's more,' Jace said. 'Because this is another high-profile case, the chief wants the two of us to work together. The usual terms. You'll continue with your death investigator duties as needed. Is that OK with you?'

This assignment change put me in an ambiguous situation. Death investigators weren't supposed to solve crimes. I wasn't quite a DI or a law enforcement officer. But I never was one for coloring inside the lines. 'Of course. I enjoy working with you.'

'You may not when you hear the rest of this. The chief says we have to wrap this case up as soon as possible. A prominent citizen is dead, under salacious circumstances – naked women, satin sheets and champagne. We have to make sure no photos of Selwyn's apartment are leaked to the media. I've already posted a uniform at the door.'

'Let's hope he's paid enough he won't let the tabloids in for a look,' I said.

'If he does, he'll be looking for another job,' Jace said. 'After we finish our coffee, we're going to have to go back to see Estelle Skipton. If word gets out about her husband's extracurricular activities, the media will go crazy.'

I had a question I needed answered. 'Why didn't you tell Estelle about her husband's love nest with the giant nude paintings when we were there?'

'I wanted her to be able to grieve the husband she loved,' he said.

'Loved? Doesn't sound like she loved Selwyn very much. She asked about his "remains." It sounds like she has to take out the garbage. You don't call your husband's body that.'

At least, that's not how I'd referred to my late husband. I was stunned when the police told me Donegan had a heart attack at age thirty-five. I rushed to the hospital to see him. By the time I got there, my beloved Donegan was dead.

'People grieve in their own way, Angela. At the very least, she liked her life with him – or the life she imagined she had. And that's gone forever. Even if we keep the photos of that love nest under wraps, the information about Selwyn's hobby will come out. You know the Forest. Gossip this juicy will spread like a bad rash.'

'The only thing she's grieving is the loss of her social position.' I felt mean when I said that, and took a long drink of coffee to hide my face.

'Her world is gone, Angela.' Jace's voice was gentle. 'She's going to need time to accept that, and learn to live with the shame her husband has brought on her. He's not only unfaithful, he's kinky, at least by Forest standards. And he had a secret sex life. He'll be the talk of the town for months, maybe years.'

I wrapped my hands around the coffee mug to warm them and said, 'Every time I think about Selwyn's apartment, and then the conversation with his wife, I feel like I fell through the looking glass. Estelle isn't even in the twentieth century.'

'Maybe it's her generation,' Jace said.

'Her generation? Estelle and her husband are in their early seventies, Jace. That makes them boomers, a generation that's supposed to be more open about sex. Estelle is too straitlaced for Queen Victoria, who liked to hop in the sack with her prince.'

Jace snorted and the coffee went up his nose, which was followed by a coughing fit. I had to pound his back to keep him from choking. He wiped his eyes with his napkin and said, 'I was just thinking about my teacher, Mrs Epstein, saying that about Queen Victoria in history class.'

'Anyway, back to the case.' He carefully sipped his coffee.

I finished the rest of my coffee. 'May I get you another cup?' I asked. 'How about a cookie?'

'No to the cookie.' Jace patted his small spare tire. 'I'm trying to keep this from getting bigger. I definitely want more coffee. I'll fire up the computer and we can start checking the files. Let's hope Selwyn didn't use a password.'

He didn't. By the time I came back with two more cups of coffee and a saucer-sized chocolate chip cookie, Jace not only had the laptop running, he'd sent half the files to my iPad.

We both went to work, sipping coffee and scrolling through files. 'I have a bunch of household expenses,' Jace said. 'The old boy was loaded, and he sure spent money on that house.'

After drinking half his fresh cup of coffee, Jace said, 'Your mother was a housekeeper, right?'

'For old Reggie Du Pres,' I said. 'The richest man in the Forest. My father worked for him, too.'

'Can I ask a personal question?'

I had a mouth full of cookie, so I nodded yes.

'Did your mom make sixty thousand dollars a year?'

I almost spit the cookie all over the table. I swallowed, and then started laughing. 'As a housekeeper? In the Forest? Rich folks are tighter than girdles at an all-you-can-eat buffet.'

I quit laughing and asked, 'So which Forest housekeeper is making sixty thousand dollars?'

'A Mrs Maybelle Warner. The notation says, "Housekeeper. Office."'

'I know Maybelle. She was a friend of Mom's. She must be keeping some big secrets to get paid that much. Are you going to talk to her?'

'Eventually,' Jace said. 'Let's see what else we can find on Selwyn's laptop.'

Jace brought another round of coffee, and we read in silence for about half an hour until I hit pay dirt. 'Jace, you won't believe this. Selwyn was a sugar daddy.'

'You mean like in the movies? A rich old guy who buys diamonds and gifts for pretty young women?'

'Sort of. Sugar daddies don't have to wait by the stage door to pick up blondes any more. Now they can find them on the internet.'

'Of course they can,' Jace said.

'Selwyn used a site called DatingDaddies.com. From what I can figure out, he's dated several sugar babies. The website says, "Sugar babies are young, attractive women paid to provide 'companionship' to their daddy." That word, "companionship," is in quotes,' I added.

'Here's the rest: "Daddies may give their sugar babies presents or help pay their rent. The degree of intimacy is between the daddy and his sugar baby."

'I can almost see the wink,' I said. 'Here's an ad Selwyn saved for a sugar baby named Tammi.' I read it out loud: '"I am twenty-one, a sweet, fun-loving business major. I want a Daddy with a kind heart. I prefer mature Daddies. I don't smoke, but I do enjoy champagne and good conversation. Color me passionate about art. I love to talk about it, especially nineteenth-century artists. Or, if you want to have a quiet evening, Daddy, I'm a terrific listener. I'll do my best to make you happy. I would love to find a business-savvy Sugar Daddy. In my free time I like to read and go for long walks." Get this, Jace. Her username is Clover Honey.'

'Is this for real?' Jace asked. His eyes were round.

'Definitely. There are a zillion sugar baby websites. Tammi uses a pretty standard headline for her bio. It says, "Let's have a secret." I see that one a lot.'

'What's the difference between a sugar baby and a prostitute?' Jace asked.

'Not much,' I said. 'But I'm old-fashioned. Sugar babies who charge outright often have "P2P" in their ads. That means "pay to play." Most just want gifts or rent money.'

'If those men give their sugar babies money, that's prostitution in my book,' Jace said.

'I'm not arguing with you, but sugar babies seem to be good at rationalization. Supposedly, many of them are college students trying to avoid student debt.'

'Right,' Jace said. 'And strippers have hearts of gold and only take off their clothes to help their sick old mothers.'

Jace was usually more open-minded. I shrugged and said, 'Just passing on the information.'

'Any photos of this Tammi sugar baby?'

'Yes, but her face is either hidden or in shadow in all three photos. In one photo she's hugging a big chocolate Labrador, and all I can see is her long, blonde hair. In another, she's wearing a teeny red bikini, and her face is shadowed by a big straw sunhat. In the third photo, she's peering through palm tree fronds. About all I can see in any of the photos is long blonde hair, long legs and a big bust.'

'How can a sugar daddy make a decision, if he can't see the woman's face?'

'From what I've read, if a daddy is serious, the sugar baby will send photos so the man can see her face.'

Jace shook his head. 'Sounds dangerous for both parties.'

'It is,' I said. 'Sugar daddies have been blackmailed and some were murdered when they quit forking over cash. Sugar babies have been raped when they didn't put out, and even killed.'

'That's what I thought,' Jace said. 'So these sugar babies have the same risks as hookers.'

'Seems like it. The sugar babies are paid well for it,' I said. 'This file says Selwyn paid Tammi eighty-five thousand dollars in six months.'

Jace whistled. 'I bet none of the women in the Forest are sugar babies.'

'Ha. You'd be surprised. I'm guessing some are. Sugar babies can be rich, bored, young women who want a short walk on the wild side, or their real daddies have cut off their allowance and the women want designer clothes.'

'That's just greedy,' Jace said.

'May I ask why you seem to hate sugar babies?'

'I don't hate them,' Jace said. 'I have more respect for women who just say they're sex workers. They don't play games.' He glanced at his watch. 'Let's go see Mrs Skipton, and ruin her day again.'

FIVE

Jace and I stood shivering on the doorstep at Estelle Skipton's home, blasted by icy snow, as we waited for someone to answer the door.

Finally, Lucille, the surly housekeeper, opened the door and glared us. 'Now what?'

'I need to see Mrs Skipton again,' Jace said. I fought to keep my teeth from chattering.

'That poor woman is in mourning.' Lucille was even colder than the weather.

'I know.' Jace was firm. 'I still need to see her. Now.'

'Mrs Skipton is in the parlor. Wipe your feet.' The housekeeper stormed off into the house and left the massive door open. Jace and I stamped the snow off our shoes, and made our way to the dimly lit parlor.

Estelle was not only in mourning, she was in her cups. Deep in them. A second bottle of Remy stood next to the empty one, and it had about an inch of brandy left. The only light was in a distant corner. Estelle was sprawled on the red velvet love seat, but she'd kicked off her shoes and removed her jacket. Her head rested on a velvet pillow and she clutched the brandy-filled water glass with both hands.

'Wha' do you want?' Estelle's speech was slurred and belligerent. She didn't greet us, nor did she invite us to sit down. Jace and I perched on the edge of the hard, tufted chairs across from Estelle.

'We'd like to give you more information about your husband and the circumstances of his death,' Jace said. 'Before you see it in the media.'

'He's dead.' Estelle's voice was flat. 'What else is there to know?'

'His downtown apartment was somewhat unusual,' Jace said. 'It was furnished with a bed, a desk and a couch and chairs—'

'Like I already said,' Estelle interrupted.

Jace continued smoothly. 'But it also has four large paintings of nude women.'

'Ridiculous.' Estelle sat up so quickly, she knocked over the bottle of Remy. Jace caught the brandy before it hit the flowered carpet.

'Are you sure you have the correct address, Detective?' she asked.

'Yes, ma'am. Also, your husband belonged to a website for sugar daddies.'

'*Sugar daddies?* Are you saying my husband had an extramarital affair?'

'Yes, ma'am. Maybe more than one.'

'I don't think so.' Estelle's voice was firm, a teacher correcting a recalcitrant student. 'Selwyn stopped that nonsense twenty years ago.'

With you, I thought.

'I'm sure he was just cuddling,' Estelle said.

'Possibly,' Jace said.

'Why are you telling me this?' Estelle demanded.

'Because your husband was strangled in an apartment with black satin sheets, champagne and nude paintings. Some people might jump to conclusions.'

'The wrong conclusions.' Estelle gulped down half the glass of brandy. I watched in fascination. That much booze would put me in a coma, yet except for a few slurred words, she seemed fine.

'We'll do our best to keep this out of the media, Mrs Skipton, but I wanted you to be prepared, just in case.'

'No one will ever believe that about my husband, Detective.'

'Where is your husband's business office, Mrs Skipton?'

'Downtown. At the Chouteau Trust Building.'

Wow. Skipton must have had plenty of bucks to play with his dough in the most expensive building in the Forest.

'Does he have a secretary?' Jace asked.

'He has an office manager. Rosalie. Rosalie Vann.'

'May we have your permission to search his office?'

'Yes, Detective. You may go now.' Estelle flicked her wrist toward the door, then poured the last of the brandy into her glass.

We were dismissed.

Jace and I let ourselves out. Now the sun was shining and the snow had stopped, typical for the Midwest's unpredictable weather. 'It's only two thirty,' he said. 'Let's talk to Rosalie at Skipton's office. And just to be on the safe side, Angela, I got a warrant for

Skipton's office. Estelle is so out of it, I'm surprised she can remember her name.'

That's why I liked working with Jace. He was a by-the-book investigator.

I followed Jace's unmarked car through the slushy snow, fishtailing more than once, to the Chouteau Trust. Built in the middle of the roaring Twenties, it was a beauty. The three-story building had a white marble facade with Corinthian columns.

I parked in front of the historic office building, and rolled my DI suitcase inside. Jace was waiting for me in the lobby.

The lobby and halls were paneled in mellow, honey-colored wood. We took the elevator to the second floor. The old-fashioned frosted door had 'Selwyn Skipton, Investments' emblazoned in gold.

The anteroom was done in the same honey-colored wood, with a muted oriental rug. Rosalie Vann, the office manager, was at her desk, typing on a desktop computer. Her red hair was the only bright spot in the office. She had the clear, alabaster skin of some fortunate redheads. Rosalie looked about forty and her outfit – an iron gray pantsuit and crisp white blouse – said she was all business. She peered over her half-glasses at us.

'Is Mr Skipton in today?' Jace asked. He did that sometimes, to judge a person's reaction.

'Do you have an appointment, sir?' Rosalie asked.

'No, but we need to talk to him.' Jace introduced both of us and showed his ID. My title, 'death investigator,' didn't seem to register with her.

'Mr Skipton hasn't come in yet,' she said. 'I've called his cell phone, but he's not answering.'

By this time, we realized that Estelle hadn't informed the office manager of Selwyn's death. The reason for Skipton's absence seemed to slowly dawn on Rosalie. Her face went dead white and her voice quavered. 'Has something happened to Mr Skipton?'

'I'm afraid I have bad news for you, Ms Vann. Mr Skipton is dead.'

'No! Not Selwyn! Was he murdered?' she asked.

Murdered? That was odd. I worked hard to hide my shock. Jace stayed cool, but he was hyper-alert. 'Why would you say that?'

Rosalie tried to backtrack. 'I don't know. I didn't mean it. No one would hurt Mr Skipton. He was a good man.'

Jace pressed her. 'Still, you said it, Rosalie.'

'It was the shock,' she said. 'I just saw him yesterday. He was in an excellent mood.' Her voice was clipped and angry. She seemed annoyed at Jace because he'd tricked her by pretending Skipton was alive.

'What time did he leave his office?' Jace asked.

'Promptly at five o'clock, the same time he always leaves. He was whistling when he left. He told me, "I may be a little late tomorrow, Rosalie."'

'Did he say where he was going?' Jace asked.

'No. I assumed he was going home.'

'Did you know that Mr Skipton kept an apartment in town?'

'Yes. In downtown Chouteau Forest. Over the chocolate shop. He brings – brought – me chocolate all the time.'

'How often did Mr Skipton stay at his downtown apartment?' Jace asked.

Rosalie stared at the ceiling as if the answer was up there. 'Maybe three or four times a month.'

'Have you ever been to Mr Skipton's downtown apartment?' Jace asked.

Rosalie's face turned beet red. 'No. Wait, yes. Yes. I was there once, I think. He called me in for some . . . uh . . . dictation. Yes, dictation.'

Even I could see Rosalie was a terrible liar.

Jace opened his cell phone and showed her a photo of a section of the fatal tie. 'Do you recognize this?'

'Mr Skipton wore a tie that color yesterday. It was a gift from one of his sons.'

'What else did he wear?' Jace asked.

The question seemed to puzzle Rosalie. She thought for a moment and said, 'A charcoal-gray business suit, white shirt and his favorite blue tie. He always wears black socks and black lace-up shoes. He has them shined at his club.'

'We have a warrant to search Mr Skipton's office,' Jace said.

Rosalie reached for the phone. 'I'll have to tell Mrs Skipton.'

'No need,' Jace said. 'She already knows. She gave us her permission.'

'His office is right through that door there.' Rosalie nodded at a frosted glass door marked 'Private.' I unzipped my suitcase, and Jace and I slipped on booties and nitrile gloves for the search.

The office was straight from the Twenties, right down to the light fixtures. A green malachite pen stand held two fountain pens. The desk had a Forties' black phone, an old Bakelite model. No papers or family photos cluttered the desk. The only modern touch was a big desktop computer.

Over the desk, the oil portrait of a grim, gray man with center-parted hair frowned down at us. From the man's features, he looked like he could be a relative of Selwyn's. He'd really be frowning if he knew what the old boy had been up to.

Jace touched the space bar on the desktop computer's keyboard and it sprang to life. We saw folders for spreadsheets and taxes, but little else. The emails were strictly business – and mind-numbingly boring.

I searched the credenza and found nothing but mundane office supplies inside. Jace found a daily business diary in the desk, filled with lunch engagements. Except Selwyn called them 'luncheon.'

'I'm calling Nitpicker to print this office,' Jace said, 'and take the computer in. I don't think she'll find anything here, but I'm being extra careful.'

After we'd finished our examination, we thanked Rosalie and left. In the elevator, Jace said, 'I suspect Rosalie and Selwyn had a fling.'

'She was definitely lying about how often she'd been to his downtown apartment,' I said, 'and I'm pretty sure it wasn't for dictation. Do you think she killed Selwyn?'

'Why do you say that?'

'If she had an affair with Selwyn, he dumped her for a younger, prettier woman.'

'We should definitely check what Rosalie was doing the night Selwyn was murdered,' Jace said.

When the elevator doors opened in the lobby, my personal cell phone chimed. 'It's a text from Chris,' I told Jace. It says, "Urgent. News for you and Jace. Call ASAP."'

Chris Ferretti is the man I love, a patrol officer with the Chouteau Forest PD. Jace and I sat on a green leather bench in the lobby, and I called Chris and put my cell phone on speaker for Jace.

Chris got straight to the point, not bothering with endearments. 'Are you two working the case of the Dirty Daddy?'

'The what?'

'Selwyn Skipton. I saw the crime scene photos.' He whistled.

'Those were some paintings the old boy had. I don't think *Hustler* would publish them, especially that one of the woman . . .'

My stomach twisted and I spoke carefully. 'Chris, who showed you those photos?'

'I don't know. They were being passed around the office. I'm at home now.'

Chris had noted my shocked silence. 'What's wrong, Angela?'

'Chief Butkus is going to shoot Jace and me. He made it clear he didn't want those photos to make it to the media and now they're being passed around the cop shop?'

'It's worse than that, Angela. I just saw a special breaking news report. The story announced Selwyn's murder as "The Death of the Philandering Philanthropist."'

Chris gave us the brutal details. 'The announcement previewed photos of that love nest, including the paintings. Black bars covered the sweet spots on three pictures, and the announcer said, "There's one more painting, but we can't show it on TV. The full report will be on the six o'clock news."'

'Good lord.' Jace gave an anguished groan. 'Chief Butkus is going to have my head – and maybe my job.'

'Was that Jace?' Chris asked.

'Yes, he's right next to me, looking very shaken. He's sitting down. Jace did everything right, Chris. He posted a guard at the door to the apartment with instructions not to let anyone in.'

'Well, obviously somebody got their hands on the crime scene photos,' Chris said. 'One of the uniforms, maybe?'

Jace put his head in his hands.

'Any idea who?' I asked.

'One person,' Chris said. 'Yesterday, Eddie Taylor, one of the new hires, was bellyaching that his vintage Mustang needed major repairs and he couldn't pay for them. This afternoon, he was all smiles. Says his girlfriend loaned him the money – three thousand dollars.'

'Thanks, Chris,' Jace said. He rose wearily and said, 'I'm going in to take my medicine.'

'I'll come with you, Jace.'

'No, Angela, that will just make it worse. I'd better let my wife know I'll be late.'

Jace went to the other side of the lobby to make the call in privacy. I said to Chris, 'Should I go with him?'

'No, he's right. Jace is in charge and he'll have to face the music alone.' Chris's voice softened. 'Now that Jace isn't around, how are you, Angela?'

'OK. It was a rough day.'

'Why don't you come over to my place for dinner?'

'Yes, you're the best thing that's happened all day.'

For the first time since I'd entered Selwyn's apartment, I was smiling.

SIX

As we were leaving the Chouteau Trust Building, Jace pointed to the left leg of my black DI pantsuit. 'Is that rice on your suit?'

I leaned down for a closer look, and my stomach flip-flopped. Maggots! Damn, I hated those critters. I tried not to scream like a girl. I knew the maggots were useful, but I still couldn't stand them.

I shook my pant leg until the wretched creatures fell off.

Jace stamped them into the parquet floor. 'I'm stamping out future flies,' he said, and managed a small smile, which was brave considering he was facing a possible firing.

My visit to Chris's condo would have to wait. I texted him that I had to make a stop first. (I didn't tell him why. Maggots and romance don't mix.)

Then I wished Jace good luck with Chief Butkus, and drove straight home, where I threw my maggot-infested DI suit into the washer and ran upstairs to shower. After I scrubbed myself and washed my hair, it was six o'clock. While I blow-dried my long, dark hair, I turned on the TV to watch the evening news.

Selwyn Skipton's murder was on all the local newscasts.

I clicked on the channel teasing the 'Philandering Philanthropist' story. Chuck Willis, the plastic fantastic news anchor, was nearly breathless with excitement as he began the story.

'Chouteau County socialite Selwyn Skipton was found strangled to death this morning at his in-town apartment above the Forest Chocolate Shoppe. We have obtained photos of the interior of this apartment, and these pictures are not for children. We'll show you them after this announcement.'

The pizza delivery and hamburger joint commercials gave parents enough time to shoo the kiddies out of the room. I guessed any children sent to their rooms would turn on their own TVs or watch the newscast on their cell phones.

That warning made sure the whole family would be glued to the screen. I sure was.

When Chuck returned, the announcer said, 'The brutal murder

was committed above this innocent chocolate shop in downtown Chouteau Forest.' The screen showed a wide shot of the shop, its windows bursting with chocolate confections.

'Few people knew there was a secret staircase to the apartment upstairs at the back of the shop,' Chuck said, as if he was confiding this information, 'and even fewer have been upstairs in the apartment.'

Now the back staircase was suddenly 'secret.' There was no video of the so-called 'secret staircase,' which told me the cop on duty did his job and kept the cameras away. I hoped that would help Jace's case with the chief. Someone at the cop shop definitely gave those photos to the press.

The announcer's voice had a salacious hush, if such a thing was possible. 'The apartment upstairs was Skipton's hidden love nest. Here are the photos of the interior.'

First, a wide shot of the room showed the massive black satin-sheeted bed, with Skipton's body blurred out.

'The super-sized bed is known as an Alaskan king,' Chuck said. 'It's nine feet square.'

'Gives you quite a playing field.' That was Andy Andover, the weatherman and Chuck's childish sidekick. The weatherman was a skirt-chaser known locally as 'Randy Andy.'

'I'm told the oil painting is a copy of *Woman with a Parrot* by Gustave Courbet,' Chuck said. The woman's private parts had a black band over them.

'If we'd studied art like that in high school, I would have never fallen asleep in class,' Andy said.

High school, I thought. That's what you two sound like. Two snickering high school boys. But I felt a twinge of conscience. I wasn't much better. I'd been making jokes while examining Selwyn's death scene. Shame burned through me again.

The rest of the 'news story' was more of the same. The station didn't attempt to show *The Origin of the World*. They showed photos of the champagne and chocolate in the apartment. 'Wow, Selwyn could do any chick in the Forest with that stash,' Randy Andy said.

More suppressed giggling. I didn't know why the station permitted such childish behavior. Ratings, I guess.

Finally, the photos ended and Chuck said, 'The late Selwyn Skipton was known for his charity to the community, helping the illiterate, the homeless, and the hungry.'

Randy Andy chimed in with: 'Selwyn obviously loved feeding women.' Muffled laughter followed, and Chuck ended the story with: 'Mrs Skipton could not be reached for comment.'

I didn't like Estelle Skipton. Not one bit. But now I felt sorry for her. The ruins of her life and marriage had been broadcast on television, and everyone in the Forest – heck, the whole state – knew it. She'd need more than two bottles of brandy to get through this.

I called Jace and asked, 'Do you still have a job?'

'So far. The chief is madder than a wet hen, and he chewed me out for ten minutes. Fortunately there was no video of the apartment's interior or the staircase, or any mention of the red "A," so he's decided it's not entirely my fault.'

'I gather the guard at the door has been cleared,' I said.

'Yes. The photos had to come from someone in the office, which means there are a lot more suspects. If the chief finds out who sold those crime scene photos to the media, they're dead meat.'

'Well, I'm relieved you're OK.'

'Not as much as I am,' he said. 'Thanks for checking, Angela. Tomorrow, I want to question Selwyn's well-paid housekeeper, Mrs Warner. Since you know her, it would help if you would meet me at her home.'

'Sure. What time?'

'Nine o'clock.'

'Good.' That meant I could spend the night at Chris's place and have a leisurely breakfast with him.

At last, I was ready to see Chris. I was freshly dressed in jeans, a dark pink sweater and knee-high black boots. I packed an overnight bag with my DI outfit – another black pantsuit, white shirt and plain black lace-up shoes. Those homely shoes were way more practical than heels, and I'd wear them tomorrow if it wasn't snowing.

On my way, I texted Chris, and ran to my car. He only lived ten minutes away, and I couldn't wait to see him.

I was devastated after my husband Donegan died of a heart attack when he was only thirty-five. I thought I could never love again. For more than two years, I drifted in a gray fog, until I met Chris. He courted me patiently. My heart began to heal, and I came to like Chris – and then love him. He was thoughtful, smart, and funny. Also, smokin' hot. And because he was with the Chouteau Forest PD, I could talk over my cases with him. I needed his insight.

I parked in his condo lot. Chris was waiting for me at the door with a glass of Merlot and a long kiss. When he held me, the horrors of the day vanished. I enjoyed the feel of his muscular shoulder and his citrusy scent.

'Mm, your hair smells nice,' he said. 'Come sit in the kitchen while I finish dinner.'

Chris had appetizers on the kitchen counter: artichoke dip, hummus, and red grapes. I spread the hummus on a cracker and asked, 'What smells so good?'

'Twice-baked potatoes and green beans with mushrooms and toasted almonds. I was waiting until you showed up to put the steaks on.'

Two-inch-thick rib eyes were on a cutting board by the stove, salted and peppered. The cast-iron pan was sizzling hot. Chris poured salt into the pan, then dropped in the steaks. He waited about two minutes and flipped the meat.

Clouds of smoke rose up from the pan. 'Flip on the exhaust fan, will you, Angela?'

I did, and asked, 'What else can I do?'

'Sit. Relax. Drink your wine. These will be done shortly. We can eat in the living room. You like your steak medium rare, right?'

'Definitely.'

The steaks were done quickly.

We carried our plates to a table by the living room window, and Chris poured more wine. 'I saw tonight's six o'clock news,' he said. 'Did Jace get his ass chewed out?'

'Not as badly as he thought he would. He still has his job, anyway. The chief is on the warpath, trying to find out who sold those pictures to the media.'

'I'll keep my ears open,' he said.

Dinner passed quickly. I tried not to gulp down my food, but I was hungry. Between bites, we talked about his day. He already knew most of the details about mine.

We were too hungry for each other to bother with dessert. We ran upstairs to his bedroom, shedding a trail of clothes. Much later, Chris brought up a decadent chocolate cake and more wine. It was after midnight when I fell asleep on his shoulder, content.

My cell phone alarm went off at seven thirty. Chris was waiting for me. After a morning wake-up session of love-making, he went downstairs to start coffee and fix breakfast, while I showered and dressed for work. The aroma of hot coffee and waffles had me hurrying downstairs.

After breakfast and more sweet morning kisses I left for the housekeeper's home.

I hadn't seen Maybelle Warner since Mom's funeral. Mom had died of cancer shortly after I married Donegan, and I'd inherited my parents' house on the Du Pres estate. Maybelle Warner lived in Toonerville, the sneery nickname for the working side of town, in a neat ranch house with green shutters. Her house looked a smidge better than her neighbors' places. The paint on Maybelle's home was fresh, the driveway had been paved with concrete instead of blacktop, and a new red Ford nestled in the carport.

Jace was parked in front of her home, waiting for me. He looked cheerful this morning, probably from the relief of keeping his job. Jace rang the doorbell, and Maybelle answered it wearing a pink velour pantsuit.

'Angela, honey, how are you?' Maybelle smiled at me. Her chin-length gray hair looked freshly styled, as if she was just back from the beauty parlor. 'It's been forever since I've seen you. What brings you and your friend here?'

Before I could explain, Jace stepped inside and showed his badge. 'I'm Detective Jace Budewitz, ma'am. We'd like to talk to you about Selwyn Skipton.'

Maybelle's smile vanished. 'I don't know what you're talking about.' Her mouth was set in a stubborn line.

'We know you were paid to take care of Mr Skipton's apartment over the chocolate shop.'

'I don't have anything to say to you, Detective.' Maybelle was pink with anger. 'I signed a confidentiality agreement.'

'You're withholding information about a murder investigation. If you don't talk, I'll lock you up.'

Whoa? Why was Jace playing tough guy with a woman in her seventies? The meeting with the chief must have really frayed his patience.

'For what? I don't have to tell you anything.' Maybelle folded her arms and set her jaw firmly. She wasn't talking.

Like a lot of women who worked in pink collar jobs – heck, most jobs – Maybelle had had a lifetime of being bullied by men, and she wasn't having it.

I stepped between Maybelle and Jace and took Maybelle's hand.

'Mrs Warner, may I speak to you, please?'

I led her to her kitchen, and we three sat down at the round wooden table, with a bowl of plastic fruit in the center.

Maybelle settled into her chair and smiled at me. 'Well, since you asked nicely, Angela, what is it you need to know?'

'You know Mr Skipton is dead. We think he was murdered.'

'I saw the news last night. I figured it was one of those girls of his – or their boyfriends. I knew this would happen. I knew it!'

'So you did know what was going on in his apartment,' Jace said.

'Of course I knew. Your generation didn't invent sex, young man!' She glared at Jace.

I leaned close to Maybelle and asked, 'Will you tell me what you did for Mr Skipton?'

'Yes. I kept the apartment clean, took out the trash, and did the laundry and changed the sheets. If he was having guests, he'd ask me to order a cold supper, usually from a good restaurant like Solange, and have it on the coffee table in the sitting area. The next morning, he would call me and tell me to come by and clean the place. I always used the back stairs. Mr Skipton paid well for my discretion.'

'When was the last time you brought a cold supper for him?'

She named the day before Skipton's body was found.

'How many suppers did you order?' I asked.

'Three.'

'And he didn't call you to clean up?' I asked.

'No. Sometimes, he just stays by himself. If he doesn't call me, I don't come by.'

'Do you know the women who stayed the night?' I asked.

'I never actually saw most of the women, but I'm pretty sure one was Rosalie.'

'Rosalie Vann, the red-haired office manager?' I asked.

'Yes, her. She left some office paperwork there one time and came by to pick it up when I was cleaning the next day. I found red hair in the bed, including hair from "down there," if you know what I mean. That woman dyed her hair. She was really a brunette.

'Before Rosalie, I'm pretty sure Mr Skipton had a fling with Irene. She was a brunette and worked in Mr Skipton's office before Rosalie. Both those women were mature – over thirty-five – and quiet.'

'How long was he seeing those two?' I asked.

'Almost twenty years. At least, that's when he hired me. Mr Skipton's generosity allowed me to quit cleaning houses and just work for him.'

Twenty years, I thought. About when Mrs Skipton said her husband lost interest.

'Did Mrs Skipton know about his activities?'

'I very much doubt that,' she said. 'I never met the lady.'

'Did you notice any recent changes in Mr Skipton's behavior?' I asked.

'Yes. Lately, he'd been seeing younger women. Much younger. Blondes, from the hair I cleaned up. They had long blonde hair. That's when I started worrying about him.'

'Why?'

'The place would be a mess – champagne bottles everywhere, wet towels on the floor, food ground into the rug. Disgusting sex thingies, like vibrators, left out in plain sight. He didn't seem to be the same man. Until recently, he was a dignified man with a mistress. He never used to go in for champagne and shenanigans.'

SEVEN

After we left Maybelle's home, Jace and I walked silently to our cars. I didn't understand his hard-nosed behavior with Maybelle, and didn't know what to say.

Fortunately his phone dinged. He checked it for a text. 'That was Katie,' he said. 'She's ready with the report on Selwyn's autopsy. She has doughnuts. We're supposed to bring coffee.'

'I'll get the coffee and meet you at her office.'

Dr Katie Kelly Stern was the assistant Chouteau County medical examiner. Our boss, Evarts Evans, the chief ME, often left the controversial jobs to Katie – long court cases interfered with his golf game. Katie was my age, forty-one, and favored drab suits and sensible shoes. Some people dismissed her as plain, but Katie's sparkling wit had captured the heart of Montgomery Bryant, the Forest's most eligible bachelor.

I picked up three black coffees from Supreme Bean and looked for a parking spot near the ME's office in the back of Sisters of Sorrow hospital. Freezing rain rattled against my car windows. The closest spot was between two black funeral home vans, but I didn't want to park between them. I didn't want to encounter any corpses, even ones in body bags.

I parked in a spot three rows away, and slid across the icy lot to the door without spilling the coffee. I wasn't sure how I was going to open the door, but an employee, so bundled up I could barely tell he was a man, was coming out for a smoke by the dumpsters. He held the door open for me.

Inside, the morgue was warm, with the harsh odor of disinfectant and hints of something less pleasant underneath. I followed the tiled hallway to Katie's closet-sized office. The door was partly open, and I could hear Katie and Jace talking.

Just for a second, I stood in the doorway of the narrow, windowless office. The wall behind Katie's desk was papered with a fall woodland scene. A grinning plastic skull was glued to the foliage. Her wall clock was a Day of the Dead skull, crowned with red roses, with a file cabinet underneath. Jace already had the best seat – the edge of Katie's desk. Behind the door was a wire contraption that passed as a chair. I avoided it at all costs.

Katie waved to me and hurried over. 'Angela, you made it. Come on in.'

She took the cardboard tray of coffee out of my hands and gave one to Jace. She pried the top off another one and handed it to me, and took the third.

'Help yourself to the doughnuts,' she said.

I took a warm glazed doughnut and used the top of the file cabinet as a table.

'How did you get three coffees across that slippery parking lot without spilling anything?' Katie asked.

'Just lucky,' I said. 'One of your colleagues helped me with the door. He was coming out to smoke a cancer stick by the dumpster. Why do people in the medical profession smoke cigarettes when they know they cause cancer?'

'We're fatalists,' Katie said, and shrugged. 'I don't smoke, but I understand how my colleagues feel. We know we can eat well, exercise and die anyway. Last week I had a young athlete on my autopsy table. He was in perfect shape, except for the brain aneurysm that blew. He was dead at twenty-five and made a great looking corpse. All that exercise and healthy eating didn't do him a bit of good. When your time's up, there's nothing you can do about it.'

I took another bite of that sweet, sugary doughnut and sipped my coffee, while Jace asked, 'Speaking of time being up, what happened to Selwyn Skipton?'

Katie instantly turned serious. 'That poor man died of ligature strangulation. Someone used his own tie to kill him. It wasn't an easy death. Strangulation is pure torture for the victim. From the bruising on his neck, it looked like the pressure was applied to his carotid arteries – the major arteries that supply blood to the brain – so he was probably unconscious. Also, he didn't claw at his neck, or have any skin under his fingernails or other defensive marks. Victims do that when they are awake.'

'Wouldn't he have at least tried to struggle until he passed out?' Jace asked.

'Like I just said, I think he was already passed out when he was strangled,' Katie said. 'Angela noticed a bruise on his forehead. It appeared he'd been whacked with a heavy round object.'

'Like a champagne bottle?' Jace asked.

'Certainly possible,' Katie said.

That was a small mercy, I thought. Selwyn didn't suffer. Usually I gave the victim's family that information. In fact, I lied and always told the families that their loved ones didn't suffer. Otherwise, the truth would haunt them. In this case, Selwyn's wife Estelle didn't seem to care.

Katie was still talking about the evidence that Selwyn was strangled. 'His tongue was swollen and he also had a broken hyoid bone and petechial hemorrhages on the conjunctiva.' I mentally translated as she talked: the hyoid was a U-shaped bone sometimes called the tongue bone and petechial hemorrhages on the conjunctiva were pinpoint red spots in the whites of the eye.

'If the decedent was strangled, wouldn't his body release feces and urine?' I asked.

'Yes,' Katie said.

'We didn't find anything on the sheets under his body,' I said. 'We suspect the original bedding and the mattress cover were removed and new sheets put on.'

'Quite likely.'

Katie sipped her coffee while Jace asked, 'Did you get any fingerprints off the tie?'

Katie brightened. 'Yes, we were lucky. We got two thumb prints. Too bad the prints aren't in the system.'

'No, but when we have a suspect, we'll know if it's the right one.' Jace reached for another doughnut, an iced chocolate with sprinkles. I noticed how tired he looked. After only two days, the pressure of this high-profile case seemed to be getting to him. And it would only get worse until we caught the killer.

My doughnut had disappeared. I reached for another in the box and asked, 'What about the red letter "A" stapled to the decedent's chest?'

'Now that was unusual,' Katie said. 'I've never seen anything stapled to a body. I also think the killer made a mistake. That spiteful act may have given us a clue.'

'Good,' Jace said. 'We can use one.'

'The red fabric was stapled to the victim's chest postmortem. The red "A" was very fine wool, a knit garment made of cashmere, which can be expensive. Cashmere fibers are difficult to obtain.'

Katie was going into teaching mode again. We were about to get a lesson on cashmere. Jace helped himself to a chocolate-frosted doughnut to get through the lecture.

Katie said, 'The fibers have to be combed from cashmere goats instead of just shearing the animals. Cashmere goats produce a small amount of cashmere wool per year. I also had the brown hair that was found on the red "A" analyzed for DNA, and we got a hit.'

Katie paused dramatically.

'It was a partial match to a Nate Alexander Gibbons, age twenty-one. He was arrested for a DUI in November. The charges were dropped but Nate's DNA remained in the system.'

Jace stood up, and I reached for my purse. We were leaving.

'Wait,' Katie said. 'Before you go charging off, I said Nate Gibbons's DNA was a *partial* match. This was female DNA. It could belong to a mother or a sister. Nate lives at twenty-two Regions Circle.'

I whistled. 'That's in the rich part of the Forest. Multi-million-dollar houses.'

Jace and I tossed our cups, left Katie's office and hurried to the parking lot. The weather was growing steadily worse. The parking lot was a sheet of ice.

'Do you want to go with me, Angela?' he asked. Ice pellets were hitting us both in the face.

'Regions Circle is only ten minutes away,' I said. 'We'll be OK if we take it slow.'

Jace and I didn't drive more than twenty-five miles an hour. The other drivers went by us at a lunatic pace. A gray Honda passed me going way too fast, then slammed on the brakes at a stop sign and skidded in a complete circle. Luckily, no one was in the intersection.

After a very long half hour we made it to the driveway of the Gibbons home. The house itself, a mishmash of pediments, pillars and Palladian windows, was surprisingly attractive.

We parked in the cobblestone drive and rang the doorbell. A slender woman of about fifty answered the door. She wore a thick beige sweater and her brown hair was bobbed.

Jace introduced us and showed her his badge.

'What brings you out in this terrible weather, Detective?' she asked. 'Is something wrong?'

Jace asked to speak to Nate Gibbons. 'That's my son,' she said. 'He's away at school.'

'Do you have a daughter?'

'Nate is our only child,' she said.

'May we come in and talk to you a moment?'

'What's this about, Detective?'

'Your family's DNA was at a recent murder scene. It will take me a minute to explain.'

The blood drained from the woman's face, but she recovered enough to say, 'I'm Ruth. Ruth Gibbons. Please come in.'

Her voice was shaky. We walked through a two-story foyer with a huge framed portrait of the family – Ruth, another brown-haired man, and a boy – all dressed in their best.

'That's my family,' Ruth said. 'My husband, Frank, and our son Nate. My boy was twelve in that portrait.' I was puzzled that she'd stopped to give us a house tour. I glanced at Jace and he shrugged.

We followed Ruth past a formal living room and into a massive open kitchen. 'Would you like some tea or coffee?' she asked. 'I just made a fresh pot.'

We both wanted coffee, mostly to warm up. Ruth poured three mugs and we sat at the vast kitchen island.

Jace explained that a brown hair had been found in a red knit sweater at a crime scene.

'The hair was a partial match for your son,' Jace said. 'The DNA was female. Do you have a red sweater?'

Ruth looked bewildered. 'No,' she said. 'I don't. You're welcome to check my closet.'

We followed Ruth upstairs to the master bedroom, a cozy room done in soothing shades of beige. Ruth opened the walk-in closet and said, 'My clothes are on this side. My sweaters are folded up in these plastic drawers.'

Ruth had sweaters in every color of the rainbow, from magenta to pale pink. But no red.

'You didn't maybe own a red sweater and give it away to Goodwill, did you?' Jace asked.

'No.'

'What about your mother?'

'Mother is deceased,' Ruth said. 'She died two years ago.'

She thought for a while, and then said, 'Wait! I did try on a red sweater at Forest Frocks and Lingerie.'

'Wow, my wife can't even afford to walk in the door of that boutique,' Jace said.

'I only go there during the sales,' Ruth said. 'I tried on a red cashmere sweater that cost one thousand eight hundred dollars. It was marked down to two hundred dollars, but it had a major pull on the back. The shop owner said I could hide the damage with a scarf, but I thought two hundred dollars was still too much for a damaged item. I could buy a perfectly good sweater for that much.'

'When was the sale?'

'Two weeks ago,' Ruth said. 'It was the shop's pre-holiday sale. That's all I can tell you.'

'You've been very helpful, Ruth,' Jace said.

Warmed by our success and Ruth's coffee, we went out into the storm. At last, we had a serious lead.

EIGHT

When Jace and I came out of the Gibbons's home, the storm was much worse. Our cars were coated with ice. The freezing wind raked icy claws through my warm winter coat. We watched a car slide sideways down the street.

'I think you'd better head home,' Jace said. 'That boutique won't be open in weather like this. I'll call you in the morning and we'll decide what to do then.'

I hung on to the railing to get down the slippery front steps and made it to my car. It took a while to get my door open, but once inside, I turned on the heater and the defroster and then sprayed the windows with de-icer.

While the car was de-icing, I called Chris. 'How are you?' I asked.

He sounded harassed. 'Dealing with idiots driving too fast. One fender-bender after another. So far, we haven't needed your services, Angela, but it's a matter of time before someone gets killed.'

'I hope you're wrong. Jace is sending me home. Want to come over when you get off work? I have chili.'

'Sounds good, but I'll be working late because of the weather. I can't give you a time.'

'That's OK. Text me when you can make it, no matter how late.'

I drove home slowly, holding my breath every time someone passed me. I saw cars spin, slide and slip sideways on the icy roads, but they all recovered and drove on. Finally, I made it home, and stowed my car in the garage.

I sprinkled salt on my slippery porch and turned on the outside lights, then prayed Chris would be OK. Loving a patrol officer was nerve-wracking. I feared one day he'd be shot during a routine traffic stop. Bad weather made his job twice as dangerous.

Chris told me I worried too much, but I knew the stats: Chris was four times more likely to be killed on the job than the average worker.

All I could do was take care of him when he was off work tonight.

I'm not much of a cook, but miraculously, I had chili, the perfect cold weather meal, in my freezer.

I defrosted it and added extra spice and beans. I don't care what the purists say, Chris and I like our chili with beans. Big red kidney beans. In the fridge, I had chili fixings: shredded Cheddar cheese, sour cream, and I diced a yellow onion. They'd taste good heaped on a steaming bowl of chili.

Last but not least, I whipped up a cornbread mix and popped the pan in the oven.

I turned the chili on low to simmer, and set the table for a buffet-style meal. Next, I tidied my home. I lived in a former guesthouse on the Du Pres estate, in a two-story, white stone house with a gingerbread porch. My late parents, who'd both worked on the estate, bought the house from old Reggie, and I inherited it from them.

There was just one hitch: Reggie owned the land my house was on, and if he wanted it back, he could boot me out and pay me what my parents paid years ago – $25,000. Reggie wasn't shy about blackmailing me. So far, I'd made it clear to him I could get a job anywhere, but now that I was involved with Chris, I wanted to keep my roots in the Forest.

No point in brooding while I worked. I took the cornbread out of the oven, then put on *Clapton Unplugged*, my favorite CD. I liked this version of 'Layla,' Clapton's song about his forbidden love for Pattie Boyd, the wife of his friend George Harrison. I could feel the passion in that song. Pattie must have too, since she married Clapton.

I listened to a lovelorn Clapton and his guitar wail while I did mundane things like dust and vacuum the living room, and clean the guest bath. Upstairs, I dusted my bedroom and changed the sheets, then cleaned the master bath. Done. And it was only eight o'clock.

I showered and changed into my gold satin robe, a long, glamorous creation that reminded me of old Hollywood.

Outside, the sleet was still pelting down, and arctic blasts rocked my stone house. The gas fireplace was realistic enough to give the living room a cozy feel.

Then I waited to hear from Chris. And worried. I flipped on the TV, but the only news was the steadily worsening winter storm and the dozens of car accidents.

Chris was going to be late. Really late. If he made it here at all.

I tried reading a magazine, but I couldn't concentrate. Restless, I went to the kitchen, stirred the chili again, then sat on the couch. Just for a moment. To rest my eyes.

My cell phone rang at eleven o'clock, waking me from a sound sleep. I fumbled with the phone, and finally answered. Chris. Relief surged through me.

'Angela,' he said, 'it's so late. Do you still want me to come over tonight?'

'Of course. Hurry over. Well, drive fast as you can. And drive safely. I love you.'

'I'm ten minutes out.'

It was more like twenty. I saw his car's lights in my drive and ran to open the door. He made his way carefully to the porch, and then he was inside, bringing the cold with him.

I didn't care. I kissed him as hard as I could, and felt his slightly scratchy five o'clock shadow. 'Come in and get warm,' I said.

Chris stamped the snow off his boots, and I hung his coat on a chair by the fire to dry. Then he wrapped me in his arms again. He must have showered and changed at the station. He smelled like soap and soft, clean cotton. I'd missed this pleasure during my long, gray twilight of widowhood: the feel of a strong man's body. His smell. And most of all, his love.

Tonight, I knew I had to feed him first.

'Hungry?' I asked.

'Starving,' he said.

Chris followed me into the kitchen. He filled a big bowl with chili, topped it with a mound of sour cream, cheese, and then asked, 'Onions?' He grinned at me.

'Help yourself,' I said. 'I like them, too.'

I cut him a big square of cornbread and handed him a beer. He sat on my brown leather couch in the living room. I fixed my bowl and joined him. We watched the flames while he told me about his day.

I tasted my chili. Not bad for a woman who usually made scrambled eggs. From the way Chris was digging in, I figured he either really was starving or he liked it, too.

Between bites, he asked, 'What is it about snow that lowers a driver's IQ? At the first drop of a snowflake, everyone has to run to the store for milk, bread, and toilet paper. Milk and bread, I understand. But toilet paper? Are they expecting mass diarrhea?'

I laughed, but I knew what he was talking about.

'Mmm.' Chris had a spoon heaped with chili, cheese and onions. 'Did I tell you how good this chili is?'

It warmed my heart to watch him eat. 'You just did,' I said. 'I'm glad you like it. Did you have lunch?'

'No time,' he said. 'Just coffee and energy bars.'

He polished off half a bowl before he came up for air again. 'Today was tiring,' he said, 'but I'm relieved no one was seriously hurt. We had a couple of close ones though.'

'Tell me,' I said, and took another bite of chili.

'Both involved teenagers. I was called to an accident caused by a sixteen-year-old girl texting her boyfriend. She lost control of her car and it slid into a ditch. The car was totaled, and it belonged to her mother. I guess that kid won't be driving for a while.'

'Texting? In this weather?'

'Yep. She's lucky all she got was a concussion and a bad cut on her head. I gave her a ticket. Liam, another teen, turned on cruise control in his dad's Beemer to be extra safe. Liam didn't realize that using cruise control in ice and snow can make the car skid or spin because it can't get enough traction. His dad's car started spinning and wiped out two parked cars and a pickup truck.'

'Yikes. Poor kid. Was he hurt?' I asked.

'He had enough injuries to go to the ER. His dad was waiting at the hospital and promised to give Liam the chewing out of a lifetime. I told Dad to go easy on the kid. Liam tried to do the right thing. He didn't know any better. People think it's safe to use cruise control, and that it can be used all the time, no matter what the weather.'

'That's what I thought,' I said.

'Nope.' Another big bite of Chris's chili disappeared. 'Drivers shouldn't use cruise control in rain, snow, hail, sleet or ice. On wet roads at the wrong speed, cruise control can cause a vehicle to hydroplane in standing water.'

'I didn't know that,' I said. I also didn't use cruise control. Chris must be really wound up to lecture me on cruise control.

We ate in contented silence until he asked, 'How's Jace doing?'

'OK, but he's not quite himself. Today, he was quite sharp when he interviewed an older woman. She bristled and refused to talk to him. That's not like Jace.'

'No, but you must have some idea of the pressure he's under,' Chris said.

'I do. The only good thing about this snowstorm is it keeps Selwyn's murder out of the local news.'

'The national news, too,' Chris said. 'This bad weather is nationwide, from California to the East Coast.'

My bowl was empty, and so was Chris's. We went back for another round, eating by the light of the flickering flames. Soon we were both drowsy. I leaned my head on his shoulder and he kissed my hair and then me. I could feel the heat, and it wasn't from the fireplace.

'Let's go upstairs,' he whispered.

We ran up the stairs, leaving a trail of clothes, and crawled under the covers. I don't spill the details about my love life, but Chris was a skilled and tender lover. Afterward, we fell asleep in each other's arms, the sleet pinging off my bedroom windows. I had my head on his chest, listening to his heart beating.

I woke up at three o'clock to a soft silence, the kind you only get with snow. Moon glow silvered the icy landscape. Chris was staring at me.

'Hi,' I said. 'What are you doing?'

'Admiring you.' He kissed me. 'You are so hot.'

'Even when I'm drooling?'

'Especially then.' He laughed and kissed me again.

'Mm, I like that.' I sighed with contentment.

He looked deep into my eyes. 'Angela Richman,' he said. 'I love you so much. I want to be with you forever. Will you marry me?'

NINE

'You want to marry me?' I was stunned. I didn't know what to say.

Chris was holding my hand as if I'd drift out to sea. 'Please say yes, Angela. I love you.'

'I . . .' Words deserted me. I felt my heart clench. I loved Chris, but did I want to marry again? My first marriage ended in heartbreak when my husband died young. Could I go through that crippling grief again if anything happened to Chris? His job was way more dangerous than Donegan's career as a college professor.

'I . . .' I waited for the right words to come. Instead, my work cell phone rang. I pounced on it. 'I have to answer my phone. I'm on call.' I was babbling. Chris knew I was on call after midnight.

There was no greeting. The caller said, 'Richman. You humping that cop?' Ugh. Detective Ray Greiman, the worst cop on the force. But right now, I was even happy to hear his insults.

'What do you want, Ray?'

'I want you to get your ass to work. We have a stiff on Ranleigh Parkway, a block south off Gravois.'

'Who is it?'

'Do you want to sit around and talk until she turns into a popsicle? Get your ass over here.'

When I first started working with Greiman, I lectured him on respect. Dead people were not crispy critters, stiffs, floaters or any of the ugly names you hear on TV cop shows. He'd laughed at me, and said I 'had a stick up my ass.'

By now, I knew there was no cure for his insensitivity, racism or misogyny. He once told a new widow that her husband had been having an affair with the passenger in her late husband's car. The man had simply given a coworker a lift home.

Complaints were useless – Ray was the Forest elite's fair-haired boy. He spoke the language and shared the prejudices of the powers that be. I had to force myself to shut up and work with him.

I ended the call and kissed Chris. 'I'm sorry. There's a fatal accident on Ranleigh Parkway.'

'Right where it joins Gravois?' Chris asked.

'A block south.'

'Dangerous place.' Chris shook his head. 'That little stone bridge at the entrance to the Ranleigh Estates is a death trap. Bridges and overpasses freeze first. Plus, this snow can hide black ice.'

'I'll go make you hot coffee, Angela. You're going to need it.'

I quickly dressed, relieved that the marriage discussion was tabled. For now.

By the time I came downstairs in boots and my warmest hooded coat, Chris handed me a Thermos of coffee and a fried egg on toast.

He gave me a torrid goodbye kiss and I was out the door and into my cold car. The temperature had dropped below zero. I drove like I was eighty years old, but I didn't dare go faster on these frozen roads. My car's interior was barely warm by the time I made it to Ranleigh Estates.

The Estates were sheltered, even by Forest standards. This postcard-pretty place, with its hundred-year-old white stone mansions and their gently sloping lawns, proclaimed 'nothing bad ever happens to people like us.' The enclave's entrance was a graceful humpbacked bridge. I'd seen it in the spring, hidden in clouds of pink cherry blossoms.

Now the pulsing crimson emergency lights turned the pale snow scene into a blood bath.

A stream about six feet deep ran under the bridge. A pale blue, squarish car had rolled down the icy embankment and was partly submerged, nose down in the water below. This was going to be bad.

A group was clustered near the wreck, mostly law enforcement.

I parked on the roadside, behind the official vehicles, dragged my black DI case out of the trunk, then lost my balance in the slippery snow, and slid down the embankment. I should have used the suitcase as a sled – I was spinning downhill on my rear end and heading straight for the water.

'Whoa, whoa!' A sturdy paramedic stepped out of the cluster of observers. He grabbed me with one hand and my suitcase with the other, before I hit the water.

I caught my breath, then dusted snow and frozen grass off my coat with shaking hands.

'Are you OK?' he asked.

'Yes, thank you. Good save.' I tried a lopsided smile. 'I'm Angela Richman, death investigator.'

'Patrick Jackson,' he said. 'Paramedic.' Patrick was six feet tall, square-jawed and muscular.

'Damn, Richman, you are such a klutz.' Greiman gave a jackass bray and swaggered over. He was wearing a puffy designer coat that had to cost at least two grand. How he could afford that on a cop's salary, I had no idea.

I ignored his rude comment and asked, 'What happened?'

'Another idiot driver.' Greiman pointed at the wrecked car. 'A woman, of course. She fishtailed at the entrance to the bridge, and crashed down the embankment. The steering column rammed into her chest, and she was nearly decapitated. She's dead at age twenty-six.'

The pointless loss of life slammed into me. 'Oh, I'm sorry.'

'Don't be,' Greiman said. 'She was too stupid to live. Hell, she was driving a 1960 Corvair. Maybe the most dangerous car ever made. Just as well she didn't have any kids. Time to put some chlorine in *that* gene pool.'

I was shocked speechless by his heartless comments. Patrick acted swiftly. He socked Greiman in the jaw so hard, he sent the detective tumbling into the ice-cold water. I heard Greiman's expensive jacket tear on a sharp piece of metal.

A furious Greiman climbed out of his ice bath, breathless with rage.

'He – he hit me!'

'No, he didn't,' I said. 'Looked to me like you tripped and fell.' I didn't see anyone from the group watching us to contradict me.

Patrick was laughing, but it had a nasty edge. He slapped the dripping detective so hard, Greiman almost fell down again. 'I heard you were a real klutz, Greiman,' Patrick said. 'Better come up to the bus and change out of those wet clothes. In this weather, you could get hypothermia and freeze to death.'

A shivering, soggy Greiman followed the paramedic up the hill to the ambulance, seething with anger. I walked carefully over to the group surrounding the car, and recognized CFPD uniform, Sammy Berger.

'Sad situation here, Angela.' I could see Sam's breath as he talked. 'The paramedic ID'd the victim as Janie Duvalle. The car is submerged up to the dashboard. We broke the window trying to get her out, but she was dead. We'll need the Jaws of Life to remove her.' The Jaws were a hydraulic rescue tool that cut through cars to rescue trapped passengers. 'I don't think you can do your investigation until the tow truck arrives and we get the wreck out of the water,' Sam said.

'So young.' I shook my head. 'Was she married or single?'

'Patrick said she was married about a year. Her husband, David, is out of town, and I guess the airport is closed.'

Thank gawd he's not home, I thought. I won't have to break the news to him tonight.

'I need to take some photos, Sam.'

'I'll clear everyone out.' Sam directed the small crowd out of the way. I opened my DI case, took out my point-and-shoot camera, and photographed the fatal accident – both long and medium shots – in the water.

Now I needed close-ups. Portable lights had been set up, and the details were revealed in their harsh glare. The Corvair was nose-down, the front end smashed, and the windshield spidered with cracks. The car had rolled at least once, and the roof was flattened. The driver's side window had been smashed in. The passenger's body was trapped between the driver's seat and the steering wheel. The victim's long blonde hair was loose and something had created an ugly red wound in her neck. The water was tinged pink.

As I repacked my DI case, Sam asked, 'Have you seen Greiman?'

'He slipped on the ice and fell in the water. He's in Patrick's ambulance, warming up.'

Sam's radio crackled. 'Tow truck will be here in about twenty minutes, Angela. You should wait somewhere warm until the truck drags the vehicle out of the water.'

'I'll be up in the ambulance,' I said.

Greiman was sitting on a stretcher in the back of the ambulance under a heap of blankets, shivering uncontrollably.

'Hi, Angela. I'm treating Detective Greiman for hypothermia.' Patrick looked cheerful.

'Is he showing all the signs?' I knew many of them.

'Yes, a classic case: shivering, slurred speech, slow, shallow breathing and a weak pulse.'

'We already know about clumsiness and lack of coordination,' I said.

'I'm leaving now, ass hat,' Greiman said with a snarl.

'So you decline treatment at the hospital?' Patrick asked.

'Hell, yes.'

'Fine with me. Sign these release forms, please.' Patrick handed the detective an iPad.

Greiman scribbled his name on the forms and rudely tossed the iPad at Patrick.

'OK, you're free to go,' Patrick said. 'Drive safely.'

'You owe me a new jacket,' Greiman said. 'And you're going to pay for it. You decked me.'

'Did I do that, Angela?' Patrick looked wide-eyed and innocent.

'I distinctly saw the detective slip and fall,' I said.

'You're lying, Richman!' Greiman glared at me.

'Patrick, isn't confusion and memory loss two of the signs of hypothermia?' I asked.

'It is, Angela.'

'And I just talked to the observers by the submerged car, Patrick. No one saw you touch Greiman.'

Greiman snorted.

'Detective, I recommend that you head home and get as warm as possible to prevent further damage.' Patrick handed Greiman a plastic bag with his dripping clothes. 'You can wear the blankets home. Here's a pair of slippers. Your boots are pretty wet. Those leather-soled boots must have cost a fortune, but they're not very practical in the snow. Might want to wear something more functional in bad weather.'

Greiman growled and stomped off through the snow to his unmarked car.

'Be careful,' Patrick called. The two of us climbed into the cabin of the ambulance and he shared a cup of his hot coffee with me.

'Between his torn coat and wet boots,' Patrick said, 'I suspect that moron lost about five thousand dollars' worth of clothes.'

'Couldn't happen to a nicer guy. If that jerk gives you any trouble, Patrick, give me a call. I'll be happy to back you up.'

'Thanks.' He took another sip of coffee and so did I. I was starting to warm up.

'Did you know the victim?' I asked.

Patrick looked sad. 'Yes, I had a crush on Janie when we were kids. She was a sweet girl, but she barely noticed me. My dad was her father's chief mechanic. Hector Duvalle.'

'The classic car collector?'

'That's the man. Old Hector had a warehouse crammed with vintage cars. He had some sweet rides: a Rolls-Royce Phantom with the swooping fenders, the kind you see in the movies.'

Patrick was practically drooling. 'He also had a 1935 Packard, a gorgeous white Cord, and some newer ones, too, like a DeLorean.'

'The car with the gull wing doors?'

'Yep, it was in that movie, *Back to the Future*. I used to hang around the warehouse on weekends with my dad because I liked cars and I was hoping to catch a glimpse of Janie.'

He shrugged. 'I didn't have a chance. She met her husband David at a party and fell hard for him. They've been trying to have a baby.'

'How did you know that?'

'It's the Forest,' he said.

'Hm.' I sounded doubtful.

Now he looked ashamed. 'OK, my mom works for Janie's gynecologist. She keeps me up to speed on Janie.'

So much for the medical information privacy laws, I thought. Now I knew why the paramedic lost his temper and slugged Greiman. If I'd known this, I would have helped Patrick beat him.

'Anyway, I didn't have a chance with Janie. We lived in different worlds. You know what that's like.'

'I do. My parents worked for Reggie Du Pres and I grew up on his estate.'

There was no need to say anything else.

'When Janie's dad had all those cars, why did she drive that old Corvair?'

'It's a classic, too,' Patrick said. 'The Corvair was the only mass-produced American car with a rear-mounted engine. Very advanced. When Janie's dad passed away two years ago, he left all his cars to her. She sold the collection, except for the Corvair. She loved that car.'

'Why? Corvairs are unsafe.'

'Don't believe it. Ralph Nader' – he spat the name of the consumer advocate – 'trashed the Corvair in his book, *Unsafe at Any Speed*. The Corvair had some problems, sure, but if you knew what you were doing, it drove like a dream. Car lovers called it the "poor man's Porsche." Janie's dad taught her how to drive it, and helped her understand its quirks. The big problem with the Corvair was its suspension, which made inexperienced drivers oversteer and lose control.

'Janie loved the feel of that car. I think she drove it to feel closer to her father.'

We stared at the partly submerged wreck, floating in a sea of bloody light.

'I guess she is now,' Patrick said. 'Closer to her father. I mean, I hope she's with him.'

TEN

Sam knocked on the passenger door to the ambulance. I rolled down the window a couple of inches, and the cold rushed in. The cop was stamping on the ground, trying to keep warm. 'The tow truck has pulled Janie Duvalle's car out of the water,' he said. 'It's being towed to the police impound garage. They'll have to use the Jaws of Life to get the body out. You can examine her in the garage. It's too cold to do a death examination outside, Angela.'

I stifled a yawn. It was four thirty in the morning. I thanked Patrick the paramedic and climbed out of the ambulance. It was so cold, my nose hairs froze and my teeth were chattering.

'What's the wind chill?' I asked Sam, as I followed him to my car.

'Twelve below. I'll meet you at the garage entrance.'

The CFPD impound garage was plain gray concrete, crammed with crime scene cars (some with blood and bullet holes), stolen cars, evidence vehicles and a few flashy seized assets that had belonged to drug dealers and other crooks. Those would be sold at auction.

On the short drive there, I thought about poor, unlucky Janie, one of two thousand Americans who died every year on icy, snowy roads. Winter was a silent killer.

Fifteen minutes later, I was at the garage. Sam had beat me there. He flashed his lights, and I followed his patrol car into the garage. The wreck was off the flatbed tow truck. A bright overhead light was trained on the fatal Corvair.

I parked my car in a nearby spot. Inside the garage, it was cold enough to see my breath, but still warmer than working outside.

Rick Hall, a firefighter in beige turnout gear and helmet, stood by, ready to pry open the wreck with the Jaws of Life. The police photographer would video the opening of the car, and I'd photograph it.

The Jaws looked like giant pliers and had a noisy motor. Rick was about six-feet-two, with thick, muscular arms. He held the bulky machine as if it weighed no more than a can opener, and used it to pry open the driver's side door. Water gushed out onto a fine screen over a drain on the concrete floor.

When the Jaws were shut off, Sam and I checked to see if anything had tumbled out. A thin, black leather purse with a Gucci logo had slid out, along with a small heap of window glass. I was responsible for everything on the body. The purse would be in police custody.

Sam gloved up and opened the purse in front of us. Inside, a black Gucci wallet had Janie's driver's license, an ATM card for a local bank, three credit cards, and a wedding photo of a smiling Janie and a dark-haired man. The billfold held three ten-dollar bills, and twenty-six cents in change.

Sam opened a zippered pocket in the purse. 'Here's her cell phone,' Sam said. 'She definitely wasn't talking on it at the time of the accident.'

Sam went back to examining the purse. A wad of damp tissues, a lipstick, and a hair brush completed the contents. The bag was videoed and I photographed it. Sam tagged and bagged the purse in brown paper. At the lab, it would be hung up to dry.

Sam brushed the broken glass on the screen covering the drain into another paper bag.

We found nothing else in the car.

'Janie kept that car pristine,' Sam said. 'No fast-food wrappers or receipts. We have no idea why she was driving in such dangerous conditions at that hour.'

Rick moved closer to the car and asked, 'Are you finished? Should I continue?'

'Go ahead,' Sam said to the firefighter.

'We're lucky to have the Jaws,' Sam said to me. 'Most counties our size can't afford one.'

'I heard this one was a donation from a family who lost a loved one,' I said.

The motor roared again, stopping our conversation, as the firefighter cut away the crushed roof of the car. We could see the steering column pinning Janie to the driver's seat. Rick worked on that next.

Once Rick cut through the steering column, Sam said, 'I think we can get the victim out now.' The firefighter agreed to help move the decedent.

I rolled my DI case over to where portable crime scene lights were set up, took off my winter gloves, put on four pairs of nitrile gloves, and spread a sterilized sheet on the cold concrete. I had an odd urge to put down a blanket to keep Janie warm, even though I knew she was past feeling anything.

'Ready?' Sam asked.

'Let's do it,' Rick said. 'Jeez, look at that wound on her neck. What if her head comes loose when we carry her?'

I found another sterilized sheet so they could put the body on it. The two men carefully, respectfully lifted Janie out of the car and onto the sheet, then carried her to me. There was no laughing or joking to break the tension. They were solemn pall bearers. The cop and the firefighter set the decedent on her sheet on top of mine. Sam straightened her coat.

It was an eerie scene. In the glare of the lights, Janie was strangely beautiful. Her pale yellow hair hid her terrible neck wound, and the broken glass fragments dusted her white skin with diamonds. Bleak shadows lurked in the corner, as if Death was waiting to collect her.

I shook my head to get rid of such fanciful thoughts. I was here for the facts of Janie Duvalle's death.

In pre-computer days, a fatal accident generated almost an inch of paperwork for the medical examiner's office. Now, since we'd adopted forms on iPads, reporting a vehicle fatality was still a hand-cramping amount of writing, but the new technology made the information easier to record and read.

Tonight, I'd stashed my iPad in my coat to keep it warm. Extreme cold made it glitchy. I opened it to the Vehicular-Related Death form and began answering questions.

The form started with: *Was the subject the driver/operator?*

Yes, I wrote.

Was the subject conveyed to a hospital? Were there any resuscitative attempts? Were there any other passengers?

No, to all three questions.

I wrote down the date and day of the accident, then asked Sam about the next round of questions.

'Do you know when the victim was pronounced dead, Sam?'

The uniform checked his notebook. 'At two fifty-five a.m. I pronounced her. Nine-one-one got the call at two eleven a.m. and I made it to the scene at two thirty-five. Patrick and the bus arrived a minute later. The car was nose-down in the water. We waded into the water to check on her. I broke the window with a tire iron. It was clear the victim was dead, and there was no way we could get her out without the Jaws of Life.'

He'd already told me this, but I wanted it exactly for the record. I wrote down Sam's name and badge number.

'Oh,' he added. 'The headlights were off and the engine wasn't running. And the temp was eight degrees, in case you need that.'

I did. All of it.

I noted other mundane facts, also provided by Sam: no pedestrians were on the road. The speed limit was fifteen miles an hour, and the Corvair did not appear to have been speeding. The car was westbound, and the road conditions were ice under snow. There were no street lights.

In Missouri, cars made before 1968 don't need seatbelts. The Corvair had been retrofitted with a lap belt, but did not have modern shoulder seat belts, much less air bags.

The form asked if the victim had been ejected during the accident. *No.*

I wondered if air bags would have saved Janie's life – or if she'd have survived if she'd been thrown out of the car.

No way to answer those questions. Because the Corvair had its engine in the back, the collision had pushed the dash and steering column forward, trapping and killing Janie.

Other questions were answered: no drugs or alcohol were in the car. The wipers had been off. No radio or CD player, and Janie wasn't using a cell phone.

At long last, I was ready for Janie's body inspection.

Her skin was pale as milk, with a slight bluish tinge. I measured her at five-feet-six-inches tall and guessed her weight at around 125 pounds. Her blonde hair was down to her shoulders. She wore a long navy wool coat with a hood, a red V-neck sweater, black jeans and black leather boots.

Wait. That wasn't a red V-neck. That was a beige sweater with a bib of dark red blood. I measured the bloodstain: eleven inches wide and fourteen inches long. Her hair and clothes were soaked with water. Her chest was oddly flattened. I suspected massive internal injuries, but the ME would discover those. I couldn't remove her clothing.

My inspection started at her head. She had a contusion (bruise) on her forehead above her right eye measuring three inches wide and half-an-inch high. Her face had a thin, bloody scratch two inches long on her right cheek. Bits of glass were on her left side, probably from when Sam smashed in the window. I used tweezers to pick twenty-three pieces of safety glass off her hair, neck and coat.

I brushed aside her hair to reveal the deep jagged wound on her neck. It started under her right ear and continued on a diagonal down to her left collar bone, right through the anterior triangle at the front of the neck. It looked like the dashboard had sliced through her carotid artery. From the angle of her neck, I suspected it was broken.

But I couldn't tell for sure. The medical examiner would have to determine what killed her.

She was wearing round diamond-stud earrings in a rose gold setting, but I couldn't say that. I described them as 'earrings with a clear round stone in a pinkish metal setting.' I wasn't there to appraise jewelry. I took close-ups of both the earrings and her wedding and engagement rings. Those were rose gold, too, and the diamond solitaire was huge. So big, I wondered why she wore the ring when she went out alone. Robbers had killed for less. Forest folks were sheltered.

Her coat was buttoned, and had a six-inch rip on the right shoulder. Her beige sweater had an eight-inch rip.

She wore knee-high black leather boots with flat heels. There were deep scrapes in the boots, which protected her legs. Not that that did Janie any good.

Sam and Rick helped me turn the body. I measured and photographed another bloody patch on the back of the coat.

That was all. Sam helped me slide Janie Duvalle in a black plastic body bag, and I called the morgue conveyance. It was nearly nine in the morning when the morgue picked up the body and took it to the medical examiner.

Once the driver signed the paperwork, I was free to go. I said goodbye to Rick and Sam and drove slowly out of the garage. As my car emerged, I was nearly blinded by the sun.

Janie Duvalle's case had distracted me from Chris's marriage proposal, but I'd have to give him an answer soon. How I answered could destroy our love.

My car lingered at the garage entrance.

I didn't know which way to turn.

ELEVEN

Before I left the garage, I texted Jace: *Called out on a case last night at 3 a.m. Just finished. When do you want me to report?*

Jace texted back: *Get some sleep and report to the boutique at ten tomorrow. This is a paperwork day for me.*

Most cops dreaded paperwork, and let it pile up. In fact, there's a legend that in the 1890s, a St. Louis beat cop found a dead horse on Pestalozzi Street, south of downtown. The cop dragged the horse around the corner to Gravois, so he wouldn't have to spell Pestalozzi.

As for Jace's suggestion to sleep, I was exhausted, but could I really sleep after Chris asked me to marry him? I expected to toss and turn for hours.

There was little traffic and the roads were plowed and salted, but it took longer than usual to drive home. The schools were closed, and hordes of kids were playing in the snow. I was going at a turtle-like ten miles an hour, when a boy in a blue knit hat zipped in front of my car during a snowball fight. I pumped the brakes to avoid hitting him, and my car nearly went into a ditch.

I slowed down to five miles an hour, and was glad I did. I was a block from the turn-off to the Du Pres estate where I lived when a little girl in a red plastic sled slid in front of my car.

I stopped, my heart pounding. The girl, about six, was crying. I got out of the car to see if she was OK, and the words tumbled out.

'Kingsley pushed me down the hill and I cut my lip.' Her lip was bleeding and her straight, dark hair had fallen out of her pale blue hood.

I pushed her hair back into the hood and asked, 'Where do you live?'

'Up there.'

She pointed to the newer two-story houses on the hill. 'The beige one with the red door.'

'Get in the car and I'll drive you home.'

'No!' The girl set her mouth in a stubborn line. 'Mommy said *never* get in a car with strangers.'

'Your mother's right.' I dug a tissue out of my purse for her bloody lip, put on the car's flashers, and locked it. 'Sit in the sled and I'll take you home.'

The cold air woke me up as I dragged the sled up the steep hill. The little girl was surprisingly heavy. She'd quit crying and chattered about Kingsley and what a bad boy he was.

'He's twelve,' she said, 'and picks on the little kids. I'm not supposed to play with him, but I wasn't. He came up behind me and pushed my sled. Real hard. It went down the hill and he ran away, laughing.' The girl asked, 'Am I going to get into trouble?'

'I think you should tell your mother what happened.'

I was puffing a bit now, and the house was in sight.

The girl jumped out of the sled and ran toward the house, shouting, 'Mommy, Mommy! Kingsley hurt me.'

Her mother, a trim thirty-something woman in jeans and a blue sweater, opened the front door.

Once again the girl's words rushed out. 'Kingsley pushed me down the hill in my sled. I wasn't playing with him. Kingsley just came up behind me. I hurt my lip and couldn't stop. My sled nearly hit this lady's car. She stopped and wanted to drive me home, but I wouldn't get in the car, so she pulled me up the hill in my sled.'

The mother seemed to understand the story. She wrapped her arms around her girl and said, 'I'm glad you're OK, Olivia. Your daddy and I will talk to Kingsley's parents. Come inside and we'll have hot cocoa.'

'With marshmallows?' Olivia asked.

'Yes. You're letting in the cold. Go into the kitchen.'

The woman turned to me. 'Thank you. Would you like to come inside?'

'Just for a moment.'

The living room was beautifully furnished in light gray and pale blue.

'I'm Olivia's mother, Emily Murphy.' She offered her hand.

As I shook it, I said, 'I gather Kingsley is the local bully.'

Emily rolled her eyes. 'His parents think their darling can do no wrong. Would you like some hot chocolate or coffee?'

'Thanks, but I need to get home.'

'Thank you for saving my girl and bringing her safely home.' Emily's lip trembled.

'You've trained Olivia well,' I said. 'She refused to get in my car.'

I waved goodbye and hurried back to my car, chased by a cold wind. Five minutes later I pulled into my drive. Chris's car was gone. I wondered if he was angry at me.

After parking in the garage, I unlocked my door and was greeted with the scent of cinnamon. The kitchen table was set for one. Chris had left this note by the place mat:

Angela, I had to go to work this morning, but I made a cinnamon coffee cake from your Bisquick (you'll need more). The cake is warming in the oven. The coffee is ready to brew. Just press the button. I'll call when I can.

Love you madly – C.

Sigh. He did love me, and he didn't sound angry. But would his love continue if I didn't marry him? Or would it wither and die?

I turned on the coffee and slathered the warm coffee cake with butter. I'd worry about Chris when I wasn't so tired. Right now I needed sleep – and lots of it – to think clearly.

I finished two fat slices of the crunchy-topped, buttery cake, and could hardly keep my eyes open. Time for bed.

I dumped my clothes in the washer, and climbed the stairs to my bedroom. Chris had made the bed. I fell asleep as soon as my head hit the pillow, and didn't wake up until seven that night.

I wished I'd slept through the night. I hated waking up like this. My tongue was furry and my head ached. I flipped on the TV and saw that the news stories were still talking about the storm damage. Selwyn Skipton wasn't in the current news cycle. That would take a little pressure off Jace.

I texted Chris my thanks for the cake and decided not to call. Maybe a short break would help me make up my mind about marriage. Chris was a playful, passionate lover. He was kind, thoughtful and a good cook. It would be fun to have him around all the time. But marriage was so . . . permanent. My brain was going in circles, and I wanted it to stop.

I fixed my go-to meal, scrambled eggs on toast, and added a slice of Chris's coffee cake for dessert. The food made me sleepy. By nine o'clock I was back in bed, sound asleep.

The next morning, I wore my best black pantsuit for the trip to

Forest Frocks and Lingerie. The temperature was up in the twenties today, and the cold was almost bearable.

Forest Frocks had been around some eighty years, and the Forest's well-heeled women shopped there. The mannequins had outdated hair styles with finger waves, and blood-red lips, but the dresses they wore were cutting edge, and at least four figures.

The saleswomen, clad in plain black dresses, had a reputation for terrifying anyone they didn't think belonged in the store. To say you shopped at Forest Frocks was a sign of status.

Jace was waiting in his unmarked car in front of the store, looking like a kid who had to see the principal. I didn't tell him that the lingerie section was at the front of the store, and despite the old-fashioned appearance of the window, the lingerie was pretty racy.

As we entered the shop, an imitation Louis XIV table was covered with piles of women's panties. A gilt sign said: *Panties with the three Ps. Pretty, pee-proof, period-proof.*

Jace blanched and made an abrupt turn – right into a display of lacy teddies. He backed away, as if the lingerie was covered in needles, and nearly knocked over a rack of 'Sheer Support.' In other words, flimsy see-through bras.

I hid a smile and grabbed his arm, steering him to the main aisle, before he blundered into the shelf of silicone nipple covers and stick-on bras for backless dresses.

A grim woman in a black dress bore down on us.

'May I help you, sir? Madam?' Ice shimmered on each word.

'No!' Jace said.

'Yes!' I said. 'We need information about one of your customers.'

Jace recovered enough to introduce us and show his badge.

'I'm Mrs Helena Stone, proprietress.' Her face was thin and pale, and she had a mole near her nose. She was as tall as me and wore chunky square-toed shoes.

'What exactly are you looking for?' It was a demand, not a question.

'A red sweater that originally sold for one thousand eight hundred dollars,' Jace said. 'It was damaged and marked down to two hundred.'

'Oh, a sale item.' She wrinkled her nose in disapproval, as if 'sale' was a dirty word. 'I can't remember who bought a sale sweater.'

'We need it, ma'am,' Jace said. 'It's connected to a murder.'

Helena straightened her spine and said, 'My clothes would never be involved in a murder. My clients are the cream of society.'

'Cream curdles,' Jace said.

I bit my lip to avoid laughing.

'Humph,' said Helena. 'I have many important clients, and I need to protect them. You'll have to get a warrant. Now, if you'll excuse me.'

She turned around and stomped into a back room.

Back outside, Jace said, 'What got into her? It's a simple request. Why is she so difficult?'

'Beats me,' I said. 'The world won't stop turning if we find out Mrs Gotrocks wears a thirty-six B bustier.'

'Maybe it's Mr Gotrocks wearing it,' Jace said.

We laughed and Jace went off to get the warrant.

TWELVE

Back in my car, I checked my texts. There was just one, from Katie: *Autopsy report on Janie Duvalle ready. Come by when you can.*
Will Greiman be there? I texted.
You're joking, right? she answered.
I took that as a no and promised to meet Katie at her office in half an hour. I swung by and picked up two large coffees, and was soon at the morgue. It was warmer inside than outside, but I never got used to the smell – industrial disinfectant with a faint hint of death underneath.
Katie's office door was open. She was working on her computer at her desk, head down while she pounded the keyboard.
'Katie?' I said.
She gave me a welcoming grin. 'Angela. Good to see you. Especially since you brought coffee.'
I handed her the cup and she said, 'I have chocolate chip cookies.'
She gave me a metal cookie tin. I helped myself and sat on the edge of her desk. The cookies were rich, buttery, and studded with fat chunks of chocolate.
Katie appraised me with shrewd eyes. 'You look tired, Angela.'
I shrugged. 'I'm OK.'
'Really? Those bags under your eyes have nothing to do with a certain hunky patrol cop?'
'Of course not,' I said quickly. Too quickly.
Katie knew something was off. 'Did you two have a fight?'
'No! Why would you say that?'
'Because my Angela lie detector is screeching.'
I looked her right in the eye and said, 'Chris and I did not have a fight. I swear on this box of cookies.' I helped myself to another.
'Hm.' She gave me an appraising look. 'You didn't have a fight, but you're acting like someone kicked your legs out from under you. He proposed, didn't he?'

'Uh.' I stalled.

'He did!' Katie was triumphant. 'Chris proposed and you said no.'

'No! I didn't give him an answer yet. I'm still thinking it over.'

'Why didn't you say yes? Don't you love him?'

'Yes.' I answered without hesitation. 'But that doesn't mean I should marry him. Marriage is out of style.'

'Really?' Katie said. 'Tell that to the sixty-one million married couples in the US. They'll be really surprised.' She zinged me with another statistic. 'That sixty-one million is an increase from forty million married couples in 1960.'

She looked so smug I wanted to throw my coffee at her. Instead, I slugged her with another barbed number. 'More Americans may be getting married,' I said. 'But the share of adults who are currently married fell – as in dropped – from sixty-seven percent in 1990 to fifty-three percent in 2019. That's a big plunge for people not taking the plunge.'

Before Katie could spend too much time pondering that fact, I slammed her with another stat. 'During that same time, the number of people living together has doubled. Doubled. Cohabiting couples are increasing. So put that in your pipe and smoke it.'

I have no idea where I came up with that childish retort. I ate another cookie to hide my shame.

'Big hairy deal,' Katie said. 'Those cohabiting numbers went up from a measly four percent to nine percent in 2019.'

'Big hairy deal?' I said. 'What are you? Nine years old?' I tossed my empty coffee cup in the trash basket.

'No, but I can dig up statistics as well as you can. And here's one thing I know for sure: married people live longer and are more financially secure than unmarried ones.'

'I do quite well for myself, thank you.' My voice was cold steel. My feminist flag was waving. 'I don't need a man to support me.' I piled on one more zinger. 'And if marriage is so great, why aren't you and Monty married?' Hah! I thought. Explain that one.

For once, Katie was speechless. 'Because . . . because . . .'

'Gotcha!' I was triumphant. Katie and I could sling stats at each other all day. I had to stop this silly conversation before I damaged our friendship.

Finally, she came up with an answer. 'Because Monty and I are not the marrying kind. You've been married once already. Marriage is a natural state for you.'

'Until it isn't.' I felt tears stinging my eyes. 'Until the man you love drops dead of a heart attack and your life is in ruins.'

Katie heard the pain in my voice. 'I didn't mean to upset you, Angela. And Chris isn't going to die. He's healthy as a horse. Now, let's get on with that autopsy report.'

She handed me the last cookie as a peace offering.

'How did Janie Duvalle die?' I asked.

'Loss of blood,' Katie said. 'The crash forced the dashboard into her neck, cutting through her carotid and her jugular. She bled out. But even if she'd survived those injuries, she probably would have died anyway. She had a flail chest.'

I looked at her blankly.

'The steering wheel hit her chest so hard it broke off a section of ribs and left them dangling. Only the surrounding meat was holding the ribs in place.'

'Ouch.' I winced.

'Ouch is right,' Katie said. 'When she tried to breathe, she had a chunk of spareribs flailing back and forth.'

The words 'meat' and 'spareribs' triggered an image of a barbecue gone wrong. In my mind, I saw a section of spareribs flopping around on the prep table. I tried to erase the image.

'That must hurt,' I said.

'No kidding. It can also be deadly, especially since she had a pneumothorax.'

'Collapsed lung,' I said.

'Very good.' Katie rewarded me with a smile, like a gold star student.

'Those injuries sound painful,' I said.

'They would be – if she survived her injuries, and there wasn't much chance of that. Oh, her fetus died, too.'

I felt a stab of sadness. 'She was pregnant?'

'About six weeks.'

'I heard she was trying to have a baby. Are you going to tell her husband?'

'The kid may not be his,' Katie said.

'What? She was cheating on her husband?' I couldn't hide my shock. 'How do you know? That can't be true.'

'But it is. The police went through her cell phone. Her husband called from New York at about five o'clock the night the storm hit, telling her his flight was delayed until the next day. She immediately texted Paul Holpen—'

'The lawyer?'

'Right. Also the man she dated in college before she met her husband.'

'How do you know this?'

'The information was all on her phone – in a series of text messages. Janie joked about letting Paul copy her notes in their American History class. She'd been having a fling with Paul for six months.'

'That's terrible.'

Katie shrugged. 'Don't be so judgmental, Angela. Going through fertility treatment is hard on a couple. It can take the romance out of any marriage. Maybe being with Holpen was the only sex she was enjoying. "Making a baby" with fertility treatments can feel like a mechanical process.'

'I guess you're right. But why did she leave Paul's house during the storm?'

'She got another text from her husband. He said he'd be home by six in the morning.'

'So she hurried home, slid on the ice, and died.'

'End of story,' Katie said. 'As for telling her husband, if he wants a copy of the autopsy report, I'll give it to him.'

'Makes sense,' I said. 'Why compound his grief with a double loss – his wife and baby.'

'Exactly. Although you won't believe how many women try to pass off the cuckoo in their nest as their husband's child.'

'And without a DNA test, Janie's husband would never know the truth.'

My cell phone chimed. 'It's Jace. I'll take this,' I told Katie. I put the phone on speaker so she could hear.

'How's the subpoena going?' I asked.

'I didn't need it.' Jace sounded triumphant. 'I'll tell you over lunch. How about if I bring Chinese?'

'Yes!' Katie shouted.

'I'm with Katie, Jace. At her office. You're on speaker.'

'Good. Kung pao chicken for Katie?'

'Extra spicy,' she called.

'Shrimp and snow peas for me,' I said.

'See you shortly.'

'Don't forget the fortune cookies,' I said, before he hung up.

Katie brewed green tea for us and I cleared her desk so we could use it as a table. Half an hour later, Jace arrived with two big bags of food. He greeted us with an extra-wide smile.

'You're in a good mood,' I told him.

'I didn't need that subpoena. Judge Lambert is the duty judge this week, and he's a pain in the neck. I'm starved. I got extra fried rice and spring rolls. Let's eat and I'll tell you the story.'

Soon Katie's desktop was covered with spicy, flavorful Chinese food. We filled our paper plates, and ate. I speared my fat shrimp and crunched on the snow peas. Katie poured extra hot sauce on her kung pao chicken. Jace wolfed down pork fried rice and regaled us with how he outfoxed the boutique owner.

'I knew Judge Lambert would make my life a misery if I asked for a subpoena, so I thought I'd try the "proprietress"' – he made mocking air quotes – 'one more time. She was just as stubborn as before. She made me feel like something she'd scraped off her shoe. "You'll have to get a search warrant, Detective," she said in that snippy voice of hers. "And I assure you my clientele" – she pronounced it clee-un-tell – "would never have anything to do with something as sordid as murder."

'I was ready to stomp out of there and do battle with Lambert when I realized that if she was hiding something, she'd have plenty of time to destroy evidence and alert the buyer. So I said, "OK. I'll get your subpoena. But when I come back, I might need your store computer and your ledgers. And I can't tell you how many days I will need it. So you tell me – how long can you afford to have your store closed? And what will you do when word gets out that you were uncooperative with the police?"'

Jace paused.

'Did the threat work?' Katie asked.

'A little too well,' Jace said. 'She gave me four bankers boxes of stuff.'

We all laughed, and promised to help him sort through the papers. It felt good to laugh. The last few days had been tense.

We'd eaten all our food, down to the last grain of rice.

Katie opened her fortune cookie, and read the message out loud. '"It could be better, but it's good enough." That's the motto of the ME's office. What's yours say, Angela?'

'Mine says, "Your reality check is about to bounce." Hah. Just when I finally got my bank account balanced. Jace, what does your cookie say?'

He cracked open his cookie and read, '"A closed mouth gathers no feet."'

'I'm going to have that needlepointed on a sampler,' I said.

My phone rang. I checked the display and said, 'It's Chris.' I moved to the other side of the tiny room to take his call. Katie and Jace kept talking, pretending they couldn't hear.

Chris sounded like he was a thousand miles away. His voice was faint and weak. 'Angela?'

'Chris, what's wrong? I can barely hear you.'

'I've been shot.'

'Shot! Shot where?' My heart was pounding so hard I could hardly hear him.

'Jasmine Trail.' His voice was almost a whisper.

'No, I mean, where were you shot? What part of your body?'

Jace and Katie were silent now, clearly eavesdropping.

Chris was struggling to talk. There were long pauses between his words. 'Angela . . . I may not . . . make it . . .'

'What? What do you mean you may not make it?' I was crying now. Tears blurred my voice.

Chris didn't seem to hear me. 'Angela . . . I love you. If I survive, will you marry me?'

I could hear a siren in the background.

'Chris, who shot you?' I was desperate to find out.

His words were slurred. It sounded like he said, 'Eat' or 'Feet.'

'Chris! Chris! Talk to me.' I was begging now.

The phone went dead.

'No!' I screamed. 'No!'

THIRTEEN

I shoved my cell phone into my purse and started running. Katie grabbed my arm and stopped me before I raced out her office door.

'Where are you going?'

I was crying and talking at the same time. 'It's Chris. He's been shot. He's at Jasmine Trail. I'm going to him.'

'Angela, you can't. He'll be brought here.'

I looked at her with dazed eyes. 'Here at the morgue?' I gulped.

'No, at the hospital. Jasmine Trail is five miles away. The ambulance will be taking him to the ER. Let's go meet them. Follow me.'

'I'll go with you,' Jace said.

Jace and I followed Katie through the maze of beige corridors, the three of us running, dodging food carts, empty stretchers, and janitors cleaning the floors. Katie's white lab coat flew out behind her like a stiff cape. Various departments flashed by – radiology, MRI, medical records, human resources. I felt like I was in one of those dreams where I kept running and running and getting nowhere.

And then we turned left, and were at the emergency room. I saw the ambulance parked at the entrance. Sturdy paramedics with serious faces wheeled Chris inside on a stretcher. I caught a glimpse of his blood-covered face, an oxygen mask, an IV line and blood. Lots of blood – on his face, hair and upper body. Mike was with him.

Horrible memories of Donegan's death came flooding back. I tried to go in after Chris, but the ER guard barred my way. He was a tall, stern, dark-skinned man.

'What's your relationship to the patient, ma'am?' he asked.

'I'm his—'

His what? I thought.

'Are you his wife? His sister? A family member?' the guard asked.

'I'm his girlfriend.'

That wasn't enough to get me admitted.

'Sorry, ma'am, you have to be family.' The guard blocked the door. I wasn't Chris's wife. I wasn't his anything. I gave a thin, wailing cry.

Through the small windows in the doors, I could see the paramedics wheeling the stretcher to Room One in the far corner. The room reserved for the most difficult cases. Chris could die in there. Alone. Surrounded by tubes and machines and impersonal strangers.

Jace held me and said, 'It will be OK, Angela, you'll see.'

I was savvy enough to know this situation wasn't good. 'I've seen dead people with less blood, Jace.'

'You know head wounds bleed more,' he said. He was still puffing slightly from his run to the ER.

Katie was talking to the guard at the entrance to the ER. All trace of my friend who'd been laughing and joking at lunch was gone. Katie was serious and in command. She came back and said, 'Angela, go to the waiting room across the hall. I'll check on Chris. Jace, will you stay with her?'

'Of course,' Jace said.

The waiting room was blandly beige with uncomfortable plastic chairs, a coffee and tea counter, and a soda machine. A TV blared overhead. I reached up and pulled the plug. I wanted quiet, not talking heads.

'Can I get you something to drink?' Jace asked. 'Coffee? Tea? A bottle of water? A soda?'

'Nothing, thanks.'

I was too restless to sit. Instead, I paced the tile floor, back and forth, back and forth, then up and down, while I watched the clock. *Clack, clack, clack.* The sound of my boot soles on the polished tile. It was two thirty, and the clock's hands seemed stuck.

'Why don't you have a seat, Angela?' Jace said.

I knew I was annoying him, but I couldn't bear to stay still. I crossed and recrossed the beige tile floor until Jace took me by the shoulders and sat me down on a chair, which was harder than a bus bench. 'Please, Angela, sit. You're going to wear yourself out.'

'How long has it been since Katie went into the ER?' I asked.

'Eight minutes.' Jace patted my hand. 'She'll have news for us soon.'

I heard the hospital operator announce, 'Code blue. Code blue.' My heart thundered. That was the emergency code for patients in cardiac arrest, respiratory failure, seizures, or other life-threatening emergencies.

'That's Chris! He's dying,' I said. 'Jace, he's dying.'

Jace's voice was soothing. 'Chris isn't dying, Angela, and that code wasn't for him. You missed the sentence that said, 'Report to the ICU. Listen.'

I relaxed and heard the operator say, 'Code blue. Report to the ICU. Code blue to the ICU.'

I took a long, shaky breath. Chris was alive. For now.

I found a well-thumbed *People* magazine from 2021 and read the ancient celebrity news. Singer Jesse McCartney married actress Katie Peterson, and their dog was the flower girl. Jennifer Lopez and Alex Rodriguez officially called off their engagement and J-Lo was back with Ben Affleck. And Meghan Markle and Prince Harry announced they were expecting their second baby.

There was something comforting about reading these old stories. I knew that Jennifer would marry Ben, Katie and McCartney were still married, and Meghan and Harry had a healthy baby girl. They were proof there were happy endings.

But what about Chris? Would he survive? Would we have a happy ending?

Finally, after an agonizing half hour, Katie came charging back to the waiting room.

I jumped up to meet her. 'How is he?'

'He's in surgery. Sit down, Angela.'

I didn't want to, but Katie's voice was a command. She softened her voice and took my hand. 'Chris has a perforating wound. In other words, the bullet entered and exited the cranium.'

'He has a what?' Jace asked.

'A gunshot wound to the head,' Katie said.

'No!' That was me. I was shaking.

'It's not as bad as it sounds,' Katie said. 'The wound is on the right side. The bullet entered his forehead, stayed high and exited in back. The wound is survivable.'

'How survivable?' Jace asked.

Thanks to my job, I knew the answer to his question, and wished I didn't.

In a shaky voice I gulped back tears and said, 'Not very. Ninety percent of the time, gunshot wounds to the head are fatal. Many people die before they even get to the hospital.'

'But Chris is alive,' Katie said. 'He's strong, Angela. He's going to make it.'

'Maybe. He *may* make it. But I know too much, Katie. I know what his chances are. Half the people who survive the gunshot wound at the scene die in the ER.'

'But he's not dead,' Jace said. 'Chris is alive. That's good.'

I refused to accept this, and dredged up more grim facts. 'Chris may wish he was dead,' I said. 'There's a fifty percent chance that he'll have seizures and need epilepsy medication. He'll also need long-term rehab. He may never be the same again.' My tears started falling and I couldn't stop them.

'That's enough, Angela.' Katie's brown eyes flashed. 'Don't go borrowing trouble. We all know perfectly healthy people who keeled over walking down the street. Here's what you have to remember. Chris is alive. He was shot in the head, but he has the best kind of bullet wound, if there is such a thing. His bullet went up – through the tip of the right frontal lobe. It will probably cause fairly mild damage, because it didn't pass through any vital brain tissue or vascular structure.'

I could almost hear the 'so there' in Katie's voice. She kept talking, trying to give me hope.

'If the bullet had gone down instead of up, the damage would have been terrible. But it didn't. Yes, Chris may have seizures, but millions of people live with them. As for Chris going back to work, how do you even know that he will want to go back? Maybe he's through with policing.

'Stop the gloom and doom, Angela. Chris needs you. You had a traumatic brain injury when you had six strokes a couple of years ago. Whether you marry him or not, you know what he's going through.'

She was right. I did. And I'd only recovered thanks to the help of my friends. Especially Katie. Now Chris needed help.

It was time to pay it back.

FOURTEEN

I sat in the emergency waiting room, staring at a poster on the wall called 'How to Properly Wash Your Hands,' as if it contained the secrets of the universe. In truth, I barely saw it. I was thinking about what Katie said, that Chris's brain injuries might be similar to my strokes, and I could help him. After a series of blinding headaches, I'd wound up in the hospital needing emergency brain surgery. I was in a coma and my recovery took months. Katie and other good friends got me through this dark time.

Would I take care of Chris while he recovered?

Yes.

Would I help him through the hurdles? If his injury was like mine, he'd have to fight crippling depression, as well as his physical disabilities.

Yes, I'd do that.

Did I love him?

Of course.

'Angela.' Katie waved her hand in front of me. 'Are you in there?'

'Yes. Sorry.'

'Let's go upstairs to the surgical waiting room,' she said. 'It's more comfortable and we can follow Chris's progress in real time.'

In the elevator to the third floor, I stood between Katie and Jace as if I was in their custody.

Katie was right. The surgical waiting room was way better. The vast room had recently been redecorated and painted a pleasant blue. Dividers filled with greenery separated the room into a maze of different zones: work zones for people with computers, talking zones for families who wanted to chat, and TV-watching areas. The chairs looked soft and well-padded.

Mrs Porter, a sweet-faced, grandmotherly woman, met us at the door. Katie introduced me as Chris's fiancée: a title I was too dumb, or too flustered, to give myself.

Mrs Porter gave me a number – fifty-one – on a slip of paper and said we could keep track of Chris's surgery on the big TV screen on the main wall. The screen was divided into several colored zones: Pink for 'pre-op,' purple for 'in surgery' and green for 'recovery.' Chris's number was in the purple section.

'When your fiancé is ready for you to see, Ms Richman, I'll announce your number,' Mrs Porter said. She nodded toward two small rooms in the corner. 'Also, the surgeon may come out and speak to you in one of the private consultation rooms. May I bring you coffee or tea, dear?'

'No, thank you.' There. I'd managed three coherent words to a stranger.

'You let me know if there's anything I can do for you,' Mrs Porter said.

Katie steered me to a conversation area, and promised to come back. Jace went with her. While I waited, I listened to bits of worried conversation, and felt like I was eavesdropping on people's private thoughts:

'Should Grandma's gall bladder surgery take this long?'

'How long does it take to remove hemorrhoids? Bill's been in there for hours.'

'I'm worried about Aunt Carol. Is she strong enough to survive this surgery? She's seventy-eight and not in the best of health.'

Katie returned with a steaming cup of coffee and a chocolate bar. 'Drink,' she said.

I took a sip and made a face. 'It's loaded with sugar.' I drank my coffee black.

'That's right. You're in shock. You need the sugar. Drink.'

I obeyed, though the coffee was so sweet the spoon could almost stand up in the cup.

'Now, eat the candy bar.'

I did, and began to feel a little better. Well enough to ask Jace a question. 'Do you know who called the ambulance for Chris?'

'Mike,' he said. A patrol officer I liked and trusted. 'Chris wasn't answering dispatch. The GPS said Chris's car was on Jasmine Trail. Chris's bod— uh, I mean Chris – was on the ground on the passenger side. He was shot in the head. Mike called for an ambulance. He said Chris was talking on his cell phone after he was shot.'

'To me,' I said. 'I think I was the last person to talk to Chris.'

'Mike will be here soon to get a statement from you.'

'Is Mike taking Chris's case?'

'Mike and I both are,' Jace said. 'On a larger force I couldn't do that since I work with you on a regular basis. But the other choice is Ray Greiman. Since I'm a crimes against persons detective, the chief said I could handle Chris's shooting. Someone with Mike's experience is just who I need.'

'Ray Greiman,' I said. 'The chief's fair-haired boy.'

'Hare-brained is more like it,' Katie said. 'Greiman is the man who nearly let the chief's mechanic go free because he was the only person who could fix Buttkiss's Mercedes. If Nitpicker and Angela hadn't insisted Greiman look at the evidence that killer would have walked away.'

'And don't forget when Greiman tried to railroad an innocent Latina because she was the obvious suspect,' I said. 'We could spend the rest of the day going on about how bad Greiman is.'

'Let's not,' Katie said. 'Greiman is a waste of breath.'

For the next fifteen minutes, I stared at the TV screen, where Chris's number fifty-one stayed stubbornly in the surgical section, refusing to move. I didn't talk to Katie or Jace. I felt so tired.

Then Chris's number jumped to the recovery section. 'Look, Katie, Chris is in recovery. Can we see him now?'

'Not yet, Angela. It may be awhile before you're called. Still, it's good news.'

Jace's phone rang, and he took the call in the hallway, then came back. 'That was Mike. Are you up to talking with him?' he asked.

'Yes. Anything to help.'

'Mrs Porter says we can use one of the consultation rooms. Katie and I will sit in with you.'

The room was barely big enough for the four of us, especially since Jace was a big guy and Mike was hefty. The glass door made the room less claustrophobic, and I could watch the TV screen with Chris's number on it, glowing in the green recovery section.

'Angela,' Mike said. 'We need your help to find out who tried to hurt Chris.' The veteran cop's kind eyes and gentle voice reassured me.

'First, how is Chris?' he asked.

'He's in recovery now,' Katie said.

'Is his condition good or bad?' Mike asked.

I shifted uneasily. I'd been wondering the same thing.

Katie patted my hand and said, 'We don't know yet, Mike.'

'You found Chris,' I asked Mike. 'Was he supposed to be on Jasmine Trail?'

'It's not in his regular patrol area,' Mike said. 'He didn't tell dispatch he was there and it took ten minutes before they called me to check. When I got there, his head was bleeding, and he was talking on his cell phone. I called for an ambulance, then dug my first aid kit out of my car and put a trauma dressing on his wound. Chris could barely talk. I heard the ambulance siren and went out into the road to wave it down. When I got back and asked him who did this, Chris said something that sounded like "peach Jell-O." Does he like peach Jell-O?'

'I don't think so,' I said. 'I've never known him to eat it.' I didn't add that Chris was a foodie and probably wouldn't touch the stuff.

'Maybe his mom used to make it for him,' I said. 'He said something like "eat" or "feet" when I asked who shot him. His words were slurred and I couldn't make out what he was saying. Shortly after that he fainted. Were there any other calls on his phone?'

'Just the usual work numbers and your number, Angela. Oh, and one more. He had a text asking him to go to Number Ten Jasmine Trail and pull over by the white fence. The text number belonged to a burner phone.'

'Did you ping the phone to get a location?' I asked.

'Not yet,' Mike said, 'but we will.'

'None of this makes sense,' I said. 'Why would Chris be on Jasmine Trail, out in the country? And who would want to shoot him? I didn't think he had any enemies who wanted him dead.'

'What did Chris say to you?' Mike asked. 'Besides mentioning "eat" or whatever he was trying to say.'

I felt my heart stutter. Could I say this? I took a deep breath and started, 'Chris said that he'd been shot and he loved me. He said – he said – he might not make it.' I was crying and I didn't want to. I tried to gulp back the tears as my words rushed out. 'He said if he survived he wanted to marry me.'

It was too much. Salt tears ran down my cheeks and I tasted their bitterness. I didn't get a chance to tell Chris yes. I wished I'd told him yes. Now, with all my heart, I wanted to marry Chris. I didn't care how sick he was. I loved him. And it might be too late to tell him.

Katie took me in her arms and let me cry on her shoulder. Despite her tough exterior, she was a good friend and surprisingly softhearted. She rocked me and said, 'Shh, Angela. It's going to be OK. Go ahead and cry. Chris will be OK.'

'How do you know, Katie?'

'I'm a doctor.'

I sat up and dried my eyes with the handkerchief Jace handed me. I realized he and Mike looked uncomfortable.

'I'm sorry, gentlemen.'

'That's OK,' Jace said. 'You've got good reason to cry. Do you think you can answer some more questions?'

'Yes,' I said.

'Good,' Jace said. 'Does Chris have any enemies?'

'No,' I said. 'Not that I know of.'

'What about his ex-wife?' Mike was asking the questions now.

'She moved away. I think she's living in Hawaii now. So far as I know she's never contacted him since they sold their house after the divorce.'

'Does Chris gamble?'

'No.' I shook my head.

'Owe anyone major money?'

'I've never seen his bank account, but he's never seemed worried about money. He told me he owned his condo free and clear. He bought it with the proceeds from his house sale.'

'Has anyone he arrested ever threatened him?'

Again, I said no.

'I'm sorry to ask this, Angela.' Mike spoke slowly. 'Has Chris given you any reason to be jealous? Is he cheating on you?'

Now I was furious. 'You think I shot Chris? I was with Jace and Katie when I got the phone call.'

'You could have hired someone,' Mike said.

Red rage burned through me. 'A hit man? You think I hired a hit man? With my luck I'd ask an undercover cop. I can't believe you asked that question. And for the record, Chris is not a gambler or a cheater. He wants to marry me. What's wrong with you two?'

Jace and Mike both looked uncomfortable. Jace said, 'Angela, Angela, we have to ask these questions. You know that. I'm sorry they upset you, but we're doing everything we can to find out who hurt Chris.'

I calmed down enough to understand they were right. 'I'm sorry. I know you're doing your job. It hurts to hear you ask those questions.'

'We have just a few more questions, Angela.' Mike was treating me as if I was a fragile piece of china.

The next questions were easy. When was the last time I saw

Chris? The last time I talked to him, besides today's phone call? Did Chris seem worried about anything? Distracted?

I answered those questions easily. Then I heard my number being called. 'Number fifty-one. Number fifty-one. Please come to the desk.'

'That's Chris,' I said. 'He's in recovery and I can see him.'

'Terrific news.' Mike stood up. 'I'll spread the word. About half the force is milling around downstairs in the ER waiting room, drinking coffee.'

I was touched. 'They care about Chris that much?'

'They do. And it's an excuse to dodge work, flirt with nurses and get free coffee,' Jace said.

'Come on, Angela,' Katie said. 'Let's go see Chris.'

FIFTEEN

I pasted a smile on my face, and told myself no matter how bad Chris looked, I would remain cheerful and encouraging. I'd recovered from a serious brain injury, and he could, too.

Except I didn't see Chris. At the waiting room's reception desk, a tall, thin man in green scrubs greeted me. 'Ms Richman, I understand that you're Officer Christopher Ferretti's fiancée.'

'Yes,' I said.

'I'm his neurosurgeon, Dr Harry Hallen. Let's go in the consultation room and discuss Officer Ferretti's progress.'

Katie squeezed my hand and said, 'I'm the assistant medical examiner and a friend of Ms Richman. I'm here with her.'

'I know who you are, Dr Stern,' the surgeon said. 'Fortunately, I haven't had much contact with you.'

I couldn't tell if the two liked each other or not.

As the surgeon opened the consultation room door, I noticed his long, beautiful fingers. Also, it finally registered in my sluggish brain that he was wearing a scrub cap covered in grinning skulls. Now I couldn't take my eyes off those skulls.

As we sat down, the surgeon noticed me staring at his cap.

'Don't be alarmed by my skull cap, Ms Richman.' He laughed at his feeble joke. 'I collect caps and people like to give them to me. I have an extensive collection – tie-dyed caps, some with flames, stars, and sharks. As it gets closer to Christmas, I'll wear my holiday caps.'

'OK,' I said. I knew surgeons, especially brain surgeons, had giant egos and eccentric tastes.

'Call me Angela,' I said. 'How is Chris? Where is he? Is he still in Recovery?'

'He came through surgery just fine. The bullet trajectory was such that it did the least amount of harm.'

'That's good,' I said. 'Right?' I was gripping my chair arms so hard my knuckles were white.

'Right. But we discovered a small issue in Recovery.'

My heart was thudding and my voice trembled. 'What kind of

"small issue"? There are no small issues in brain surgery, Doctor. Tell me what's going on. This is torture when you draw it out.'

Katie jumped in. 'Angela is a Chouteau County death investigator, Dr Hallen. She's familiar with most medical terms, so you can talk to her.'

'The news I have is difficult for even medical people to absorb,' he said.

I wanted to slap the surgeon's pompous face, but I hung on to my chair.

Not Katie. She pounded her chair arm. 'We'd both like to know what the hell is going on. With no pussyfooting.' Ah, that was the Katie I knew and loved. Smart and angry.

'I was trying to break it to Angela gently,' Dr Hallen said.

'This is your idea of gentle?' I said. 'This is death by a thousand cuts. And the cuts weren't made with a scalpel, either.' My restraint snapped. 'Tell me what's going on! Now!'

'Officer Ferretti did not wake up in Recovery.'

My heart dropped. I couldn't breathe. Katie took over. 'Is he in a coma?'

Coma. That four-letter word chilled me.

The surgeon was still waffling. 'We're not sure. We've moved him to the ICU and we'll know more over the next several hours.'

We, I thought, as in the royal we. Unless he had a mouse in his pocket.

'Is he on a ventilator?' Katie asked.

'Yes, we felt that was necessary.'

'Does he have a drain in his head?' Katie asked.

'No.'

'What caliber bullet was he shot with? A twenty-two, a forty-five, a thirty-eight?'

'We don't know,' the surgeon said. 'We didn't recover anything, since it was a through-and-through wound. But a thirty-eight would be a safe guess.'

'So what's next?' I asked.

'We'll continue to monitor him. He could wake up and be just fine. If he is in a coma, he could stay in it for days or weeks or—'

Katie cut him off before he could say 'years.' 'What happens if it's long term?' she asked.

'Officer Ferretti is young and strong and healthy,' the surgeon said, 'and he could wake up with no damage. But the longer he's in the coma, the less likely his chances for full recovery.'

I stood up on shaky legs.

'I want to see Chris.'

'He's in the ICU, Angela,' the surgeon said. 'You can only visit him for ten minutes every hour.'

'I want to see him.' My voice was stronger, powered by fear. 'I want to go now.'

'I'll take Angela.' Katie stood up with me. 'Let's go.'

I followed her out of the surgery waiting room and down the hall to the ICU at the other end of the floor. We walked briskly, dodging patients in wheelchairs, impatient families waiting for elevators, and hulking food carts loaded with trays.

'Is it dinnertime already?' I asked.

'It's five o'clock,' Katie said.

Once we cleared the high traffic area, I asked, 'Is this Dr Hallen any good?'

'Yes. Chris was lucky to get him. If I ever need neurosurgery, he's the man I'd choose. But he's such a jackass, I only want to deal with him if I'm under anesthesia. His so-called skull cap is just one example of his bedside manner. But if you want someone to save Chris's life, he's the man.'

'That's good, I guess.'

Katie used her hospital keycard to open the ICU doors and said, 'Let me handle this, Angela.'

She told the duty nurse we were there for Chris. 'He's in Room one B, across the hall,' the nurse said. 'Visits are limited to ten minutes every hour.'

'OK, Angela,' Katie said. 'Prepare yourself. A patient just out of brain surgery is not pretty. Be brave.'

I thought I was brave. I thought my work as a death investigator had prepared me for every awful scene. I'd dealt with decapitations, rotting corpses, and auto accidents that turned humans into horror shows.

But nothing prepared me for the sight of Chris in that bed, in a coma.

He seemed smaller, and paper white. IV lines were taped to the back of his hand, and led to a metal tree hung with clear bags of medicine. Tubes and wires snaked away from his body. His thick brown hair was shaved on the side of the surgery, and the wound was red and raw. The rest of his hair was matted. His face was red, swollen and bruised. Machines beeped and whirred.

Worst of all, the ventilator mask was strapped on his face. The breathing machine made a horrible whooshing sound.

Except for the machines, Chris was still and silent as a marble figure on a tomb.

I looked at him and whimpered. I couldn't help it.

'Chris is fine, Angela,' Katie said. 'He's supposed to look like this.'

'But his face is so swollen and distorted.'

'The surgery and the drugs did that. You looked much worse, and you're fine now.'

I sat in the chair next to his bed and held his hand. 'Chris,' I said, softly. 'It's me, Angela. I love you. I want to marry you. Until then, I will be here and help you get well. Please, Chris. Get well. And wake up. Please?'

I kissed his cold forehead.

The nurse was back. 'Your time is up, Ms Richman.'

Outside the ICU, I said, 'Katie, can I stay in Chris's room tonight?'

'I've got some pull, Angela, but I can't overrule ICU edicts. No long-term visitors in the room. It's for Chris's safety. If there's an emergency, the staff can't waste time shooing you out.'

'But what if Chris wakes up? Or something goes wrong?'

'The best I can promise is you can crash in my friend Dr George Miller's sleep room. He owes me.'

'Oh, thank you.'

'Don't thank me yet. The SOS sleep rooms make monks' cells look like the Ritz. I'll call and clear it with him.'

Katie went to a cell phone area to make her call and soon came back. 'All clear. I'll give you the numbers to unlock the door.'

She showed me the room, which had a wobbly brown nightstand and an old hospital bed with the head slightly raised. 'It's permanently stuck in that position,' Katie said. The bed had a thin pillow and a thinner hospital blanket.

'There's a patient welcome kit with a toothbrush, toothpaste, soap, washcloth and comb in the nightstand. And you can sleep in this lovely hospital gown.' Katie held up a patient gown, the kind that left the patient's rear end exposed.

'This room is good, Katie.'

'If I leave now, will you be OK?'

'I'll be fine,' I said.
'Promise me you'll eat dinner in the cafeteria.'
'You're asking a lot,' I said.
She gave me the evil eye, and I said, 'I promise, Katie.'
'I'll tell the nurses what you're doing. Now try to get some sleep.'

I visited Chris twice more that evening before I went to the SOS cafeteria. I ate the special, but had no idea what it was. For all I knew, it was cardboard cordon bleu. Considering the hospital cafeteria's reputation, it could have been.

Each time I told Chris I loved him and prayed for him to wake up. I didn't get so much as the flicker of an eyelash.

At 8:05 p.m. the night nurse caught me leaving Chris's room and said, 'Why don't you try to get some sleep, honey? Give me your cell phone number, and I'll call you if there's any change, good or bad.'

I unlocked the sleep room, and rested my eyes. I woke up at two thirty a.m. in a panic, wondering where I was. Then I remembered. The horrors of yesterday came crashing down on me. I couldn't sleep. I slipped out to check on Chris.

The night nurse felt sorry for me and bent the rules so I could go in and see him for five minutes.

He was still in the coma. Once again, I told Chris how much I loved him and begged him to please wake up. Once again, there was no response.

By then I was so tired I could hardly sit up. I went to sleep, not bothering to change into the hospital gown.

At seven thirty that morning, Katie unlocked my door and woke me up. 'I brought you breakfast.' She handed me an insulated lunch bag. 'I made the egg sandwich myself and there's a Thermos of hot coffee.'

'Thanks,' I said. 'I didn't want to drink the hospital dishwater.'
'Nobody does.'
'How's Chris?' I asked.

'I checked on him and then checked with the nurses. He's definitely in a coma, but he's doing well. There's no swelling in his brain, and that's good news.'

'If he's doing so well, why doesn't he wake up?'

'We don't know, Angela. The three pounds of brain are complex, and we still don't know how they work. I can tell you the vital parts – the midbrain, the pons, which has four of the twelve cranial nerves, and the brain stem – were not harmed. Chris will wake up when he's ready,' Katie said.

'What should I do while he's in the coma?'

'Talk to him. Tell him you love him. Hold his hand. Read to him. Does he have a favorite author?'

'Lots of them, but he likes Joseph Wambaugh, because he used to be a real cop and he gets the details right.'

'Then read him Wambaugh.'

'For ten minutes at a time?'

'Yes. He may or may not be able to hear you, but some part of his brain may recognize your voice and find it soothing.'

'Then that's what I'll do.' I stood up.

'Wait,' Katie said. 'First, you're going home to shower. Your clothes look like you slept in them. And you stink.'

'I what?'

'You stink, Angela. Fear has its own sour smell, and it overrides the best deodorant. I say this as a friend. Go home, clean up, and come back refreshed. Then read to Chris. You have to take care of yourself as well as him. I'll stay here until you return.'

'And you'll call if he wakes up?' My voice was trembling.

'Yes. Now go.' She shooed me out of the room.

SIXTEEN

The next three days were lost in the beige haze of hospital life. Katie brought me breakfast and watched Chris while I went home to shower and change.

I was impressed by the care the ICU nurses gave Chris – especially Stacey, a statuesque black woman on the day shift. I stopped by Supreme Bean for a large container of good coffee and enough cookies for the nursing staff. When a doctor tried to help himself to a cup of that coffee, the nurses shooed him away. 'Get your own coffee,' Stacey told him.

I visited Chris for ten minutes every hour, and read to him from Wambaugh's *Echoes in the Darkness*, a book I knew Chris liked.

Jace stopped by each day to check in on Chris. The detective was worried he was making no progress in the Selwyn Skipton murder. Mike came by to update me on the progress with Chris's shooting.

'I wish I had good news for you, Angela,' Mike said, 'but there's nothing. We didn't find any useful clues at the scene.'

'Did you recover any brass?' I asked.

'That's going to be difficult. The area is covered in poison oak and poison ivy. We'll have to wait till the snow melts and then wear protective suits.'

'What about footprints and tire tracks?' I asked.

'The ambulance and paramedics stomped all over them.' Mike shook his head. 'Chris's patrol car has been towed to the impound garage. The techs are taking it apart.'

'What about the call from the burner phone? Any word on its location?'

'All we can find out is the call came from downtown Chouteau Forest,' Mike said. 'That's not much help. But we'll find something, Angela. Don't you worry.'

I wanted so much to believe him.

I racked my brains trying to come up with useful information. Why was Chris at Jasmine Trail in the middle of nowhere? Had he ever mentioned it before? Did anyone he'd arrested threaten him?

Could the burner phone belong to a CI, a confidential informant? So far as I knew, Chris didn't have any.

Cops stopped by for short visits with Chris, usually two at a time. Some stood awkwardly around his bed, listening to the hissing, beeping machines and, I suspected, seeing their own mortality.

I went back for more bland cafeteria meals and hopeless sessions by Chris's bed.

On the fourth day, Katie blew up my new routine, bursting into my borrowed sleep room at seven in the morning and shaking me awake. 'Angela! Wake up! The soup has hit the fan.'

'The soup?' I was groggy after two hours of sleep.

'You know what I mean,' Katie said. 'I'm trying to clean up my language.'

Katie fulminated four-letter words, until her lover Monty had asked her to tone down her language. Now she found inventive ways to express herself.

Katie stood over my bed and glared at me. 'Here, take a look at this.'

She plopped a fat tabloid on the nightstand, sending it rocking. 'That's today's issue of the *National Scandal*. Our shame is now coast to coast.'

The *National Scandal* was one of the scaliest tabloids on the newsstand. It made the *National Enquirer* look like the *New York Times*. Readers loved its smutty stories.

I reached for the paper and saw these headlines screaming from the front page:

Hijinks in the Heartland.
Selwyn Skipton, pillar of Chouteau Forest, Missouri, kept secret bower of bliss stocked with champagne, chocolate, and lusty paintings.
Local bigwig murdered after romp on black satin sheets.
Decor was a mix of gentility and genitalia . . .

At the top of the page, a portrait of Selwyn frowned down disapprovingly at the main color photo on the front: the living room part of his apartment with the Courbet painting, *Nude Reclining Woman*.

I quickly skimmed the salacious story, lighting on choice phrases, including this one: 'Skipton's love nest turned into a hornet's nest when he was murdered on a mattress as big as a bedroom.'

Nine feet square was a bit small for a bedroom, I thought, but kept reading.

'Apparently Mrs Skipton didn't know about her horny hubby's hidden hobby, and says the room must be a mistake. The police remain as clueless as his widow.'

'Poor Jace,' I said. 'I bet the chief is livid.'

'Livid doesn't begin to describe it,' Katie said. 'I thought the chief's head would explode. The whole town is up in arms. One of their own has been attacked.'

'Worse, he's being laughed at,' I said. The elite was notoriously thin-skinned.

Katie handed me a cup of coffee and sat on the edge of the bed. 'Wait till you hear the rest of it. Our esteemed boss, Evarts Evans – the human hemorrhoid – has delegated me to tell you that you have to go back on call again as a death investigator.'

'He what?' I was outraged. 'Doesn't that jerk know that Chris is in the hospital?'

'He certainly does. Evarts said – and I quote – he "couldn't support you spending so much time at the hospital because you and Chris are living in sin."'

'What century is this?' I said.

'As far as I'm concerned, the bat fastard can take a flying leap,' Katie said. 'Monty says he'll be happy to sue Evarts's socks off.'

'Maybe later,' I said. 'Right now I want to keep my connection with the police while we look for whoever tried to kill Chris.'

'Eat your breakfast,' Katie said, handing me an egg sandwich.

'You know this is the only good food I get all day,' I said. 'Thanks for making time for me.'

'Mm.' Katie was checking a text on her phone.

'What else is wrong?' I said. 'You're holding back. What is it?'

'It's Jace. He has something to tell you. He's in the building and will be right up.'

Anxiety twisted my stomach. 'Is it bad? I hate surprises.' I also hated sounding so whiny, but this had been a rough couple of days.

'It's not really that bad,' Katie said. 'But he has to tell you. Why don't you wash up before he gets here?'

I shined myself up in the bathroom down the hall, even adding lipstick. By the time I returned, Jace was in my sleep room, and it was definitely crowded. 'Let's go to the family lounge down the hall,' Katie said.

I doubted if anyone could lounge in that room. The small couch and two boxy chairs looked uncomfortable, and the single end table was decorated with nicks and scratches. On the TV, blow-dried talking heads were babbling. I reached up and unplugged the boob tube.

Katie and Jace waited until I settled down. Now that I had a chance to study him, Jace looked worried. His hair was mussed and he had dark bags under his eyes.

'You saw that tabloid story,' he said.

'It was pure trash,' I said.

'Trash everyone in the Forest is taking seriously. Trash that will come crashing down on my head if I don't solve Selwyn Skipton's murder. That's why the chief still wants you to help me on this.'

'OK.'

'No!' He added quickly, 'You don't have to, Angela. I can say you're helping me and you can stay right here with Chris. No one will know. I'll work on my own.'

'No, I'll help,' I said. 'Bring me the boxes of those store receipts and I'll go through them. I can do that while I stay with Chris.'

'You know there are four bankers boxes of receipts. And each of those boxes is one foot square.'

'I know what a bankers box is and how much it holds,' I said. 'I'm still volunteering. It will give me something to do while I wait to see Chris.'

Jace looked relieved. 'That would be a huge help. I'll bring them around this afternoon.'

I started to stand up, but Katie said, 'There's one more thing. I know you don't want to leave Chris alone. If you have to leave to work a case, one of us will stay here with him. Monty and I will work out a schedule. Jinny Gender, Monty's office manager, has volunteered, too. If there's any change, good or bad, we'll call you.'

'That's so kind.' I felt tears filling my eyes and tried not to cry. Katie pulled a handful of tissues out of the box on the table and said, 'Go ahead and cry. It's good for you.'

'I'm fine.' I stubbornly wiped my eyes and refused to break down.

Katie and Jace walked me to the ICU and left. I spent the next ten minutes with Chris, holding his hand while I read to him. I looked for some kind of change, but he was exactly the same.

I walked around the hospital until the next hour rolled around, when I found two uniforms, Pete and Scott, waiting by the ICU. Pete looked as uneasy as a guilty schoolboy.

'Hi, Angela, is it OK if we go in and see Chris?' He looked at his shoes as he asked.

'You can, but Chris is still in a coma.'

'We know that,' Pete said, 'and the nurse said it would take away from your time, but maybe someone different talking to Chris will help him wake up.'

'It's not a bad idea,' I said. 'I'll go down the hall to the nurses' lounge and get a cup of coffee.'

The ICU nurses' lounge had fairly decent coffee and Stacey gave me special privileges since I'd brought coffee and cookies for the staff.

I was in the lounge filling a mug with coffee when I heard a loud, blaring alarm and running feet. What room was that coming from?

I stuck my head out the door and saw Nurse Stacey running for Chris's room.

'No!' I left the mug on the counter and raced down the hall to Chris.

I met Stacey coming out of Chris's room.

'What's wrong?'

'It's OK, honey.' She patted my hand. 'Chris is OK. His ventilator was unplugged. Officer Scott said he must have accidentally stepped on the cord.'

'I'm really sorry, Angela,' Scott said. 'I didn't mean to scare everyone.'

'No problem,' Stacey said. 'It happens.' She smiled at Pete and Scott.

Pete edged toward the door, saying, 'We'd better leave. We've caused enough trouble. Sorry to upset you.'

'Think nothing of it,' Stacey said.

But I thought about it – a lot. Chris had had several visitors and none of them unplugged the ventilator. Was someone still trying to kill Chris? Mike said the burner phone call came from downtown. Too much was there: shops, restaurants, office buildings, the jail and police station. Were the cops involved?

I didn't believe Chris's ventilator was accidentally unplugged. Did Scott or Pete yank it out of the wall? Or let in someone who did?

SEVENTEEN

Despite Stacey's claim that Chris's ventilator could be unplugged by accident, I wasn't reassured. The ventilator was plugged into the row of outlets over his bed, and the excess cord dangled behind the headboard. Yes, the cord was on the floor, but to step on it, a person would have to move the machine. I was convinced someone deliberately pulled that plug out. This was another murder attempt.

Suddenly I was so frightened, I could hardly breathe. I called Katie. She didn't answer, and I left her a frantic message.

Jace texted me at noon that he was on his way with the boxes. Twenty minutes later, I met him at the elevator by my sleep room. He had all four boxes strapped to an enormous dolly.

'Where do you want these, Angela?'

'In my sleep room. The door locks, so there's no chain of custody problem.'

Jace followed me down the hall, the wheels on the dolly squeaking. I unlocked the door and he stacked the boxes inside. The sealed boxes overwhelmed the cramped room.

'There's barely space to move,' he said.

'It's OK. Do you want me to organize these receipts?' I asked.

'No, just photograph each box, then photograph it again when you open it. I gotta tell you, Angela, most of this stuff is junk. If you do find anything useful, photograph it and put it in a bag. Then call me.'

He gave me a stack of evidence bags. 'Not a problem.' I didn't add that Jace was being overly optimistic. I'd be lucky if I used one bag.

'Oh, and would you wear gloves?'

'I was going to do that.'

Jace produced a foam container. 'I brought you a present.'

I eyed the big white box. 'Wrong color to be from Tiffany's.'

I lifted the lid. 'My favorite. A turkey club with avocado. And the turkey is real, not that processed stuff. Where did you get it?'

'New deli just opened. But wait, there's more.' Jace presented me with a large cup of hot coffee and a giant chocolate chip cookie.

I batted my eyes and clasped my hands like an old-time movie heroine. 'My hero. You saved me from another cafeteria lunch. Seriously, Jace, thank you.'

'You're welcome. Call me if you find anything.'

First, I sipped coffee and demolished my club sandwich. It tasted as good as it looked. Then I found my point-and-shoot camera in my DI case, which I'd stashed under the bed.

I photographed the first bankers box from several angles, then again after I broke the seal and opened the box. I pulled out a fat handful of assorted papers. What a mess.

On top was a stack of old dry-cleaning receipts. Next, a lunch order for two tuna sandwiches on sourdough bread and a turkey wrap with no mayo. Business cards held together with a rubber band. A supermarket ad circular for June. A UPS shipping receipt. A candy wrapper. Junk mail for new credit cards. There was more, much more, but it really did feel like 'proprietress' Helena Stone had dumped a waste can into the box. Finally, I hit pay dirt – a big clump of receipts. The shop used old-school receipts, with the buyer's name and address handwritten at the top.

These receipts were from October, which was outside our targeted time period. I rummaged through them anyway – and soon saw why Helena didn't want us nosing around in her store's business.

One was a receipt for $689.75. Hale Lambert, the duty judge Jace regarded as a pain in the neck, had bought frilly lingerie in extra-extra-large sizes. I knew his young wife was stick-thin. She would swim in those sizes, and his mother and mother-in-law were dead. Was His Honor exploring his sexuality? I kept that receipt to show Jace.

A quick check of my cell phone told me it was time to visit Chris. I sat by his bedside again, holding his hand and reading to him. There was no change. At the end of my visit, I kissed him, and took a walk down the hall to stretch my legs. Then I went back to work.

The second box also had nothing useful for Jace, but I found more Forest secrets. A prominent attorney bought a lacy black size-two bustier – and I knew his generously proportioned wife was at least a size sixteen. Was the skimpy lingerie for a girlfriend? It wasn't the sort of thing he'd buy for his daughter.

A snooty matron paid three hundred dollars for four pairs of incontinence underwear. I wouldn't show that receipt to anyone, but I'd remember it next time she looked down her long nose at me.

By the time I'd finished the second box, it was time to visit Chris again. I held his hand while I read to him, and begged him to wake up. Nothing. No answer. Nobody was home. The only sounds were the soft beeps of the machines and the inhuman hiss of the ventilator.

I went back to my room, feeling discouraged, and found Katie waiting for me. On the wobbly table was a vase filled with colorful Gerbera daisies. 'Did you bring those?' I asked.

'I thought the room, and you, could use some cheering up,' she said.

I moved the third unopened box off the bed, and we used the bed as a couch.

'You sounded frantic when you called,' Katie said. 'Are you OK?'

'No.' I told her about Chris's unplugged ventilator cord. 'Stacey said not to worry about it, but I think someone pulled that cord on purpose.'

'Stacey's a good nurse,' Katie said. 'Why would you doubt her?'

'She's a little too flirtatious with the cops.'

'So what? She's not some feather-headed dingbat. Stacey always puts her patients first. And devices do get unplugged. People knock into an IV pole or hit an infusion pump, and cords get tangled. That's one reason why the ventilator has an alarm. And Stacey didn't waste any time – she was there immediately and fixed it. So, no harm was done.'

'But it could have happened,' I said.

'And the ceiling could fall in, or a plane could crash into the ICU wing, or the hospital could be hit by an asteroid. But it's unlikely those will happen.'

'Why won't you believe me, Katie?'

'I do believe you, but you're making yourself sick when Chris is getting top-notch care. If you're really worried, ask the nurses to call you when Chris has visitors. Then you can watch Chris yourself. In fact, let's do that now.'

I felt better with a plan. Katie and I walked to the ICU nurses' station, where Stacey was working at a computer. The station was a square area with gray Formica panels topped by a tall plastic glass barrier. Stacey saw me and came out from behind the barrier, her brown eyes concerned.

'Are you OK, hon? I know that alarm really scared you.'

'Yes, it did.'

Stacey was as cheerful as ever. 'You've got nothing to worry about. I checked Chris's vitals after you left. He was fine. The swelling is decreasing a bit and that's good news.'

'Thank you,' I said. 'Could you let me know when Chris has visitors? He doesn't have any family except me. Most of the people coming to see him are people he works with and I'd like to greet them.'

'No problem. I have your cell number.' She smiled at me. 'He'll wake up soon, Angela. Trust me.' I gulped down the lump in my throat.

Katie and I walked silently back to my room, while I fought to hold in my tears. Once inside, I lost the battle. I was crying, and I hated it.

Katie said, 'Sit down.'

She rummaged in her purse for a bottle of water, and snapped the cap open. 'Drink.'

It was a command. I sniffed back my tears and sipped the warm water. Katie glared at me. I knew I was in for a tough-love session. She spoke slowly and her voice was lightly tinged with anger.

'Angela, what's wrong?'

'Everything. I think someone is trying to hurt Chris, and I can't figure out who would do that. That's why I try to stay with him. What if something happens to me? Who's going to watch Chris?'

'I will,' Katie said. 'And Monty. And Jace. You'll both be OK. You have good friends who will take care of you. Don't forget that.'

I sniffed back my tears and started crying again. 'I'm sorry,' I said.

'There's no reason to be sorry,' Katie said. 'The man you love is in a coma. You have a job where you look at dead bodies, and most of them died horribly. If you don't let go and cry, you're going to crack. And who's going to take care of Chris then? You're a smart woman, but when it comes to taking care of yourself, you're dumber than dirt.'

I was really crying now. Hard. Katie rocked me in her arms and said, 'It's OK. It's not good to stay bottled up.'

'Once I start crying, I'm afraid I won't be able to stop.' I was still sobbing. My phone rang, and I answered with a watery, 'Hello?'

'Angela, it's Stacey. Chief Butkus is here to see Chris.'

'I'll be right out,' I said.

I blew my nose, then checked the mirror on the wall, ran a comb through my hair and put on lipstick. I told Katie, 'Buttkiss is here.'

'I noticed the waterworks dried up when you needed them to,' Katie said. 'So much for losing control. I have a small bit of good news about the Selwyn case. We got a DNA hit on one of the two hairs.'

'Who is it?'

'All I know is what I told you. Now go see Buttkiss. I'll hide in here while you talk to him. I want to stay away from that bozo.'

The last time I'd worked with the chief was a double murder case that resulted from a formal dinner. The chief had been wearing a monkey suit, and Chris had looked impossibly handsome in his tux. Don't go there, I thought. Don't think about how Chris looked that night.

I hurried down the hall, steeling myself to greet Buttkiss.

'Chief,' I said. 'How kind of you to stop by.' I pasted on a smile and hoped he wouldn't notice my red eyes.

The chief was in uniform today, and khaki was not kind to his chubby physique. He stuck out his chest and swelled up like a bullfrog.

'I just had to make sure one of my men was getting the best care.'

Four days after Chris was shot, I thought. When almost everyone else in the department had already been to see him.

Buttkiss gave me a funeral-sad smile. 'My wife sends her best wishes. I'm so sorry to hear about Officer Ferretti. Shall we go in and see him?'

He sounded like we were going to approach the casket at a funeral home. Inside the ICU room, Chris was still the same: deathly white and surrounded by hissing, beeping machinery.

'Why is his face so fat?' the chief said.

I wanted to scream, *The only fat in here is your fat head.* Instead, I parroted Katie: 'That's because of the surgery and the drugs. The swelling will go down.'

'When do you think he'll be back to work?' he asked.

'Knowing Chris, as soon as he wakes up. And the ICU nurse says that will be soon.'

'Angela,' he said, 'I'm so sorry this happened to Chris. He's a good officer and a good man. I wanted to let you know that I'm taking Detective Jace Budewitz off the case.'

'Why?'

'He needs to devote himself full-time to the Selwyn Skipton murder. That family needs closure.'

And you need the bad publicity to stop before you lose your job, I thought.

The chief grasped both my hands and said, 'Don't you worry, Angela. We'll find out who did this to Chris.' He gave me a toothy smile. 'I've put my best man on the case.'

'Your best man.' I repeated his words in a flat voice, hoping he wasn't going to name the person I feared he would.

'Yes,' he said. 'I'm putting Detective Ray Greiman on the case.'

EIGHTEEN

Back in my room, Katie reacted just the way I thought she would. 'Buttkiss gave the case to *Ray Greiman*?'
'That's what he said. Because Ray's the best man for the job.'
She tried to pace around the room, but it was too small. Instead, Katie sat on my battered bed and raged.
'Ray Greiman, protector of the Forest's fat cats,' Katie said. 'The man who believes everyone who is poor is guilty until proven innocent. The only thing Ray excels at is smooching the chief's well-padded posterior. That so-called best detective couldn't figure out how to pour water out of a boot with the directions written on the heel.'
I started laughing, interrupting Katie's tirade.
'What's so funny?'
'I wish I'd recorded those sentences for Monty. They'd be proof-positive you'd improved your speech. "Well-padded posterior" is the perfect euphemism. And my dad liked to use boot-pouring to describe someone who was dumb, but he didn't use water. The liquid was a lot less socially acceptable.'
Katie laughed, too.
'I didn't just clean up my act for Monty,' she said. 'I made one of the nuns at Sisters of Sorrow hospital blush with my language. She promised to pray for me.'
Katie's phone dinged, and she checked a text. 'Duty calls,' she said. 'I'm being summoned by Evarts.'
'Thanks for the flowers,' I said, as she ran out the door.
The colorful bouquet brightened the plain room. I went back to work, exploring the third box. This one had four months of receipts, right on top. A big clump was stuck together by something dark and sticky.
A spilled Coke? A latte?
Ick. I was glad I was wearing gloves.
I gently pried the clump apart. The receipts were all from September. Useless. I dug down into the box, until I came to receipts from the week before Selwyn was murdered.

And there it was. At long last – a receipt for a red designer sweater that originally cost $1,825.

I'd read that $2,000 sweaters were the new status symbol, right up there with pricey purses and shoes. Some fashionistas were buying hand-knit sweaters that cost $4,500. My entire wardrobe didn't cost that much, but no fashionable woman would be caught dead in my practical black DI suits and sensible lace-up shoes.

This sweater was supposedly made of genuine cashmere. Stapled to the receipt was a tag, bragging about the purity of said sweater:

> Congratulations. You are the proud owner of a 100% cashmere sweater. Cashmere comes from Mongolian goats' innermost downy layer of hair. This hair is harvested and combed to produce fine fibers. It takes one goat four years to shed enough wool to create this cashmere sweater. Enjoy the exceptional softness of this fine garment.

All that luxury, gathered from a Mongolian goat, to wind up stapled to an old goat's chest.

Enough. I went back to examining the receipt. The sweater had been marked down to $200. Stamped on the receipt was: *Final Sale – no refund, no return*.

In small, neat printing was another message:

> This V-neck sweater has a 27-inch snag below the rear neck opening. The buyer acknowledges the damage to this garment and understands that it is nonreturnable.

I couldn't read the scrawl underneath, but the buyer's name and address were perfectly readable on the receipt.

The damaged sweater had been sold to Chloe Westbrook, and her address was in the Forest: Unit 717, Peacock Luxury Apartments, 12 Peacock Way.

Gotcha!

I sealed the receipt in an evidence bag, and called Jace with the good news.

'I've found it,' I said. 'I have the name of the woman who bought the sweater.'

'A break at last,' Jace said, after I gave him the name and address. 'I'll see if she has a sheet.'

'I'll see what I can find about Chloe Westbrook online.'

Jace sounded hopeful and energized. 'I'll text you when I'm ready to come over,' he said.

I opened my iPad and started googling Chloe Westbrook. I soon found out Chloe was blonde. Was that her blonde hair left at the crime scene?

Chloe was twenty-one, and had a twin sister named Zoe. Both were seniors at Chouteau University in the Forest. The *Chouteau Forest Gazette* said Zoe won a full scholarship in engineering. The photo showed a pale, studious blonde wearing horn-rim glasses and a plain, beige dress. Zoe reminded me of those old movies where the hero removes the staid secretary's glasses to kiss her and suddenly, she's beautiful.

There was no doubt that her twin, Chloe, was beautiful. A photo of her as queen of the university's Homecoming dance showed that. Chloe had waves of golden hair and huge blue eyes. Her shoulder-baring dress accented her creamy skin and curvy figure.

Chloe was a business major at Chouteau University.

So why did Zoe live in the spartan Peterson dormitory on campus while her sister lived in luxury off campus?

My phone dinged a reminder. Time to see Chris. I brushed the dust from the box search off my black DI suit, and went to see him.

My routine was the same. I read to him, talked to him, and kissed his cold forehead. Discouraged that Chris was showing no signs of recovery, I walked slowly back to my room, where I saw Jace pacing impatiently outside the door.

Jace rushed into the room, eager to tell me what he'd found. 'Chloe is a twin,' he said. 'She's a real looker. Lives in a fancy apartment. Drives a BMW. Never been in trouble with the law. Not even a parking ticket.'

'What about her sister, Zoe?' I asked. 'She could be just as pretty. She lives in a dorm at the university. What does she drive?'

'A ten-year-old Kia.'

'Why do the twins live so differently?' I asked.

'Let's go find out,' Jace said.

I was on call that day, and Katie was on stand-by to watch Chris if I had to work. I texted her and she answered, 'I'm on my way over.'

I rolled my DI case out to my car, which freed up more space. Now I could stash the bankers boxes under my bed.

Outside, the cold air felt good. I'd been spending too much time cooped up in the hospital. Jace and I hurried to our cars, and I followed him to the Peacock Luxury Apartments, about twenty minutes away.

The setting was impressive. Turning in to a winding drive, I saw a huge antebellum style building with Corinthian columns.

We parked in visitor spots in front, and Jace said, 'Looks like *Gone With the Wind* on steroids.'

'Either that, or someone abducted a courthouse,' I said.

We walked into a lobby carpeted in peacock blue. Ferns on stands, blue couches, and a stained-glass mural of peacocks were elegant additions.

We were greeted by a smiling, red-haired receptionist. Her name tag said 'Maria.' Double computer screens showed camera views of the property, inside and out.

'We're here to see Ms Chloe Westbrook,' Jace said.

'Is she expecting you?' Maria the receptionist asked.

Jace flashed his badge and the receptionist's smile disappeared. 'Oh, my. Yes. I'll call her now.'

We heard the phone ring and ring, but no one picked up. 'Have you seen Ms Westbrook leave her apartment today?' Jace asked.

'No,' Maria said. 'I haven't seen her in several days.'

She checked a computer screen and said, 'That's her car in the garage. Also, newspapers are piled up in front of her apartment door. That's not allowed here.'

'She could be sick. Maybe we should do a welfare check on Ms Westbrook,' Jace said.

'I'll call the manager. He has a key to her apartment.'

Five minutes later a soft-faced balding man in his forties hurried out of an Employees Only door. The name tag on his navy suit read, 'William Newton.'

'How may I help you?' he asked.

Jace introduced us. We followed a worried-looking Newton to the elevator. As we got off on Chloe Westbrook's floor, an older woman with dyed black hair poked her head out of her apartment. 'Finally, Mr Newton!' she said. 'I've been complaining about those newspapers piled up by that door for days.'

'Yes, Alice.' Newton sounded tired. 'I've noted your concern. I'm going to talk to Ms Westbrook now.'

'And talk to her about the screaming, too. I can hear that all the way down the hall!'

Alice was out in the hall now, wearing toe-squeezing spike heels that looked painful, and a dress splattered with big red roses. Her hands were on her hips.

'Now you're finally going to do something about my complaints,' Alice said. 'That young woman is nothing but a prostitute, I tell you, and doesn't belong in this building. She lowers the tone.'

'Yes, Alice. I hear you.'

Alice stepped back, but kept watching us from her apartment door.

William Newton unlocked Chloe Westbrook's door. When it swung open, the unmistakable odor of death poured out. Newton turned as white as his shirt and looked like he was going to throw up.

'Stand back,' Jace warned the manager. 'Don't go in there, sir. Better yet, go downstairs.'

Newton fled down the hall, grateful to be dismissed.

'Chloe is dead,' Jace said to me. 'Or at least a young woman with a lot of blonde hair is dead.'

Alice had slipped down the hall and was standing by Jace. She said, 'What's going on, Officer? Is she dead?'

'It's detective, ma'am, and I need you to go back to your apartment, please. We'll get to you as soon as we can.'

'Good!' Alice said. 'Because I have a lot to say about that one!'

'I bet she does,' I said, as I watched Alice's retreat.

'That's good,' Jace said. 'Busybody neighbors are a gift.'

'I'm on call today,' I said. 'Should I get my DI kit?'

'Go ahead,' he said. 'I'll call this in and let the powers-that-be know what's going on.'

By the time I came back down to the lobby, a frantic William Newton was talking to an anxious knot of residents. Most were older, with gray or white hair, and I saw at least two walkers.

'Yes, ladies and gentlemen,' Newton said. 'The police are here in the building. It appears that a resident may have met with an accident.'

'An accident?' said a white-haired man. 'I heard she'd been murdered.'

'We don't know what happened,' Newton said. 'Her body has just been discovered.'

A frail white-haired woman in a pale blue pantsuit said, 'We could all be killed!'

'No, Mrs Sanders.' Newton mopped his sweating forehead with a white handkerchief. 'I don't think that's possible. I do not believe any residents are in danger. That's all I can say for now. I will inform you as I know more. Thank you.'

He scurried back into the Employees Only area.

Meanwhile, Maria the receptionist was looking decidedly more harried than when I last talked to her. She answered the phone at high-speed. A lock of red hair hung down over her eyes. Every time she hung up the phone, she brushed the hair out of her eyes. It fell right back.

I ran to my car, yanked out my DI case, and hurried upstairs. I could hear sirens. The police were arriving. Upstairs in the hall, I pulled two pairs of booties out of my case so Jace and I could cover our shoes.

Only then did I enter the apartment to see the elusive Chloe Westbrook.

Was she the woman who'd murdered Selwyn Skipton? If she was, then who killed her?

NINETEEN

The clusters of worried residents were still in the lobby, but now they were besieging poor, harried Maria. I made it upstairs with my DI case without anyone noticing. Jace ushered me inside Chloe's apartment.

'I've cleared everything with the bosses. You've been assigned this case,' he said.

I'd work this murder along with Selwyn's, but I hoped it wouldn't be as difficult.

Alice pushed her way inside the apartment. 'Ma'am,' Jace said, 'you can't go in there.'

Alice ignored him. 'That's her,' she said. 'That's Chloe Westbrook.'

'You're sure?' Jace asked.

'Yes. I'd know her anywhere. Even like that. What happened to her?'

Jace didn't answer. He stiff-armed Alice and walked her out the door. 'Come in here again, and I'll arrest you.'

Alice left, sashaying indignantly down the hall.

'Does that count as an identification?' I asked.

'Yes. We'll get dental records to confirm it, but we can consider this woman Chloe Westbrook. It will save her sister from making a formal ID.

'Now, as I was saying, Mike is on his way to keep sightseers like Alice away. A police photographer will be here shortly. Nitpicker will be working the scene.'

I heard an ungodly screech.

'What's that?'

'A parrot.' Jace nodded toward to a huge birdcage near the living room window. Inside the cage, a gray bird with bright red tail feathers was perched on a bare tree limb.

The bird screeched again.

'I think it's hungry,' Jace said. 'The water dispenser and seed dishes are empty. Help me find the parrot food until everyone gets here.'

The parrot gave another screech. The sound was like an ice pick in my ears.

'I wonder if that's the screaming Alice was complaining about,' I said.

'Let's find the food before that bird does it again.' Jace headed for the kitchen in the back of the apartment.

There were no closets in the large living room. It was furnished in subtle shades of gray with red, black and white accents, much like the parrot itself. The stylish room had a light gray couch with red and white throw pillows, a vibrant red rug, and two comfortable black chairs. A long hall led to a bedroom, again in shades of red, black and gray. Next to the bedroom was a home office. I heard Jace rummaging through the kitchen cabinets for parrot food.

Chloe was lying on her back in the living room. A heavy red pottery vase was next to her head, smashed to pieces. Pulled tightly around her neck was the black leather strap of a Kate Spade purse. Was Chloe strangled with her own purse?

I slipped on a pair of gloves, and opened the hall closet. The parrot supplies were right in front of me: bags of seed, treats, toys, cuttlebones and more.

The parrot gave another earsplitting screech.

'Found it, Jace,' I said. 'Here's the food.'

'Good thing,' he said. 'That bird is getting on my nerves.'

'I almost have some sympathy for Alice,' I said. 'Almost.'

I filled the metal seed cups, and Jace put more water in the dispenser. At last, the bird was quiet.

Mike was the first to arrive at the scene. He would keep the crime scene log. 'Man, that's some parrot,' he said.

Then he turned his attention to the blonde victim. 'That poor girl,' he said. 'She must have been pretty. What a waste.'

I wasn't sure if Mike was talking about the waste of her life or her good looks.

Todd Winter, the police videographer was next, a silent, six-foot man who seemed to blend into the scene. He nodded at us, and immediately went to work photographing the crime scene, starting with the living room.

By the time Nitpicker arrived, the videographer was working on the rest of the apartment. Mike handed the crime scene tech booties and she stepped into the living room.

I was glad to see her, even under these circumstances. Nitpicker is our best tech. A tireless worker, she made our grim job easier. Today her hair was a vivid green.

Like Mike, she talked about the parrot first. 'That bird is living in style,' she said, placing her case on the floor. 'My aunt Selma used to keep parrots. Those birds need a lot of care and attention. This owner knew what they were doing.'

Nitpicker carefully crossed the living room to study the bird. 'I think that's an African grey parrot. Sure looks like the one Aunt Selma had.'

Now her voice was soft with awe. 'Beautiful creature. A work of art. Look at the details on those feathers on its head. See the white edges on the feathers? And the white feathers around the eyes? And the strong black beak?'

'You really like that parrot,' I said.

'I'm crazy about parrots. African greys can live fifty or sixty years. The only thing I want to inherit from rich Aunt Selma is her parrot. Has this one said anything? African greys are great talkers.'

'Just screeched his head off,' Jace said.

'Must be upset,' Nitpicker said. 'These birds are smart and easily bored. Its owner has lots of toys in the cage – ropes, mirrors, ladders to climb.' She pointed to wooden shapes hanging from a string. 'Those are chew toys. This parrot may talk when it feels better. If it's attached to its owner, the bird could be traumatized by her death.'

Jace gently reminded both of us what we were doing there. 'While we're talking about a traumatic death, we should work the scene.'

Chastened, Nitpicker and I went to work. I unzipped my DI case and started taking photos – long shots, medium and close-ups – of the decedent. Then I gloved up.

Nitpicker kneeled down by the body. 'How long do you think this poor woman has been dead, Jace?' she asked.

'I'd say four or five days. The parrot was out of food and water and she took good care of it.'

'African greys can live four days without food,' Nitpicker said.

She examined the broken red pottery vase by the victim's head, photographing it in place, then began dusting the larger pieces.

'Fingerprints! Hope these are useful,' she said. 'I got fingerprints off this chunk here. There's a small amount of blood on the vase. Do you think the killer whacked Chloe on the head to knock her out, and then strangled her?'

'It's possible,' I said. 'The ME can tell us for sure. I don't see any scratch marks on Chloe's neck, so it appears she wasn't fighting for her life.' Hanging and strangulation victims will scratch themselves trying to escape death.

'I hope for her sake she was unconscious,' Nitpicker said. 'Ligature strangulation can be a long, slow death.'

'That's the same way Selwyn died,' I said. 'Think these deaths are connected?'

'That's what we need to find out,' Jace said.

Ligature strangling, or garroting, is killing someone with a cord or a wire. In this case, the killer looped a leather purse strap around the victim's neck and pulled.

Everything on the victim's body goes to the medical examiner's office. That included the purse. I asked Nitpicker to print it.

'There's a chance we may get prints off this leather,' she said. 'Let's hope the killer wasn't wearing gloves.'

Once she finished fingerprinting the purse and its strap, I spread out a clean sheet to examine its contents. I photographed the purse closed, complete with the designer logo, then opened it. The contents included a black make-up bag crammed with foundation, eyeliner, eye shadow, false eyelashes, and a bouquet of brushes.

'How did she get so much in that little make-up bag?' Nitpicker asked.

The purse also held a hairbrush, tissues, breath spray, a tampon holder with two tampons, and a plastic compact for birth control pills. After the pill case was printed and photographed, I opened it. 'She stopped taking her pills four days ago,' I said.

The last thing was a hot pink Kate Spade wallet with $1,527 in cash.

'If the killer left behind that much folding money,' Nitpicker said, 'this probably wasn't a robbery.'

There was no driver's license, just a Visa card, as well as a health insurance card and a Starbucks coffee card.

'Did you find a phone?' Jace asked.

'No such luck,' Nitpicker said. 'I'll keep looking.'

While she worked in the living room, I photographed and bagged the purse's contents, then began the death investigation.

I opened my iPad, and checked the room's temperature – seventy degrees – then photographed the thermostat, which read seventy-one degrees.

Finally, I started the Body Inspection form.

The first questions were: *Is the body fresh?* (No).

Beginning to breakdown? (Yes).

Insects present? (Yes). I used tweezers to collect insect samples.

Then I started at the decedent's head. Chloe's pale blonde hair was long and thick. Her eyes were blue, and strangulation made her eyes and tongue protrude slightly. She also had petechiae – pinpoint red spots – in the whites of her eyes and on her face.

She was wearing black yoga pants and a black sweater, and her clothing was not disturbed. Her feet were bare. There were no injuries on her hands or feet. Her nails and toe nails were painted bright red, and the nails were not chipped or broken.

I placed her hands and feet in clean paper bags and sealed them with evidence tape.

Nitpicker had moved on to the bedroom. 'Jace! Angela!' she called. 'I found something. Come in here.' We clustered around the vast bed with the black, satiny duvet.

'There's an open book on this bedspread.' She pointed to a copy of *Scaling Up Excellence: Getting to More Without Settling for Less.* On the nightstand was a bowl with some kind of brown snack and a bottle of Fiji water.

'It looks like she was reading, drinking water and eating roasted chickpeas when she suddenly stopped,' Nitpicker said. 'Was she interrupted by the killer?'

'If so, she must have known the person,' Jace said. 'She let them in. Maybe the receptionist has a record of the visitor.'

'And by the way, that's a Scandia Home duvet cover,' Nitpicker said. 'Retails for about nine hundred bucks. The pillow shams bring the price to more than a thousand dollars.'

Jace whistled.

'This woman definitely lived well for a college student,' Nitpicker said.

'We think she supplemented her income,' Jace said.

'On her back,' I said. 'She may have been a sugar baby.'

'To each her own.' Nitpicker shrugged.

I saw a pair of black ballet flats by the bed and wondered if Chloe had padded to the door barefoot.

I went back to my body inspection. Now the form asked if the decedent was wearing jewelry.

Chloe was wearing diamond stud earrings, at least a third of a carat and possibly set in platinum. I noted them as 'stud earrings with round clear stone, set in silver-colored metal.'

Around her right ankle was a silver anklet with a delicate silver bow. I listed it as a 'silver-metal anklet, brand name Tiffany & Co.' She wore no other jewelry.

I spread out a sterilized white sheet from my DI case, and Jace helped me turn the body. When Chloe was strangled, her bladder and bowels released.

Jace shook his head. We both felt sad. 'The killer stole this young woman's life and her dignity,' he said.

Chloe had a small amount of blood on the round part of the back of her head, the parietal bone. I felt the area with gloved fingers and found what felt like a depressed fracture. The skull was sunken in from the hit. Could she have survived the injury? I didn't know.

I measured and photographed the bloodstain and the injury to her head, then photographed the rest of the body. It was time to send Chloe to the morgue.

Jace helped me get her into the body bag, and I called the morgue conveyance. That black van would really send the residents into a tizzy.

'After you hand over the body,' Jace said, 'want to go with me to interview Alice?'

'If Chris is OK.' I texted Katie and she replied, *He's fine, Angela. No reason to worry.*

'Yes, I can go, Jace. Will you go with me to inform her sister?'

Death notifications were part of my job, and they could be tricky. Sometimes the family member was stoic, or collapsed into tears. A few just collapsed, and needed medical care to handle the bad news. Others tried to attack me in a classic 'kill the messenger' move. I didn't like to do this chore alone.

'Of course,' Jace said.

Nitpicker came running into the room, her green hair sticking out in all directions.

'I found the cell phone!' she said. 'It's in the nightstand drawer.'

A fancy iPhone in a red case was in the open drawer. 'It's been photographed,' Nitpicker said. 'I think you need a password or a fingerprint to unlock it.'

'Can we use Chloe's fingerprint?' I asked.

'No, she's been dead too long. Unlike what you see in the movies, dead people's fingerprints usually don't work.'

'Why not?'

'We all have a little bit of electricity running through our bodies.

The phone's sensors use that electricity. When someone dies, the electricity stops, and the sensors don't work.'

'Maybe Chloe's sister knows the password,' Nitpicker said.

'She's a twin sister,' I said. 'Too bad we can't use the twin's fingerprints to unlock the phone.'

'Even identical twins have different fingerprints,' Nitpicker said.

'Another movie trope busted,' I said.

'Reality is no fun,' Nitpicker said.

TWENTY

Chloe Westbrook left her apartment for the last time in a black chlorine-free body bag with a curved zipper and six built-in handles. The morgue attendants placed her on a gurney and were solemnly rolling her body down the hall when Alice darted out of her apartment and began photographing the body bag with her cell phone.

Jace grabbed her cell phone. 'What are you doing?' he asked.

Alice's eyes narrowed. 'I'm taking photos to show everyone in this building that the slut is gone for good. Give me my phone back.'

Jace stood in front of Alice, shielding her view. His voice was a low growl. 'No. There is no slut,' he said. 'This is a young woman dead before her time, and I'll ask you to show some respect.'

'Humph,' she said. 'I know what I know.'

'If you know so much, then we want to talk to you,' Jace said.

Alice glared at Jace and ignored me. Her dead-black dyed hair turned her aging skin yellow and emphasized every wrinkle, including the lines around her unhappy mouth.

'Come in.' It was a grudging invitation.

Judging by her living room, Alice liked flowers. In addition to the red flowers splattering her white dress, she had a pink-flowered couch, pale blue cabbage roses on her curtains and multicolored flowers rioting on her wallpaper. Silk flowers were tightly imprisoned in cut-glass vases.

The effect was more claustrophobic than cheerful.

Alice sat on her couch and coquettishly crossed her legs. 'I want my phone, Detective.' She batted her eyes at him.

'Only if you delete those photos.'

'I don't see why.'

'Out of respect for the victim's family, who haven't been informed of her death yet.'

Alice deleted the photos, and then showed Jace her phone's photo gallery to prove they were gone.

'If any photos of that body bag turn up on the internet, Alice, I'll come back and arrest you.'

Jace took out his notepad and asked Alice for her full name. She said, 'I am Alice Marvin-King. My last name is hyphenated.'

Once uncorked, the words poured out of Alice in a torrent. Like all good interviewers, Jace let her talk while he jotted notes.

'I moved in here after my husband Lawrence King died of a heart attack seven years ago. You may have heard of him. He was a prominent attorney. I have one son, Barron.

'The Peacock Apartments was an ideal place to live until *she* moved in. That woman.'

'Which woman?' Jace asked.

'Chloe Westbrook.' Alice poured real venom into those words. 'This has always been an exclusive address. She ruined everything.'

'Ms Westbrook?' Jace asked. Now he was trying to rile her.

'Yes, of course. Who else are we talking about except that lowlife whore? And don't look at me like that. I'm in my own home and I can say what I please.'

'Why do you think Ms Westbrook was engaged in prostitution?' Jace asked. 'Did she bring men back to her apartment?'

'No.'

'Did she engage in lewd behavior?'

'She wore sluttish shoes. What young people call hooker heels.'

Jace looked unimpressed. 'So she liked high heels. That doesn't say she's a hooker.'

'Oh, those shoes said it, all right. In fact, they screamed sex. She was also on that disgusting website.'

'What website, ma'am? There are lots of them.'

'It's called Dating Daddies and the women on it claim to offer companionship.'

'Nothing wrong with that,' Jace said. 'People get lonely.'

'Sex-u-al companionship,' Alice said, drawing out the first word.

'How do you know that, ma'am?' Jace's voice was mild. 'Are you on the website?'

I bit my lip. Hard.

Alice looked like she might explode. 'Of course not! I am a decent, law-abiding woman.'

'Yes, I'm sure. But I am curious. How do you know about that website?'

Alice was trembling with suppressed rage. 'My son showed me!'

'And how does Barron know? If Ms Westbrook is indeed on that site, the young women use pseudonyms and their photographs are so vague your son would have to see the women in person. Did your son ever meet Ms Westbrook for companionship?'

'Of course not. He's happily married. He found out from a friend of a friend.'

'Ah. The famous friend of a friend.'

Alice missed Jace's sarcasm.

'Let's move on,' Jace said. 'Did you have any other problems with Ms Westbrook?'

'You saw one of them today.' Alice folded her arms. 'She lets newspapers pile up outside her door for days at a time. That's strictly forbidden. I repeatedly told management, but they didn't listen.'

'Anything else?' Jace asked.

'Yes, that parrot. It screeched all the time. And I wasn't the only one who complained about the noise. She also played loud music. Once, it was so loud I knocked on her door and asked her to turn it down. She had that parrot on her arm. She said they were dancing. Then she turned up the music even louder.'

'When was the last time you saw Ms Westbrook?' Jace asked.

'Four days ago. A long-haired blonde knocked on her door. At first, I thought the woman was Chloe's twin sister. Now, that Zoe is a nice young woman. Completely different from her sister. Quiet. Well-behaved. Very studious. Then I realized the visitor wasn't Zoe.'

'How?' Jace asked.

'This woman was just a little different. She was slightly taller, maybe an inch or so, and a little heavier. But the two looked enough alike to be twins. Even had the same hair color. Chloe invited her in.'

'Do you know this woman's name?' Jace asked.

'No.'

'When did she leave?'

'I have no idea, Detective. I have better things to do than watch that woman's door. Do you have any other questions?'

'No,' Jace said.

Alice stood up. 'Then if you don't mind, Detective, I have a bridge game I must attend.'

I waited until we were outside in the parking lot before I burst out laughing. 'Jeez Louise, Jace. I could hardly keep a straight face.'

'She made me mad,' Jace said. 'Where does she get off calling Chloe Westbrook a slut?'

I didn't remind Jace that he'd dissed sugar babies like Chloe because they weren't honest prostitutes.

'I was goading her on purpose, Angela, and she gave us some good information about Chloe's last visitor. Shall we give Chloe's sister the bad news?'

'After I check on Chris.' He was always in my thoughts these days. I texted Katie and once again she assured me he was fine.

I couldn't delay any longer. We had to inform Zoe Westbrook. I followed Jace to Zoe's dorm at Chouteau University. We arrived about four in the afternoon and parked in the visitor lot.

The dorm belonged to the Fifties' shoe box school of architecture. The rectangular, featureless building was born ugly and didn't get better looking with age.

Zoe was studying in her room and answered as soon as Jace knocked. She looked exactly like her dead sister, if Chloe had worked to make herself unattractive. Zoe's long blonde hair was scraped back into a low ponytail. She wore a drab gray sweater and baggy brown pants.

Her narrow room had beige cinder-block walls and a scuffed tan tile floor. There was barely room for the few pieces of furniture: a narrow bed, a black leather office chair, and a plain wooden desk piled with books and papers. A tall wooden bookcase overflowing with thick tomes took up one wall. Nothing brightened the cheerless room.

Jace identified us and Zoe paled. Before he could say anything, Zoe said, 'My sister? Is she dead? Did someone kill my sister?'

'Have a seat, Zoe,' I said.

She stayed standing. 'Please,' she said. 'Just tell me. Don't make me wait.'

'I'm sorry, Zoe,' I said. 'We believe your sister is dead.'

'No!' Zoe howled and began pounding her head against the cinder block wall. 'No! No! No! That can't be true. This is my fault. My fault.'

Jace gently pulled her away from the wall, and forced her to sit down on the bed. He put a box of tissues beside her.

While Zoe wept bitter tears, I ran to a small alcove near the door that had a sink, a mini-fridge and a narrow shelf. I found tea bags, filled a mug with water and popped it in the microwave. When the tea was hot, I added a lot of sugar and a healthy slug of Smirnoff vodka.

'Here.' I handed her the vodka-laced tea.

Zoe made a face when she tasted the drink, but she gulped it down, then rocked back and forth to comfort herself.

When she'd cried herself out, Zoe said, 'Wait a minute. You *believe* she's dead? You don't know for sure?'

'We're ninety-nine percent sure the dead person is Chloe,' I said. 'We need her dental records to confirm. Will you give us permission?'

'Of course. Her dentist is Dr John Stone.' Dr Stone was the best dentist in Chouteau Forest.

'Why can't I see her? I can identify my sister.'

'It would be better if you didn't,' said Jace. 'You should remember how she looked.'

'If I want to remember how she looked, I can see myself in the mirror,' Zoe said.

I handed Zoe the paperwork to get her sister's dental records. She signed it.

'Chloe was murdered, wasn't she?' Zoe said.

'Yes,' Jace said.

'How?'

'She was strangled.'

'Did she suffer?' The question all loving family members asked.

'No,' I lied.

'Do you know who would want to harm your sister?' Jace asked.

'Yes, that awful old man, Selwyn something.'

'Did you know about him?' Jace asked.

'Chloe's my twin. She tried to recruit me to be a so-called sugar baby. I told her no. I said she was nothing but a prostitute, and we fought. Chloe wouldn't speak to me for two months.'

'Did Chloe think of herself as a prostitute?' Jace asked.

'Of course not. She said Selwyn was a "friend with benefits." The benefits included the rent on her apartment. He also bought her a BMW. Used, like her.'

Zoe's answers made me think she was still angry at her sister.

'Her sugar daddy made sure she had all the latest styles, and lingerie. That man had a kink for lingerie. Chloe said he liked to give her little gifts and she returned his affection. In bed! I said that was plain old prostitution no matter how she tried to justify it. She said I was too judgmental. It was just a job. Well, it wasn't a job. It was a profession. The oldest! I was ashamed of her. I said our parents would be mortified. She was raised better than that.'

'Where are your parents?' Jace said.

'They died. In a car accident on I-55 when we were in college. Freshman year. After we sold the family home, we both had enough to finish school and a little extra. We were getting by working part-time jobs, but Chloe was unhappy. She's always had a taste for finer things.

'A girl in her class told her about the sugar baby website and the next thing I know Chloe moved out of the dorm. She was living in an expensive apartment, and wearing designer clothes. I was embarrassed, but she didn't see anything wrong with what she was doing. She said sex was a commodity. Her body was her chief asset and it was depreciating every year. She had to make the most with what she had while she could.

'Eventually, we made up. She was my sister and I love her, even if she was wrong. But then she did something I . . . I couldn't forgive.' Zoe burst into tears again. 'I should have. I should have reached out to her. Instead, I drove her away.'

'What happened, Zoe?' Jace asked.

'Three weeks ago, my sister said she had a good way to make more money. Easy money. Her sugar daddy, Selwyn, had a secret desire to have sex with twins.'

I stifled a gasp.

'She wanted me to join her. Chloe said he'd pay twenty-five thousand dollars, and I could have half. That was enough money to get me through the rest of the year. I could quit my job working in the school cafeteria.

'I was shocked. Chloe said that it was only one night and Selwyn was so old it was hardly sex at all, and over in a minute. I refused. I was angry and humiliated. I told her to go away, and she did. And now she's dead.'

Zoe's weeping tore at my heart.

'Do you know if she went through with the threesome?' Jace asked.

'Chloe said if I wouldn't do it, she'd get her friend, Wendy Raymond, who looked a lot like her. Selwyn was vain and wouldn't wear his glasses when he was with her. He wouldn't know the difference. My sister and Wendy would split the money. Chloe thought she was doing me a favor.

'I should have stopped her,' Zoe said. 'She's the only family I had.'

'Zoe,' Jace said. 'You do know that Selwyn Skipton, your sister's sugar daddy, is dead. He was murdered. Before Chloe died.'

'How?'

'He was strangled. It was all over the news.'

'Between work and school, I don't have much time to follow the news,' Zoe said.

'Do you think that threesome went wrong somehow, and Chloe killed her sugar daddy?'

'No. Absolutely not. My sister would never kill anyone. Never.'

'Did you ever think she would be a sugar baby?' Jace asked.

'No,' Zoe said. 'Never in a million years.'

'People can surprise us,' Jace said.

TWENTY-ONE

Finally, Zoe cried herself out. She dried her tear-reddened eyes with a tissue and sniffled a bit. Jace and I had been waiting for her to stop crying. It seemed to take forever, but Jace was more patient than me.

In a gentle voice, he asked, 'Zoe, can you help us find your sister's killer by answering some questions?'

She nodded her head yes.

'How many people did your sister date from the website?'

Zoe twisted the tear-stained tissue in her hands as she talked. 'At first, she went out on lots of dates – as many as ten in a month. If the men weren't generous – by that, I mean if they didn't give her money or buy her gifts – she dropped them.'

'Did any of those men threaten your sister when she didn't see them again?' Jace was jotting notes.

Zoe thought for a minute. 'No. She never mentioned anything to me. I don't think she formed an attachment to any of them. When she turned them down, it wasn't a big deal. There are so many women on that website, it didn't make much difference. The men would move on.

'Then Chloe met Selwyn, and they made some kind of arrangement. She would only date Selwyn. As I said, he paid her rent and gave her generous gifts. She said it wasn't demanding work and it paid well.'

'Did she know that Selwyn was married?' Jace asked. He kept all trace of disapproval out of his voice.

'They're all married, Detective.' Zoe said that with a hint of scorn, as if Jace was naive. 'My sister said that site was a place for married men to hook up. Selwyn said he was in a loveless, sexless marriage.'

'Selwyn was telling the truth,' Jace said. 'We talked to his wife. Mrs Skipton said her husband was finished with sex.'

'No, *she* was finished with sex,' Zoe said. 'At least according to my sister.'

'Did your sister say anything else about her time with Selwyn? Anything that stands out?'

Zoe thought for a moment. 'Well, she told me he had a private apartment over the chocolate shop in downtown Chouteau Forest, and she had to go in by the back entrance. The place had a huge bed and paintings that looked like museum art. He liked black satin sheets. The apartment was stocked with champagne and chocolate and he always had a cold supper for her. Selwyn wanted her to wear lingerie that he bought for her. My sister said it was an elegant life and way better than shoveling fries in the hot, greasy school cafeteria.' Zoe shrugged her shoulders. 'I couldn't argue with that, but I couldn't see how she could be a kept woman.'

Zoe started to cry again, and reached for more tissues. I hurried to find a bottle of cold water in the mini-fridge and handed it to her. When she quit crying, she sipped the water while she talked.

'Can you tell us more about your sister's friend, the one who looked like her?' Jace asked.

'You mean Wendy Raymond? I think she was about our age – twenty-one or twenty-two. She lived near my sister in the Bellingham Apartments.'

'Pretty ritzy address,' Jace said.

'It is, but Wendy shares the apartment with a roommate.'

'What kind of car does this Wendy drive?' Jace asked.

'A little white convertible. Chloe talked about how cute it was, but she never told me what the make was.'

Jace brought out a cell phone in an evidence bag. 'We think this is your sister's phone. It's locked and we need to get into it. Do you know if she used a password or a fingerprint?'

'Password,' Zoe said.

Jace and I both relaxed. We'd just been saved hours of phone company paperwork and applying for court orders.

'Chloe made calls outdoors in the wintertime and didn't want to take off her gloves to unlock her phone,' Zoe said. 'Try our old house address – 2325.'

Jace typed in the numbers with gloved fingers, and the cell phone opened.

'It's charged,' Jace said.

He opened the photo gallery, and thumbed through the pictures. One showed Chloe and Zoe smiling in front of a white house with black shutters and a wide green lawn. Both girls wore long pastel dresses. Next to them were two awkward boys in badly fitting tuxes.

'That's our prom photo,' Zoe said. 'We were high school seniors and our parents were still alive.' Her eyes filled with tears, but she didn't cry.

The next three photos showed the girls posing with a handsome couple in their early forties. 'That's Mom and Dad,' she said. 'We'd just turned thirteen. We were official teenagers.'

In the photos Zoe was just as pretty as her sister. Did she tone her looks down when Chloe became a sex worker? After their parents died? Or both?

Next came a photo of Chloe in skimpy black lace, her arms wrapped around a nude Selwyn's scrawny chest. She looked like a nymph embracing a troll.

'Ugh,' Jace said. 'That photo of Selwyn makes me want to scoop out my eyes with a melon baller.'

'Then don't look at the next three photos,' I said.

Moving past the photos of Chloe and Selwyn, I saw photos of two blondes in black lingerie. One was Chloe. The other looked like her at first glance, but this woman was curvier, her face was broader and her nose a bit longer. With her blue eyes, come-hither smile and long, wavy hair, she was definitely a beauty.

'That's her,' Zoe said. 'That's Wendy.'

'Good,' Jace said. 'Now we know what she looks like.'

He opened the video section and called up the first video. We heard a loud squawk, and Jace turned down the sound. Zoe watched the video for a moment, and then smiled for the first time. 'That's Buddy! Oh, my gosh, how could I forget about Buddy?'

'And Buddy is?' Jace asked.

'Our African grey parrot. Dad gave Buddy to my mom, but we all loved him. Chloe took him after our parents died. In her new apartment, she had the room and the time to care for him. African greys need lots of attention. Is Buddy OK?'

'Yes,' Jace said. 'We've made sure he had plenty of food and water. One of our techs, who loves parrots, is taking care of him at your sister's apartment until you decide what to do.'

'Thank you,' she said. 'Buddy's really smart and talks a blue streak. Did he talk for you?'

'Just screeched a lot,' Jace said.

'He must be upset. Do you think he saw Chloe being . . . being killed?'

'He may have,' Jace said.

A Scarlet Death

'Buddy loved my sister. Open that video.' Zoe pointed to another one.

We heard disco music and saw Chloe in black sweats, with the parrot on her wrist. 'Come on, Buddy,' she said. 'Let's get down.' The two bobbed their heads to the music as Chloe swooped gracefully around the living room and the parrot flapped his wings.

'Stop, please,' Zoe said, and Jace shut off the video.

'It hurts too much to watch them,' she said. 'I'm afraid I'll start crying again. When this is all over, could I have her phone back?'

'Of course,' Jace said.

She pointed to another video. 'That one there,' she said. 'You'll see Buddy talking. He's at our house. I mean, our house when we were still a family.'

Buddy was perched on a wooden stand outside his cage in a bright, sunny room. He hopped back and forth on the stand and said, 'Buddy's a good boy. Buddy's a pretty boy.' His words were easy to understand.

The bird whistled, then said, 'Hello. Hello. Good morning. I love you. Give me a kiss. Give Buddy a kiss.'

Jace said, 'He's got quite a vocabulary.'

'We had to be careful what we said around Buddy, because he'd pick it up,' Zoe said.

The bird stopped for a moment and began counting to ten. Then he screeched, 'Chloe! Zoe! Get down here this minute and explain yourselves. What are these charges doing on my credit card?'

'That's Daddy,' Zoe said. 'My sister and I sneaked Dad's credit card to do some unauthorized clothes shopping. He wasn't happy. We spent the summer working off those charges.'

The bird whistled and chirped, then said, 'Dammit, Chloe! You borrowed my white shirt and ruined it. You got spaghetti sauce on it and it won't come out! Stop ruining my clothes.'

'Buddy picked that up from me,' Zoe said. 'I was mad at my sister.'

Buddy barked like a dog, meowed like a cat, and imitated a motorcycle, whistling and chirping between his sounds. He finished with: 'Buddy's smart. He's a smart boy.'

Then the bird said, 'Young lady, I'm asking you to pick up your newspapers. You leave them piled up outside your door. That's against the rules and you know it. If you continue, I'll report you to the management. I mean it.'

'Is that Chloe's neighbor, Alice?' I asked.

'Sure sounds like her,' Zoe said. 'My sister must have taken that recently. I haven't seen it before. That old crab didn't get along with my sister.'

'Nasty old bitch,' Buddy said. 'Nasty old bitch. Buddy is a bad boy. Bad boy. Nasty old bitch.'

All three of us burst out laughing.

'Do you think Alice killed your sister?' Jace asked.

'Alice? Never. Chloe and I didn't like the old biddy, but Alice would never kill my sister. She enjoyed complaining about Chloe too much. That gave her empty life purpose and something to talk about at her bridge games.'

'Who do you think killed Chloe?'

'Either Selwyn's wife, Estelle, or his secretary, Rosalie Vann. Selwyn told my sister that he had a fling with his secretary and then quit seeing her. Selwyn said he split with Rosalie when she started hinting that he should divorce his wife and marry her. Selwyn told my sister that he would never divorce Estelle. He wanted Rosalie to understand that right from the beginning.'

'Why wouldn't Selwyn divorce his wife?' Jace asked.

'Divorces were messy and expensive. Also, Estelle was important to his social life, and his position in Forest society. His secretary, Rosalie, knew Selwyn had another woman at his apartment, and she resented Chloe. My sister was younger and prettier. Rosalie sorta stalked them. She knew which nights Selwyn went to his in-town apartment. One morning, Rosalie was waiting in her car in the alley when Chloe left the apartment. Rosalie followed my sister home.'

'Did Rosalie know your sister lived at the Peacock Apartments?' Jace asked.

'Yes. Chloe was worried. She saw Rosalie as a desperate older woman who thought Selwyn was her last chance to marry. My sister told Selwyn that Rosalie had followed her home. He said he'd talk to her. Chloe told me she was still worried about Rosalie.'

'So your sister was worried that a jealous Rosalie might kill her?'

'Yes. She was also afraid of Mrs Skipton. Estelle knew Selwyn was a sugar daddy.'

Jace showed no sign of surprise. He had an impressive poker face. I kept my head lowered in case Zoe could read my surprise.

Estelle Skipton claimed she'd never heard of the sugar daddy websites.

'How did Mrs Skipton find out about her husband?' Jace asked.

'I don't know,' Zoe said. 'But she had a key to his apartment. Estelle barged in one night. She was dead drunk. So drunk she could hardly talk.'

That sounded like Estelle, all right.

'Mrs Skipton caught Selwyn and Chloe in bed. She scared my sister half to death. Called Chloe every name in the book, from harlot to floozie, and swore she'd kill her. Then she turned on her husband. Estelle said she'd tell everyone at church, and he'd be ruined. She said she'd never divorce him – she'd kill him first. She turned around and marched out. More like wobbled out, really. My sister said she was really drunk.

'Chloe couldn't stop crying that night. Selwyn told her not to worry. He said Estelle would never do anything like that – she loved her social life too much. That's when he told Chloe he had a secret desire to have sex with twins. Chloe tried to recruit me, and I refused.'

'When did Mrs Skipton come to Selwyn's in-town apartment?' Jace asked.

'When did he die?' Zoe asked.

Jace told her the date.

Zoe said, 'Estelle Skipton confronted her husband three weeks before he died.'

'Anyone else?' Jace asked.

'No, not that I can think of. When can I bury my sister? I want her to be with my parents.'

'We'll let you know,' I said. 'Is there someone who can stay with you?'

'My friend, Betsy. She's down the hall. She'll let me stay with her. Her roommate moved to an off-campus apartment.'

'Can we call her for you?'

'No, thanks,' she said. 'I'll call her as soon as you leave.'

'Are you sure you're all right?' Jace asked.

'As well as I can be, with my whole family dead.'

TWENTY-TWO

When Jace and I left Zoe's dorm, the dark winter night closed in on us, black and hopeless. The cold slapped me in the face. I dread the dark days of December.

As we hurried to our cars, I said, 'Do you think that parrot could tell us who killed Chloe?'

Jace stared at me. 'Do I look like Dr Dolittle? What am I supposed to say, "Polly wanna cracker? Wanna tell me who killed your owner?"'

My face was hot with embarrassment. 'OK, OK, it was a stupid idea. What's next?'

Jace said, 'It's six o'clock. I want to visit that Wendy Raymond. Do you want to come along?'

'Let me check on Chris.' I texted Katie and she answered, *Chris is fine. No change.*

'I can go with you,' I said. 'Wendy's apartment is nearby.'

The Bellingham was a red-brick building adorned with urns, scrolls and assorted white terra-cotta doodads. The dark marble lobby had a receptionist, a burly African-American man whose name tag said he was Lucas. As soon as Jace flashed his badge, Lucas told us Wendy's apartment number and let us into the elevator.

We knocked on the door, and a young brunette in navy sweats answered. Barefoot and eating a bowl of cereal, she didn't seem to have the slightest fear about opening her door.

She put the cereal bowl on the small table by the door, which was already piled with scarves, earrings, lipstick and one high heel.

Jace identified himself.

The young woman's brown eyes widened and she flipped back her long brown hair. 'You're really a police detective? I've never met one before. I'm Skye.'

Jace introduced me, and when she heard my death investigator title, all Skye could manage was 'oh.'

'Come in,' she said. 'The place is a bit of a mess.'

The small room was chaos, with sweaters tossed on the couch, sweats and underwear puddled on the floor, and shoes everywhere, even on the coffee table. An eyelash curler sat on the TV stand, and make-up brushes were scattered on every surface. The only reading material was *Vogue* magazine.

'We're looking for Wendy Raymond,' Jace said. 'Do you know her?'

'Oh, yes, we're roommates.' Skye seemed proud of that.

'Is she here now?'

'No, Wendy's in Chicago, staying at the Drake Hotel, lucky dog.'

'She goes to Chicago in the winter?' I asked. 'It's freezing up there.'

'It is, but the shopping is outstanding. Their clothes are so much more advanced than what you can find in St. Louis.'

'When did Wendy go to Chicago?' Jace asked.

'Four days ago. She should be home in about two days.'

'Where does Wendy work?' Jace asked.

'The new PR firm in town, Cool News 4 U. On Gravois. She loves that job. Anything you'd like me to say to her when she gets back?'

'No need,' Jace said. 'You answered all my questions. Nice meeting you.'

Once we were outside, Jace said, 'Skye was helpful. I can't wait to talk to Wendy when she comes home.'

'What's next?' I asked. I was so cold my teeth were chattering.

'It's six thirty,' Jace said. 'Too late for us to talk to Rosalie Vann and Mrs Skipton.'

'Estelle lied to us,' I said.

'Yes, she did. We're going to have a talk about that.' I could see Jace's breath. He looked like he was breathing fire. 'I hate being played for a fool.'

'I can't go now, anyway. I want to see Chris,' I said. 'I'll get only one more chance tonight.'

'How is he doing?' Jace asked.

I felt tears stinging my eyes. 'The same. No better, no worse. I'm afraid if he doesn't improve soon, he'll never wake up.'

Jace hugged me, an unexpected but appreciated move. 'He will get better, Angela. And we'll do everything we can to help. Do you want to go with me tomorrow when I see those two women?'

'Can I help?'

'Yes. You always help. But if you need to stay with Chris, I understand.'

'I'll be fine,' I said. 'I must see him in the morning, but working with you helps keep me occupied. Unless there's a change, of course. Then you won't be able to pry me out of his room.'

'Got it,' Jace said. 'Then I'll meet you at Estelle's home at ten o'clock tomorrow. I'm bringing my rubber hose.' I knew Jace was joking, but he was also angry – with himself – for being such a sap.

'Thank you, Jace.' I waved goodbye and escaped to my car before I started crying. I missed Chris badly. He was my love and my refuge at the end of a difficult day, and my life felt empty without him. I said a prayer to St Jude, the patron saint of hopeless causes, for his recovery, and returned to my temporary home, Sisters of Sorrow Hospital.

Inside the hospital, the harsh glare of the hallway lights was far from comforting, and the cacophony of code calls and announcements was confusing. When I opened the door to my room, Katie was sitting on the bed. Instead of her lab coat and a suit, she wore jeans and a warm beige sweater.

'How's Chris?' I asked.

'He's fine,' she said.

'Any change?'

'Not yet.'

'Is he ever going to get well?' I could hear the tears in my voice. I hated them.

'Yes, he will.' Katie sounded firm. 'Go see Chris. When you get back, I'll have dinner ready.'

I hurried down the hall to Chris's ICU room.

The room was dark and cool, and Chris was still as a statue. The only sounds were the horrible hisses and beeps of the machines keeping him alive.

I held his cold hand and whispered, 'Chris, I love you. Come back to me. Please. Do you remember the day we drove to St Charles, and walked all over the town's historic district? That was fun, wasn't it?'

I recalled as much as I could about that trip this fall. It was one of our best days together, though it seemed so far away now in this chilly room, with lines and wires attached to Chris. He looked different, too. His lean, handsome face was still swollen and bruised from the surgery, and his thick brown hair had been shaved off on one side of his head.

I heard the warning announcement that visiting hours were over, and kissed him goodbye.

When I returned to my room, a grease-stained bag was perched on the nightstand. 'Do I smell food?'

'You just noticed?' Katie asked. 'When's the last time that you ate?'

'I don't remember,' I said.

Katie raised an eyebrow. 'Angela Richman, the woman who is always hungry, can't remember when she last ate? Never thought I'd see the day. Yes, you smell food. I brought us dinner from Gringo Daze.'

'My favorite,' I said. 'The best Mexican restaurant in the Forest.'

'Also, the only Mexican restaurant,' Katie said.

She opened the big bag of food. We used the bed as a dining table. Katie spread a towel over the coverlet, and that was our tablecloth.

'First, we have guacamole and homemade chips.' Katie opened a wax paper bag of homemade chips, and a container of guac.

'Next, carne asada. That's grilled flank steak marinated in a cilantro-beer sauce.'

'Yum.' My stomach growled. I was hungry.

'And rice and black beans.'

'Perfect.'

'Not quite. We also have flan for dessert.'

She brought out a bottle of red wine. 'Here's a bottle of zinfandel. It will stand up to the savory beef. Besides, you can use a drink.'

'Can I ever,' I said. 'It's not like I have to drive home.'

Katie produced china plates and silverware from another bag, and two plastic wineglasses. She poured me a stiff drink of wine, and heaped my plate with the food. I dug into the guacamole, first with salty corn chips, then went for the carne asada with rice and black beans.

As I wolfed down the food, I told Katie about the death of Chloe, Alice the awful neighbor, and Buddy the dancing parrot. I needed another drink when I told her about how Jace and I had told Zoe of her sister's murder.

'I've done death notifications before,' I said. 'But that one was especially heart-wrenching. Chloe was the last of her family, and the twins were on bad terms.'

'Because Chloe was a sugar baby?' Katie asked.

'Yes. Also, Chloe wanted her twin to join her in a threesome with Selwyn.'

Katie whistled. 'That's taking sisterly love a little too far.'

'It was. Except now Zoe is overwhelmed with guilt and regret that she didn't forgive her sister.'

Katie took my empty plate and refilled it, and I started on my second round of carne asada. The hearty food revived me.

'Considering Chloe's profession,' Katie said, 'I can see why her twin had problems dealing with her.'

'Too bad Zoe's blaming herself,' I said. 'I'd find that hard to forgive, too.'

Katie refilled my wineglass again, and then took my empty plate. 'Try this flan,' she said.

The creamy flan was laced with vanilla, and the caramel top was just right. I finished the last bite, feeling contented and sleepy.

'Thank you so much, Katie. This meal was a wonderful surprise.' I stifled a yawn, but Katie saw it.

'Angela,' Katie said. 'Time to get ready for bed.'

'Let me help clean up.'

'There isn't room. Go get ready.'

She shooed me away. By the time I was washed and in my nightgown, Katie had packed up the dishes.

'Let's plug in your cell phone and iPad to charge,' she said. 'What time do you want to get up tomorrow? Seven thirty?'

'Yes. I want to see Chris before I go to work.'

Katie tucked me into bed. It felt good, being cared for. As I drifted off to sleep, I heard Katie shut off the light and say, 'Goodnight, Angela.'

Maybe it was the food, or the wine, or the help of my friends, but I slept well that night, and woke up half an hour before my alarm went off – at seven the next morning.

Sitting on my nightstand was a cup of hot coffee and a homemade ham-and-egg sandwich wrapped in foil. Taped on the sandwich foil was a note from Katie. It said:

Hope you slept well. Monty will look after Chris today. He'll call if there's any news. I have the sugar baby's autopsy.
Text you later.
Katie

PS: Eat your breakfast. It's the most important meal of the day. And don't forget lunch.

I ignored my breakfast sandwich and gulped down the coffee. As soon as I was dressed, I hurried off to see Chris. It was a new day, and after my good night's sleep I was filled with hope. I raced into the room and said, 'Chris. Chris. It's me, Angela. Are you there? Are you awake?'

The only answer was the inhuman hiss of the ventilator and the mechanical beeping. I kissed him, but my sleeping beauty didn't wake. So I went back to our routine, reading from the Wambaugh book and telling Chris how much I loved him. When our time together was up, I went for more coffee, then back to my room.

I didn't feel like eating, but I forced down Katie's breakfast sandwich and went for a walk through the hospital halls. I envied everyone I saw: the thirty-something man trying to walk with crutches. The skinny old man struggling to make it out of his room using a walker. The young woman in a pink bathrobe being pushed in a wheelchair. They looked bruised and battered, but they were moving, and they were conscious. I wanted that so badly for Chris. I wanted him to wake up.

It was time for my second visit to Chris that morning. Sadly, it was a repeat of the previous visit. While I held his hand, I wondered who had tried to kill him, and if they would come back to finish the job. I couldn't think of anyone who would hate Chris that much. I had to protect him.

When my time was up, I left, once again discouraged. While I tidied my room, my cell phone dinged. It was a text from Katie: *Remember, I'm here for you. And I have wine.*

As always, she made me smile. I was lucky to have friends who took care of me. My job was to take care of Chris.

TWENTY-THREE

When I parked outside the Skipton mansion that morning, I saw Jace pacing in the driveway and mumbling to himself.

'What's wrong?' I asked. 'It's too cold out here to be doing that.'

Jace looked at me with furious eyes. 'I'm trying to cool off, Angela. Estelle Skipton played me. I was stupid to give that woman the benefit of the doubt, and she lied to me. Well, not this time.'

He stomped up the steps to the Skipton home, and pounded on the black front door. Lucille, the housekeeper, answered the door and glowered at us.

'Mrs Skipton can't—' Lucille began, when Jace interrupted her.

'I don't care if Mrs Skipton is on her death bed. I want to see her. Now. If you won't get her, I'll arrest her and drag her scraggy derriere down to the station.'

Lucille was outraged. Hands on her hips, she shouted, 'Arrest Mrs Skipton? What for?'

'Impeding a homicide investigation. Obstruction of justice. Looking at me cross-eyed. And anything else I can think of.'

Lucille used her sturdy body to block the door.

'And if you don't let us in,' Jace said, 'I'll arrest you, too.'

Lucille stood aside. 'Mrs Skipton is in the front parlor.' The housekeeper looked like a hen with ruffled feathers. 'I'll show you.'

'Never mind,' Jace said. 'I know the way.'

He pushed past Lucille, his anger following like another person. I trailed behind Jace. I remembered that cramped parlor, crowded with uncomfortable red velvet furniture. This morning, Estelle was lounging on a velvet love seat, drinking a martini. She wore a long black hostess gown. Her red lipstick brought out the fine network of red lines on her face.

'Detective,' Estelle said. 'You didn't tell me you were coming for a visit.'

Jace sat across from her, overwhelming the spindly tufted velvet chair. 'And you didn't tell me that you had a key to your husband's apartment, and confronted him and his girlfriend there. In fact, when

I talked to you, you pretended you didn't know what a sugar daddy was, or what the inside of your husband's apartment looked like when you'd been inside. Why didn't you mention that?'

Estelle set her martini glass down on a small, carved table. 'Because it wasn't any of your business, Detective.'

'Your husband was murdered, Mrs Skipton. That makes it my business.'

'I couldn't possibly have murdered my husband, Detective. I wasn't in town at the time. I was at the four-day Church Women's Prayer Retreat at the St Giles monastery in the Lake of the Ozarks.'

'How did you get there?'

'Our church chartered a bus. Including travel and the stay at the monastery, the trip cost two hundred dollars. I can show you my credit card receipt. Pastor Berger will vouch that I was there the whole time.'

'Get me the receipt,' he said. 'Now.'

'If you insist.' Estelle stood up, slightly wobbly, and hurried up the stairs as fast as she could without tripping on her long gown. She was back seven minutes later with a folder containing a brochure for the prayer retreat, featuring photos of the monastery and views of the lake. The retreat promised 'prayer, fasting, fellowship and contemplation.'

She also had a receipt for two hundred dollars for the bus ride and prayer retreat with the dates. It was marked 'paid.'

Selwyn's widow settled herself back on her love seat and pounded down the rest of her martini.

'Did you pay someone to kill your husband?' Jace asked.

'Now why would I do that?'

'Because your husband was unfaithful, and he lied to you.'

Estelle gave Jace a world-weary look. 'Husbands wander, Detective. It's a wife's duty to forgive them and welcome them back.'

'Your husband spent a lot of money on women,' Jace said.

Estelle shrugged. 'My husband had a lot of money, Detective.'

Now she sat up straight. 'I did not kill my husband, Detective. His death has been keenly embarrassing. I saw the tabloid headlines, calling him a dirty daddy. I would never deliberately subject myself to that kind of humiliation.'

'Bull!' Jace said. 'You were mad enough to go storming into your husband's apartment.'

'That was private,' she said. 'Between us.'

'And Chloe Westbrook. Who was there, too. She's also dead. Did you kill her?'

Estelle laughed. 'His little chippie? Not worth killing, Detective. He would have tired of her soon enough, and then found another interchangeable blonde. She wasn't a threat.'

'So why threaten your husband?'

'He missed an important dinner that night. He was supposed to attend it with me. I was angry, and rightfully so.'

She rang a small silver bell on the carved table, and Lucille materialized.

'Lucille,' Estelle said, 'please show the detective out. And I'll have another martini.'

We left. Or rather, Jace left and I followed. I'd been invisible to Estelle. Outside, I said, 'Do you think Estelle killed her husband?'

'I don't buy that baloney about her being a good wife,' Jace said. 'She was mad enough to show up at his love nest in person and yell at him.'

'Mad enough to kill him when he forgot to take her to a dinner?' I asked.

'Maybe not,' Jace said. 'But she could have hired someone to kill him.'

'That retreat in the Ozarks is a five-hour drive from the Forest,' I said. 'She could have rented a car, killed her husband, and driven back to the retreat.'

'I need to do more research,' Jace said. 'I'll talk with her pastor and check credit card records to make sure she didn't rent a car.'

'What about Chloe?' I asked.

'I'll check video at Chloe's apartment, and see if Estelle was there,' Jace said. 'We've done as much here as we can.'

Jace was still hot under the collar, but he seemed in control again. 'Let's move on to Selwyn's office manager, Rosalie Vann.'

Jace and I both found a parking spot outside the Chouteau Trust Building, the site of Selwyn's office. Soon we were in Selwyn's third-floor office. Rosalie was in the anteroom, dressed in a honey-brown pantsuit that looked good with her flaming hair. She was packing law books into cardboard boxes.

She greeted Jace and me with a smile. 'Detective and Ms Richman. So nice to see you again.'

'Ms Vann,' Jace said. 'You're still working here?'

'Yes.' She taped a moving box shut. 'Mrs Skipton is employing me until the end of the year to pack up and close her husband's office.'

'What will happen to Selwyn's things?' Jace asked.

'They'll go in storage, in case his sons want them.'

'I'd like to ask you some questions,' Jace said.

'Certainly. Let's go into Selwyn's office. Would you like coffee? Water?'

'No, thank you,' Jace said. I followed his lead and also declined. Jace would skip refreshments when he was asking tough questions. He took out his notepad, pen at the ready.

Jace and I sat on a brown leather chesterfield sofa. Rosalie sat in front of us in a leather club chair, hands folded in her lap, legs crossed at the ankles, a model of deportment.

That was shattered by Jace's first question. 'I understand you had an affair with Selwyn Skipton.'

The color drained from Rosalie's face. 'I . . . what?'

She stumbled and stuttered until Jace said, 'Don't deny it, Ms Vann. I'm not the marriage police. When did you have the affair?'

'Uh, about four years ago.'

'And how long did it last?'

'Around two years.'

'And where did you meet Mr Skipton?'

'At his in-town apartment.'

'Why did you tell me that you'd been there to take dictation?' Jace asked.

'That's what I was doing. In a manner of speaking.' She tried a weak smile, but it slid off her face.

'You told me that you'd only been at the apartment once.'

'I'm sorry, Detective. I didn't tell the truth. I was there once a week. Sometimes twice.'

'Were you expecting Selwyn to marry you?' Jace asked.

Rosalie's answer was tinged with bitterness. 'Men like Selwyn don't marry women like me.'

'Selwyn was in a loveless, sexless marriage,' Jace said.

'Selwyn didn't marry for love or sex, Detective. Men on his level don't. He married a woman who had the right pedigree and what she called "breeding." She knew how to run his household and arrange his social calendar so he would prosper. She volunteered for all the right charities and committees.'

Rosalie was a teacher, giving a lesson to a backward student. 'Estelle was attractive, but not too good-looking, or she'd offend the horse-faced biddies who ran the Forest. Once she gave Selwyn two sons, her bedroom duties were over, and she could devote her life to her favorite hobby – drinking.'

'Mrs Skipton said her husband wasn't interested in sex,' Jace said.

Rosalie gave a loud, humorless laugh. 'Selwyn enjoyed the pleasures of the bedroom, Detective, even if his wife didn't. For him, sex was another service, like getting his hair cut or his shoes shined, and he was willing to pay for it.'

'And how did that make you feel?' Jace asked.

'I knew what I was getting into,' she said. 'My eyes were wide open.'

But did she really know? How would an attractive woman feel if a rich man used her for two years?

'Did Selwyn pay you?' Jace asked.

'Yes. Quite well. For my skills at the office and in his bed.' Rosalie stared defiantly at Jace. 'In addition to my generous pay as his office manager, he gave me annual bonuses. Five-figure bonuses. He made me financially independent, Detective.'

'You didn't want to marry Selwyn?' Jace asked.

'Weren't you listening? I just explained why Selwyn would never marry me. Never, ever. I have no need to marry. I don't want to share my life with anyone on a long-term basis.'

'So you weren't upset when your affair ended with Selwyn?' Jace asked.

'I was relieved. He was a so-so lover. I have other, better choices. I am an independent woman. When I finish this job, I will sell my home and move to Florida. I've always wanted to live by the ocean.'

'Where were you when Selwyn was murdered?' Jace gave her the dates.

'I was home. Alone. Probably watching Netflix. But I can't prove it. You'll just have to trust me.'

She smiled at both of us.

'What about Chloe Westbrook?'

'I don't know who that is,' she said.

'Chloe was Selwyn's current sugar baby. You stalked her in the alley behind the chocolate shop.'

Rosalie shrugged. 'I didn't stalk anyone. I had a hard time finding a parking spot downtown and drove around looking for one. I didn't have any change for a meter.'

'Chloe was strangled about four days ago,' Jace said.

'I'm sorry to hear that.' Rosalie didn't sound sorry. She sounded like she didn't care. 'You must realize young women like her are in a risky profession. Anything else?'

'Not right now,' Jace said.

Another pointless interview. When we were in the lobby, Jace asked, 'Want to grab some lunch?'

We walked to the New York Deli half a block away, and we both ordered the same deli classics: matzoh ball soup, corned beef sandwiches and cream soda. Our booth was tucked in the back corner of the deli. Like many cops, Jace was most comfortable in the seat facing the door. We munched our food for a bit. The corned beef was incredibly tender and the rye bread had a nice, crunchy crust. The cream soda had a strong vanilla flavor.

Jace slathered his sandwich with mustard, but I thought mine was too good to change.

Jace sighed. 'Today was a bust, Angela. I don't think either woman did it, but I'll check out Estelle Selwyn's alibi with her pastor and that St Giles retreat.'

I ... ored a spoonful of soup while Jace asked, 'Who is St Giles?'

'A French hermit who lived about thirteen hundred years ago. Supposedly Giles lived off deer milk. That makes him the patron saint of breastfeeding.'

'Huh,' Jace said. 'You'd think a woman would get that job.'

'As a kid, I used to love reading about the lives of the saints. One of my favorites was St Drogo, the patron saint of ugly people. Drogo was a rich noble who gave away his worldly goods. Then he caught a disease on a pilgrimage that made him repulsive. He lived as a hermit, and gave spiritual advice to people. After he died, he was put in charge of ugly people. Oh, and coffee, hernias and gallstones.'

'Personally, I think Giles got a better deal,' Jace said.

'We may need the help of St Rita and St Jude for this case,' I said. 'They both handle lost causes, and Selwyn's murder seems to be impossible.

'What's next?' I took a big bite of my sandwich.

'Something I've put off for too long, Angela. The uniforms gathered all the video they could from the surrounding businesses for the three nights preceding Selwyn's death. I need to go through all of it.'

'I can help,' I said. 'I'll be glad to.'

'I'll take you up on that,' he said. 'It's going to be a real bear.'

'Start emailing me the videos,' I said. 'I'm going outside to check on Chris. Monty's staying with him today.'

I didn't have to call Monty. The minute I stepped outside, Monty called me. I heard the triumph in his voice. 'Angela! Angela! Chris is starting to wake up,' he said.

'What! Are you kidding!' A thousand-pound burden slid off my back. My heart felt like it would burst.

'I'm on my way.'

TWENTY-FOUR

I ran back into the deli, shouting, 'Jace! Jace! Chris is waking up.' The other diners looked up from their meals and stared. I didn't care.

Jace had finished his lunch and packed our dishes on a tray. 'That's wonderful,' he said. 'Can I drive you to the hospital?'

'I'm fine. I can drive myself.' I was twitching with impatience.

'OK, but you seem a little . . .'

'Delirious? Drunk? Overjoyed? I'm all of those things, except drunk.'

'I'm worried about you driving,' he said. 'Why don't I give you an escort? That will keep you out of trouble if you speed.'

'With lights and siren?' I asked.

'The whole shebang. I'll escort you to SOS and then go home.' He left our lunch trays on a wooden stand. 'Let's go, Angela.'

And go we did. I'd never had a police escort before. Jace's unmarked car had a siren and flashing red lights. It made the traffic disappear like snow on a summer day.

Jace cut the lights and siren when we were a block from the hospital. I found a spot near the front door, waved goodbye to him, and ran inside.

I dodged and weaved through the hospital foot traffic, nearly running down a young woman with a cast and a cane. That earned me some dirty looks. 'Sorry,' I shouted, and kept running toward Chris.

Katie and Monty were waiting for me outside Chris's ICU room. They made a handsome couple, Katie in her white lab coat and Monty in his lawyer suit.

I peppered them with questions. 'How is Chris? What did he say? What does he remember? Is he in pain? When can I see him?'

'Whoa, whoa,' Katie said. 'I was afraid you'd react like this. Let's go where we can talk a minute.'

'My room?'

'Too small for three of us.'

I followed her and Monty into the family room at the end of the hall, and sat on a small gray sofa, which felt like an upholstered rock. Katie and Monty sat opposite me.

Katie handed me a bottle of water and said, 'Drink.'

'All of it?'

'Enough to make a dent.'

I drank about a third of the water before she said, 'Now that you've calmed down, here's what happened.'

Monty started. 'I visited Chris every hour on the hour. I stopped by for the two o'clock visit, and Chris's eyes were wide open. He was trying to talk, but he was on a ventilator, and that's hard to do. He said something like, "Eat! Eat!" and then "No, no!"'

'So he sounded upset,' I said.

'I can't be sure,' Monty said. 'The ventilator distorted what he was trying to say. I hit the call button, and Nurse Stacey came rushing in. I told her what happened and she called the surgeon, and soon doctors and nurses were swarming into Chris's ICU room. They shined lights and did other examinations, and decided this was good news.'

'Very good news.' Katie smiled at me. 'If Chris continues to improve, Dr Hallen will take him off the ventilator, and Chris will be transferred to the step-down ICU.'

'How did Chris react to his news?'

'He didn't, Angela,' Katie said. 'He fell back asleep.'

I was so disappointed, I wanted to cry. Katie patted my hand. 'Hey, there, you were in a coma yourself. You know what it's like.'

'Actually, I don't. When I woke up after I had the strokes, I was in a fog.'

'That's where Chris is,' Katie said. 'Coming out of a coma isn't like you see in the movies, where the person suddenly sits up, smiles and starts talking a blue streak. You certainly didn't. For a while, you didn't make any sense at all. You babbled words that didn't connect. You talked to dead people and scared the stuffing out of us.'

'Did you hear that, Monty?' I said. 'Katie said stuffing instead of—'

'What I used to say,' Katie said.

Monty leaned over and kissed Katie. 'And I'm proud of her.'

'I'm not eight years old, you two.' Katie was annoyed. 'Stop it. As I was saying, the surgeon thinks Chris is starting to wake up from the coma, Angela, but it may take time. Days. Weeks even. It

'How do you feel?' I asked.

'Tired,' he said. 'I'm so tired.' Once again, his eyes shut. Visiting hours were over. Katie had warned me that Chris would talk to dead people, but I was still unnerved. I told Stacey what happened, and she reassured me that Chris would be fine. 'His brain is sorting things out. I know it's upsetting, but he will be OK.'

I haunted the halls for another hour, watching patients glued to the early televisions and other patients sleeping, until I was too tired to think. Then I went back to my room, restless and frightened. I'd prayed for Chris to wake up and my prayers were answered. Now I had to pray he'd return to the land of the living.

will be a slow process, and it will require something you don't have much of.'

'What's that?'

'Patience,' Katie said.

I was starting to get angry at this lecture, but I knew Katie was trying to help.

'Look, Angela,' she said. 'You can't force Chris's recovery, no matter how much you want. He'll heal on his own time. But he will heal.'

'You're sure?'

'I'm positive,' she said.

'It's almost three o'clock. I'd like to see Chris.'

'He's all yours.'

'Thank you both for putting up with me.'

I walked back to Chris's ICU room, my heart pounding. Despite Katie's warning, I wasn't sure what to expect. My spirits sank when I saw the same thing I'd seen for the last several days: Chris on a ventilator in a cold, dim room, surrounded by hissing, beeping machines. I gently touched his eyelids, but they stayed shut.

'Chris,' I said. 'Come back to me. Please.' I held his hand and laid my head on his pillow. But the man in the bed didn't smell like my Chris. He smelled like rubbing alcohol and Betadine and adhesive tape.

I must have closed my eyes because the next thing I knew the nurse, Stacey, was shaking me awake. 'Angela,' she said. 'Ms Richman. You fell asleep.'

'What time is it?' I was groggy with sleep.

'Eight o'clock. Visiting hours are over. I let you stay with Chris, but now you should get some sleep.'

'I have been sleeping,' I said.

'I mean real sleep,' Stacey said. 'Your neck must hurt from being in that position.'

'It does.' I rubbed the back of my neck, and fiery pain shot down it and into my arm.

Stacey saw me wince and said, 'Wait here.' She came back with a warm towel. 'I put this in the microwave. Wrap it around that neck and you'll feel better in no time.'

The warm towel was soothing. I was too tired to eat dinner. I took Stacey's advice and went to bed and slept well that night. I woke up at six the next morning, grabbed coffee and a bagel in the hospital cafeteria, then got dressed to see Chris. I wore my black DI suit, in case I was called out to work. If I didn't have a death investigation, I planned to spend the day helping Jace by watching CCTV footage from cameras near the chocolate shop.

Stacey was waiting outside of Chris's ICU room, all smiles.

'I have a surprise for you,' she said. 'A good one. Chris is off the ventilator. We just took him off it about half an hour ago.'

'That's wonderful,' I said.

'First, I need to talk to you.'

Stacey saw my face fall and said, 'It's not bad news, just things you need to be aware of. When someone's on a ventilator, that can affect their mind and body.'

'How?' I sounded wary.

'Chris could have physical weakness and brain fog.'

'So his thinking could be affected?' I asked.

'Yes. He may have trouble thinking, as well as remembering and reasoning. He could have trouble recalling words, performing basic math and concentrating. He could also have bad dreams and hallucinations. If he does have these, he'll find it very frustrating. So will you. Just be prepared, Angela.'

'What can I do to help?'

'Show him photos of things you've done together, and talk about places you visited to refresh his memory. That will help orient him. Now, he may not have any of this. Just be prepared.'

Stacey squeezed my hand.

Once in Chris's ICU room, I could finally see Chris's face. His whole face. The swelling was going down. He definitely needed a shave. But I could see my Chris again.

'He's asleep.' I couldn't keep the disappointment out of my voice.

'Yes, he is,' Stacey said. 'But he's much more comfortable. He'll start waking up more. I've seen a lot of coma patients. Chris will be OK. If he does well off the ventilator, the surgeon is transferring Chris to the step-down ICU.'

'I hope you're right,' I said.

'I usually am.' She smiled. 'About this kind of thing.'

'Do you live at the hospital, Stacey?' I asked. 'You were here at eight last night.'

'Feels like it sometimes, but I'm working twelve-hour shifts. Extra money for the holidays. Call me if you need anything, honey.' She waved goodbye.

TWENTY-FIVE

Chris continued to improve. The next morning, he was awake when I stopped by. Nurse Stacey said his vitals were good. But he had long, imaginary conversations with his dead parents.

These were one-sided, but I could still figure out what was going on. Chris's mother gave him his love of cooking. This morning, she showed him how to brine a chicken, while Chris asked her questions about her technique.

'I still don't see why I have to soak a chicken in salt water, Mom,' Chris said.

Pause.

'Well, your chicken is always tender, so I'll do it. How long should the meat sit in the fridge?'

Pause.

'That long, huh?'

Pause.

'No, I won't forget to rinse the chicken and pat it dry. Hell, I'll buy it dinner and a movie if it will taste like yours.'

Pause.

'Ow! That's child abuse, hitting me on the head.' He was laughing, and he fell asleep smiling, so I knew it was a good memory.

When I came back an hour later, Chris was having a lively discussion with his father about the St. Louis Cardinals and 'the good old days, when Anheuser-Busch beer owned the team.'

I couldn't quite follow, but the names of old baseball heroes were batted around: Lou Brock, Tim McCarver, Bob Gibson, Curt Flood and Stan 'The Man' Musial.

The talk ended when Chris said, 'We can agree on one thing, Dad. The team hasn't been the same since the days of Gussie Busch. Yeah, I know about Pujols, but Gussie loved that team.'

With that, he fell peacefully back to sleep.

These imaginary conversations made the hair stand up on the back of my neck. They were creepy. He was talking to dead people.

On the other hand, the talks were oddly comforting. Chris and his parents had loved one another. I felt like I was watching a window into his past. He seemed so happy there. But what if he never fully woke up? He'd be lost forever in another, imaginary time.

Back in my room between visits, I tried to work, but I had trouble concentrating. At last, I finished a file. I called Jace and told him, 'I've gone through the Lemon Drop Gift Shoppe files. Didn't find a thing.'

'Same here,' Jace said. 'I was looking at videos from the Royal Burger. Zippo.'

'So what's next?'

'Are you asking for more work?' he said.

'No, I'm begging for work.' Anything to keep me brooding about Chris spending so much time with his dead parents. And who tried to kill him. What if the killer came back to finish the job? If I watched videos, I'd be close to Chris, and Stacey would call me if anyone came to see him.

'Then let me pile it on,' Jace said. 'Did you get the footage from the camera on the garage behind the chocolate shop?'

I checked my files. 'That's a private garage belonging to the Kellerman family?'

'Right. Watch those files for me. That camera catches the door to Selwyn's love nest. I want a list of who goes in and who goes out. And who doesn't come out. Write it down.'

'Aye, aye, sir.'

'How's Chris?' Jace asked.

'Well, he's awake, but he's talking to his parents. They've been dead for years.'

Silence. Then Jace said, 'Is that supposed to happen?'

'I've been told yes. But it's unnerving. Like he can't quite cross over to the land of the living. I just want to get him on this side of the River Styx. Do you know anything about Greiman's investigation into who shot Chris?'

'Sorry, Angela. Greiman's keeping a tight lid on it. I can't even pick up any scuttlebutt. Hang in there, Angela. And call me if there's anything I can do.'

'You've already done it.'

I opened the video from the Kellermans' garage camera, and scrolled through endless hours of boring gray.

I watched a trash truck go down the alley. And cars, lots of cars.

A homeless man dug around in the dumpster behind the chocolate shop, and left disappointed. Twice the Kellermans took their Volvo out for a spin and brought it back loaded with packages.

In between, I took hourly breaks to visit Chris, followed by coffee. During all my visits, Chris slept. I checked in with Stacey, and the nurse said she was being extra careful about Chris's visitors. 'I promise, honey, no one will get near him.'

I worked, mainly to fight off despair. Finally, I reached the day of Selwyn's murder. Before I checked that section of video, it was time to see Chris.

He was awake. I steeled myself to see what his first words would be.

'Angela.' He smiled at me.

'Chris, it's you. It's really you.'

'Who else would it be?' His crooked grin warmed my heart. 'You're here.'

I threw my arms around him and kissed him – carefully. On the undamaged side of his head.

'Of course, I'm here. I've always been here.'

'What happened?' he asked.

'You don't remember?'

'No. I remember being on patrol. The next thing I knew, I woke up here, with you watching over me like a guardian angel. My head hurts.'

He felt the side of his head with the surgery and said, 'Yeow! What's that big lump here?'

'You were shot,' I said. 'Mike found you on the side of the road and called it in. You've had surgery and you've been in a coma. Are you sure you don't remember what happened?'

'Nothing. Just driving my patrol car and then waking up in here.'

He rubbed his head again. 'Where's my hair?'

'The doc had to shave that side of your head for the surgery. But your hair is growing back.'

He started to stand up, holding onto the bed frame.

'Chris, what are you doing?'

'I've got to find who did this to me.'

He was still tethered to the machines. The disturbed machines screamed. I rang for a nurse and Stacey came rushing in. She looked a lot calmer than I felt, and quickly took command.

'Officer Chris,' she said with a smile. 'It's nice to see you awake. I'm Stacey.'

'Hi, Stacey. Where are my pants?'

She and I both pushed him back down on the bed.

'Sorry, Officer,' Stacey said, 'you're not ready to go anywhere. You have to rest up first.'

'Angela can drive me,' he said.

'No, I can't,' I said. 'Please stay in bed.'

Stacey helped settle him back on his pillows. I tucked the covers around him.

Chris refused to rest. 'I've got to go. If you love me, Angela, you'll help me.'

'I do love you. That's why I'm going to help Stacey keep you in bed.'

Stacey left for a moment to call the surgeon. Chris settled down, but he was still restless. 'I've really got to solve this, Angela,' he said.

'I know you do. But sleep first. Once you recover, we'll find who did this.'

'You won't leave me?' He was grasping my hand, begging me.

'Never.' I kissed his forehead.

Chris closed his eyes and seemed to relax. By the time Stacey came back, he was asleep.

I stepped out of the room to talk to her. 'Is he OK?'

'Yes,' she said. 'When people come out of a coma, sometimes their judgment is impaired. That's why he wanted to run out and catch whoever shot him. Angela, you look worried,' she said.

'I am.'

She patted my arm. 'This is progress. I know it doesn't feel like it, but he's getting better. Dr Hallen prescribed some medication to help him sleep if he gets agitated again. He wants to evaluate Chris and possibly move Chris to the step-down ICU.'

'When?'

'Whenever the doctor can stop by. He has two emergency surgeries today. There was a terrible car accident on I-55.'

'Stacey, are you worried that Chris could get out of bed again?' I asked her.

'It's possible,' she said. 'We can put an alarm on his bed.'

'Can I stay with him? I'll bring my work in and keep out of your way.'

'Well, it is against the rules, but I'll ask my supervisor. Why don't you get some coffee and meet me back here in ten minutes.'

I gulped down a cup of coffee, then gathered my laptop, praying that Stacey's supervisor said yes, and headed for Chris's room.

Stacey was waiting, with a smile. 'She says yes, but wants you to sit here' – she pointed to a chair in the corner – 'so you can't be easily seen by the other ICU visitors.'

'Works for me.' I would still be close enough to hold Chris's hand. And make sure no one tried to murder him.

Chris slept peacefully for the rest of the day, while I watched videos from the garage camera.

On the day of the murder, I saw Maybelle Warner, Selwyn's housekeeper, unlock the door to the entrance of the love nest at three fifty-two that afternoon. She was muffled in a heavy, shapeless dark coat and dragging a bulging bag that seemed to hold cleaning supplies. She came out an hour later, at four fifty-one, and locked the door behind her. At five thirty-seven Maybelle was back, this time carrying a heavy bag that said 'Solange' on the side. That was the name of the best restaurant in the Forest. Was Maybelle delivering the cold supper for Selwyn? His last supper?

She was back downstairs at five forty-eight. It was growing dark, but the alley was well-lit, and there was a light directly over the entrance to Selwyn's pied-à-terre.

At six twenty-eight, we finally caught a break. Two young blonde women came up the alley, laughing and talking. Both wore fur-collared coats and spike-heeled leather boots. As they stood under the light by the entrance, one looked like Chloe Westbrook, and the other could have been her twin. That had to be Wendy, the woman Zoe said took her place in the threesome. Chloe and Wendy both carried big leather purses, which could either be fashion accessories or hooker handbags. This must be the night of Selwyn's threesome. The one Zoe mentioned.

Chloe had a key and unlocked the door, and both women entered.

Where was Selwyn?

He unlocked the door and went inside at seven oh one, wearing a topcoat and hat.

I kept scrolling through the video, hour after hour, seeing nothing but an occasional anonymous car. Then, at two seventeen in the morning, both women came out, bundled up in their warm coats. No laughing now. They were dead serious. Their big purses bulged like pregnant ponies, and each carried a fat, flowered, rolling shopping bag. The folding kind that were easily bought online.

Did those bags and purses hold the missing bedding and Selwyn's clothes and shoes?

Chloe locked the door and the two blondes lugged their burdens down the alley, looking harried and unhappy.

I heard the rattle of the food carts in the halls, and realized it was six o'clock. Stacey came in with a hospital dinner on a tray and said, 'You forgot to eat again, didn't you?'

'Yes.' My traitorous stomach growled.

'Hah. I thought so. This is spaghetti, and the hospital version is fairly edible.'

'That's practically four stars,' I said.

'Eat.' She looked mock serious. 'And then go for a walk. I'll keep an eye on Chris.'

The food was, as Stacey said, fairly edible, but I was hungry. I ate the spaghetti, part of a limp salad, and a few bites of white bread that tasted like bleach. Dessert was chocolate ice cream. I finished every bit of that, and even drank the lukewarm milk.

I felt full and sleepy. I set the tray on the floor. I'd go for that walk in a minute.

'Angela, Angela, wake up.'

'Huh?'

It was Stacey, holding my dinner tray. 'You fell asleep again, honey. Visiting hours are over. Time to go back to your room. Chris will be fine, and if there's any news, we'll call you.'

My mouth felt like it had been stuffed with cotton. My nap had really slugged me. 'Thanks, Stacey. I'll go to my room.'

'You do that. And try not to worry. Dr Hallen says he'll stop by around noon tomorrow to evaluate Chris. I expect you'll be getting good news.'

Back in my room, I called Jace on my cell phone. I didn't even bother to say hello. 'I've got news,' I said. 'I've got Chloe and Wendy coming out of Selwyn's apartment the night of the murder. Well, technically, the day after, since it was after midnight. It was two seventeen in the morning, and they had big purses and rolling shopping bags, stuffed with things.'

'Flowered bags?' Jace asked.

'Yes! How did you know?'

'Because I've been watching video of the city parking lot, a block away. At two twenty-five in the morning, Chloe and Wendy rolled their stuff into the parking lot. Chloe drove off in a BMW. Wendy dumped her bags in a white Mini Cooper convertible. They both drove off at two twenty-seven.'

'And Selwyn never appeared,' I said.

'You got it. Can you do an early morning visit to Ms Wendy with me?'

'As long as I'm back at the hospital by noon.'

'See you in the parking lot of her apartment at seven a.m. This may be over soon.'

TWENTY-SIX

Despite three cups of coffee, I was still yawning when I met Jace in front of the Bellingham Apartments at seven the next morning. Only a few lights were on in the ornate old building. The morning was dark and still, and it was cold enough to see our breath.

Jace wasn't sleepy at all. In fact, he was energized. Annoyingly so, considering the early hour. We held a whispered conference outside his car.

'I got good news last night,' he said. 'The lab got prints off Selwyn's tie. That's hard to do on fabric. One set belonged to Chloe. I'm going to get Wendy's prints and see if she's the other set.'

'So each woman pulled on an end of the tie and strangled Selwyn.'

'If we're lucky, we'll be able to prove that,' he said. 'And I can get the chief off my back.'

'What about the two hairs?' I asked.

'Again, one belonged to Chloe and the other person was Ruth Gibbons, who has no connection to the murders.'

'Do you think Wendy still has the folding shopping bag?'

Jace patted his jacket pocket. 'We can search for it. Based on the videos, I was able to get a search warrant. Also, I checked video at Chloe's apartment. No sign of Estelle Selwyn. She didn't kill her.' Jace's phone dinged, letting him know he had a text. 'The photographer, Nitpicker, and three uniforms will be here in ten,' he said. 'Let's go get Wendy.'

A drowsy guard was on duty in the lobby. Jace badged the man and warned him, 'Don't call Ms Raymond or her roommate, Skye.'

In the elevator, Jace asked, 'How's Chris?'

'He seems to be having bad dreams. At least two last night. The nurse said he thrashed around and then called out, "No, no!" and something that sounds like "eat" or "feet." Chris was awake when the nurse came in to check on him, and he didn't remember anything. The nurse stayed with him both times until he fell back asleep.'

'Those dreams must be frustrating for Chris,' Jace said.

'They are. He wants to catch the guy who tried to kill him, and when he wakes up, he can't remember anything. Any word yet from Greiman's investigation into the shooting?'

'I'd tell you if I did,' Jace said. 'Greiman's being very secretive, and he's having long conferences with the chief in his office. He looks very smug when he comes out. I don't trust him.'

'Me neither,' I said. 'I'm supposed to talk to Chris's surgeon at noon. I'd like to be back at SOS for the meeting. OK with you?'

'Fine by me,' Jace said.

The slow elevator stopped at Wendy Raymond's floor, and opened with an unsettling clunk. The dimly lit hall was absolutely still – no televisions or other morning sounds leaked from the apartments.

Jace knocked on Wendy's door. No answer. He rang the doorbell and pounded on the door until he heard an exasperated, 'Just a minute.'

A sleepy Wendy, with a haystack of blonde hair and a ratty green chenille bathrobe, answered the door. She had raccoon eyes from her make-up.

'Ms Raymond?' Jace asked.

'What do you want?' Wendy sounded surly. Before Jace could answer, she glared at him. 'Who are you and why are you pounding on my door at this heinous hour?'

'I'm Detective Jace Budewitz,' he said. 'And this is my associate, Angela Richman. We want to talk to you about Selwyn Skipton.'

'Who?'

'And Chloe Westbrook.'

'Never heard of them.'

Jace had had enough. He stepped forward into her space. She backed away. 'Wrong answer, Ms Raymond,' he said. 'Can we come in?'

'And if I say no?'

Another wrong answer, I thought. Playing tough would not work on Jace.

'Then I'll drag you down to the station house. Your choice.'

'All right, come in.'

If anything, the apartment was a bigger mess than the last time we saw it. A black suitcase was open on the coffee table, dumped on top of the shoes, scarves and make-up that were already there. An ORD airline luggage tag dangled from the suitcase handle, showing Wendy had flown out of Chicago O'Hare International Airport.

I removed a pile of clothes, including a lacy pink bra, from the couch, so Jace and I could sit.

'Now, care to tell us about your threesome with Selwyn Skipton?' Jace asked. 'And if you lie, I will take you in.'

She shrugged, and the bathrobe slipped down to reveal a stained gray T-shirt. Why did Wendy have all these expensive clothes if she wore a raggedy bathrobe and an old T-shirt?

'Selwyn's a sweet old guy,' Wendy said. 'My friend and I visited him. He wanted companionship.'

'Which friend?' Jace asked.

'Chloe Westbrook.'

'And what kind of companionship did you offer this sweet old man?' Jace asked. 'Bible reading? Assembling jigsaw puzzles? Playing Scrabble? Watching movies?'

'We had sex.' Wendy stared at Jace resentfully. 'All three of us.'

If Wendy hoped to shock us, she failed.

'That must have been tiring.' Jace kept his voice mild. 'So when did you and Chloe decide to kill the old man?'

'What? Selwyn's dead? I had no idea.'

Wendy wasn't going to win any Oscars with that unconvincing performance.

'When was the last time you saw Chloe Westbrook?' Jace asked.

'The day after we left Selwyn's apartment. We had lunch together, and I left right after our meal for Chicago. I got home late last night.'

'Where did you stay in Chicago?'

'The Drake Hotel.'

'What was the purpose of this trip?'

'Shopping,' she said. 'I like to shop for clothes in Chicago. St. Louis is a hick town compared to Chicago. The fashions here are out of date.'

'So were you in Chicago when Chloe was murdered?'

'Chloe's dead, too?' She sounded like an actress in a high school play.

'We'd like permission to take your fingerprints,' Jace said.

'Why?'

'So we can catch the person who killed Selwyn and Chloe.'

'What happens if I say no?'

Jace shrugged. 'Nothing. I could get a judge to sign a warrant for your prints, but this is much easier.'

I held my breath. If Wendy refused, this could get sticky.

'Yeah, sure, go ahead.'

Jace's cell phone had a portable fingerprint scanner app. He called it up, and said to Wendy, 'Just place your fingers there on the screen. You don't have to get ink on your fingers.'

When he finished, he sent the prints to Nitpicker, who'd compare them to the unknown prints found on Selwyn's tie.

While he waited to hear back, Wendy said, 'If Chloe and Selwyn are dead . . .'

'No ifs about it,' Jace said. 'They are both definitely dead.'

'That makes two of us from that night. I'm the only survivor. I could be in danger. Selwyn's wife may be trying to kill all three of us.'

'Did Mrs Skipton threaten you?' Jace asked.

'No. But I don't feel safe. There's a killer loose.' She widened her eyes, trying to look fearful.

Jace's phone dinged. Nitpicker had returned his text. He nodded at me, and then spoke to Wendy. 'I know how to make this town much safer,' he said. 'Wendy Raymond, you're under arrest for the murder of Selwyn Skipton.'

Wendy looked genuinely surprised this time. She opened her mouth, but no sound came out.

Jace read Wendy her rights. Finally, Wendy managed four words. 'I want a lawyer.'

Jace asked, 'Angela, would you get some clothes for Ms Raymond to wear so she can be booked?'

I checked the bathroom, which didn't have any windows. No way she could escape. I looked for razors or something she could use as a weapon, but didn't find anything. If she tried to bonk me with a can of hair spray, Jace could take care of her.

Next, I rummaged in the suitcase and found clean jeans, a sweater, socks, underwear and shoes, and piled her clothes on the bathroom sink.

'You have ten minutes to dress,' Jace told her. 'Then you're leaving, no matter what you're wearing.'

She slammed the door. I waited outside the bathroom.

'I'm leaving with a uniform to book her,' Jace said. 'Nitpicker and the videographer are here, along with more uniforms. They'll help you search the place. Leave when you need to so you can be at SOS to meet with Chris's doctor.

'And call me before you go back to work here.'

By the time Wendy was ready, the two uniforms had arrived. Skye stumbled out of a bedroom in a sheer nightgown, giving the officers an eyeful. 'Hey, what's going on?' she asked.

'Your roommate is being arrested for murder,' Jace said.

'Who did she kill?' Skye asked. I was sure my mouth dropped open.

'Selwyn Skipton,' Jace said.

'Oh, the old dude who gave you all that money.' Skye looked at Wendy, then yawned and stretched. The cops were bug-eyed.

'Shut up, Skye.' Wendy looked venomous.

'If you're going to jail, how are you going to pay your half of the rent?' Skye asked.

Wendy didn't answer.

'I'm cold,' Skye said. 'I want to get dressed.'

'Good idea,' Jace said. 'Angela, will you go with Skye?'

'Why?' she asked.

So you don't destroy evidence, I wanted to say.

'Procedure,' Jace said.

Skye accepted that explanation.

I followed Skye into her bedroom, which looked like it had been tossed. 'Pick out some clothes, Skye, and you can dress in the bathroom.'

'Good,' Skye said. 'I don't want to dress in front of you. You're not my type. No offense. I have to go to work this morning.'

'Where do you work?' I asked.

'Firebird. I'm a sales associate.' That was a hip new clothing store. 'I get a fifteen-percent discount. Believe it or not, I spend most of what I make on clothes.'

'Do you and Wendy wear the same size? Do you swap clothes?' I asked.

'Oh, no,' Skye said. 'I'd swim in Wendy's clothes. I'm a size zero or a size two. Wendy is a six or an eight.' Both were fairly small sizes, as far as I was concerned, but it would make our search easier.

I escorted Skye and her clothes to the bathroom. Fifteen minutes later she emerged, wearing a black lace sweater, leather pants and a black leather biker jacket.

'We're going to execute a search warrant for your apartment and Wendy's car.' Jace showed Skye and Wendy the warrant. Neither one was interested in reading it.

'I'm required to read you the warrant,' Jace said.

The warrant was deadly dull, and Jace read it all, including the scintillating sections called 'affiant's qualifications' (Jace was the affiant), 'location to be searched,' 'probable cause,' 'opinions and conclusions' and 'items to be seized.' Skye sat like a child listening to a bedtime story. Wendy looked bored.

When Jace finished, Wendy gave a sarcastic slow clap.

Jace ignored her and asked, 'Skye, do you have a place you can stay tonight?'

Skye shrugged. 'I guess I could stay with my mom.'

'You don't have to, Skye, but it would be easier if you'd leave here for tonight and maybe tomorrow,' Jace told her. 'You may want to pack a few things. Here's my card. You can call me and I'll tell you when you can come back.'

'OK. I'll start packing.'

'And we'll supervise your packing,' Jace said.

'Can I get coffee first?' Skye said. 'I can't do anything without coffee.'

Jace let her fix a Keurig K-cup – Wild Mountain Blueberry coffee. Blueberry flavored coffee? I wasn't sure I could handle that in the morning.

Jace said, 'Angela, let me introduce you to our two new officers, Demetrius Kennedy and Robert Dolan.' Both were African American. Demetrius was a heavily muscled man, about six-and-a-half feet tall, with his hair in a buzz cut. Robert was six feet tall and slender, with a short Afro. Both men greeted me politely.

'Demetrius and Robert will help with the search,' Jace said. 'Ted will go back to the station with me.'

'I've had my coffee and I'm ready to pack,' Skye said. I followed Skye back to her room. While she packed a suitcase, she asked, 'Is Wendy in trouble?'

'It's possible.' I couldn't quite figure Skye out. Was she an air head? A friend of Wendy's? Or someone slyly stabbing her roommate in the back?

'You knew about her evening with Selwyn Skipton?' I asked.

'Yes.' Skye picked two sweaters off the floor, folded them, and put them in the suitcase, along with a leather miniskirt.

'Wendy said it was easy money, but I thought doing the deed with that geezer was gross, no matter how much he paid her and Chloe.'

'How much was Wendy paid?' I asked.

'Don't know.' Skye shrugged, and tossed her sheer nightgown in the suitcase, along with a cotton robe and some underwear. 'Except it was supposed to be five figures. I'm not sure she got all the money, though. She came home really pissed about three in the morning. Slamming doors and throwing things around. I was afraid to ask her about it. The next afternoon, Wendy took off for Chicago and she got home last night.'

'Was she planning that trip?'

'Oh, yes. She takes a shopping trip up there every winter.' She fished a chain belt out of a drawer, threw in a hair dryer and scraped a handful of earrings off the dresser top.

'How long have you two been friends?' I asked.

'I wouldn't call us friends,' she said. 'Not exactly. I mean, we don't hang together. But she puts up with me as a roommate. Most people won't because I'm kind of a slob, but so is Wendy, so we get along fine.'

She left the room and came back with a pink toiletry bag and a black make-up bag. I opened both bags. One held a toothbrush, toothpaste and deodorant. The other bag simply had cosmetics. Skye tossed the bags in the suitcase. Then she rummaged in the bottom of the closet and pulled out a pair of red heels, and added a scarf. She stared at the pile for a minute and said, 'Guess that should keep me for a day or two.'

Skye rolled her suitcase toward the door. She held up Jace's card. 'I'll call you, Detective, and find out when I can come back,' she said. 'Help yourself to some coffee.'

'Thanks,' we said, and waved goodbye.

Once Skye was gone, Jace turned to Wendy. 'Let's go,' he said.

'What about my coat?' she said. 'It's cold out.'

I pulled a practical black puffer coat out of the hall closet.

'I want my coat with the fur collar,' she said.

I shook my head. Jace knew that was the coat she wore the night of the murder.

'No, ma'am,' Jace said. 'That coat is evidence.'

Wendy made a small, impatient yip, like a stepped-on dog. I gathered she was angry. Once she put on her coat, Jace cuffed her with her hands behind her, an uncomfortable position. She should have been more polite to the detective. Ted the uniform and Jace escorted Wendy out the door.

Soon after, the doorbell rang, and Demetrius the uniform let in Nitpicker. Her eyes widened when she saw the messy apartment.

Nitpicker looked around the room. 'What happened here?' she asked. 'Did a dress shop explode?'

'Yeah,' I said. 'And we have to find evidence for a murder in this mess.'

TWENTY-SEVEN

Todd, the police videographer, arrived to photograph the apartment and the search. Todd rarely did more than nod politely, but even he couldn't keep silent when he saw the chaotic rooms.

'I wish I had half the money these two spent on clothes,' he said.

'I could get a new car,' Nitpicker said.

'Or the down payment on a house,' Demetrius added.

Robert stayed silent. He looked overwhelmed.

While Todd worked, Demetrius asked, 'What exactly are we looking for?'

'A pair of high-heeled black boots,' I said, 'women's dress pants in size six or eight, parts of a red cashmere sweater, or any red fibers from that sweater, bloodstains, a flowered rolling shopping bag, gray or white hairs.'

'What do women's dress pants look like?' Robert asked. 'And how will I know what the size is?'

'The size should be inside,' I said. 'If you have any questions, ask me or Nitpicker.'

'Where do we start?' Robert asked.

'I'll take the living room,' Nitpicker said.

'I'll work Wendy's bedroom,' I said.

'Robert, you take the kitchen, including the cabinets,' Nitpicker said. 'And Demetrius, you take Skye's bedroom. Search the room clockwise. Starting with the door and working your way around.'

'What are we going to do with all this stuff on the floor and the tables?' I asked. 'How will we keep it straight?'

She handed each of us a roll of trash bags. 'Stuff them in there,' she said. 'And don't forget to photograph everything, even though Todd is already doing it. Oh, and please glove up. When you finish, I'll vacuum the room for hairs and fibers. Good luck everyone.'

We were going to need it. I brought out my camera, then gloved up and picked up all the clothes on Wendy's bedroom floor first. Some were dirty, some clean and others still had the tags on. The items included club clothes in red or black with cutouts that would embarrass a Kardashian, along with jeans, modest button-down shirts and designer scarves. These filled eight bags.

The shoes, boots and booties left on the floor filled three bags. I found four pairs of black high-heeled boots, and bagged them as evidence, along with two pairs of charcoal-gray dress pants. The lab would examine them later.

After forty-five minutes, I could see the beige carpet. I spent half an hour picking up odd bits on the carpet, including boarding passes for a recent round-trip flight to Chicago and a parking garage receipt for the St. Louis airport. I bagged those as evidence, too. I also found credit card receipts, old bills, apple cores, orange peels, pistachio nutshells and a snowfall of used tissues. When I finished the floor, I took a break. It was nine thirty. Two hours before I had to leave to meet with Chris's doctor.

Nitpicker was stuffing a white fisherman's sweater into a bag when I walked into the living room. 'These women should pay us for what we're doing,' she said. 'Making any progress?'

'I uncovered the bedroom floor,' I said. 'First time it's been exposed in ages.'

'Find anything useful?'

'Some black boots, two pairs of dress pants, bills, credit card receipts, boarding passes for the Chicago trip, and a lot of old Kleenex.'

'Yuck. You're wearing gloves, I hope.'

'I should be wearing a hazmat suit. What about you? Any luck?'

'I went through the hall closet first,' Nitpicker said, 'and packed up Wendy's fur-collared coat and a pair of black leather high-heeled boots. I found two pairs of black wool dress pants, size six. That's it. What I don't understand is why do these two have all these clothes? I don't see any evidence that they have an active social life.'

'No information on their phones yet,' I said. 'Jace checked their social media. Both like to go to concerts and hit the clubs. Wendy has some club clothes, but most of what I've found so far she could wear to dinner with her grandmother. Skye said she likes to buy clothes at a discount from the shop where she works. I haven't seen any photos of either of them with close friends or lovers.'

'These two women are hoarders,' Nitpicker said. 'Or compulsive shoppers.'

'You ready for some coffee?' I asked. 'Skye said we could have some of hers.'

'I don't want anything from here,' Nitpicker said. 'There's a little coffee shop around the corner. Let's grab a cup and some breakfast there. We can walk there.'

'I'll ask Demetrius and Robert if they'd like anything,' I said.

The walk in the chilly air helped relieve the kinks and soreness from stuffing trash bags full of clothes and crawling around on the floor.

The coffee shop itself was vintage Seventies, with booths recycled from church pews and macrame plant holders. We ate hot coffee and Canadian bacon-and-egg sandwiches, and ordered coffee to-go for Demetrius and Robert.

Half an hour later, refreshed and refueled, we returned to the apartment with coffee for the two uniforms. Robert reported that he'd finished searching the kitchen and agreed to start on the bathroom. Demetrius was still slogging through Skye's room.

'She has a lot of clothes that are size zero,' he said. 'Is that a real size?'

'Yes,' I said.

'If you're a Barbie doll,' Nitpicker said.

Demetrius looked confused, and Nitpicker had to explain she was joking.

I spent the next hour going through Wendy's dresser drawers, where I found nothing useful, and then started on her closet. I took all the clothes out of the closet, one by one, and piled them on her bed.

About halfway into Wendy's closet I found another pair of black dress pants and a black turtleneck sweater that had three pieces of red yarn, each about an inch long.

Yes!

'Todd, Nitpicker, come in here. I think I've found something.'

The tech and the photographer came rushing in, and I showed them the yarn. It was photographed and videoed, and then Todd photographed Nitpicker using tweezers to pluck the yarn off and put it in an evidence bag. The black sweater went into another bag.

'That's it.' I was excited. 'I'm sure those are the threads from the sweater that was stapled to Selwyn's chest.'

'I hope so,' Nitpicker said, 'but don't get your hopes up. The yarn could just be the remains of a sweater she gave to Goodwill.'

'What do you mean the sweater was stapled to the victim's chest?' Demetrius asked.

'I mean someone cut a scarlet letter "A" out of a wool sweater and used a stapler to stick it on Selwyn Skipton's chest,' I said.

'Man, those chicks are sick,' Robert said.

'And not in a good way,' Demetrius said.

'Just be glad you didn't see it,' Nitpicker said.

The four of us went back to work. By eleven thirty, I'd emptied Wendy's closet. The shelves were bare, and so was the closet floor.

'It's time for me to leave for the hospital,' I told Nitpicker. 'The nightstand in Wendy's room has to be emptied. Everything else is done.'

I made it back to the hospital with time to spare. Naturally, Dr Harry Hallen was late. I waited in Chris's ICU room, talking to him and reading from his favorite book. Chris slept peacefully, untroubled by frightening dreams. I prayed that he would wake up, but he slept on.

It was going on one o'clock when the tall, thin neurosurgeon stalked into Chris's room, wearing green scrubs and a surgical cap covered with flames, so the top of his head looked like it was on fire.

Oh, right, this was the doc with the weird cap collection.

'How can I help you, Miss?' Dr Hallen looked at me blankly. He didn't remember me.

'I'm Chris Ferretti's fiancée,' I said. 'I'm supposed to talk to you about his condition.'

He peered at me over half-glasses. 'Oh, right, right. We've met before. Forgive me.' I heard the unspoken rest of that sentence: *I'm so busy with important things.*

'Let's go down to the family conference room, shall we?'

I followed Dr Hallen down the hall to the little room with the rock-hard couches and sat down. Carefully, so I didn't break any pelvic bones.

'I evaluated Chris this morning,' he said. 'We talked for more than five minutes. He was quite lucid.'

'Oh.' I was overwhelmed with relief. 'So he wasn't talking to dead people?'

'No, no. I'm very much alive.' Dr Hallen gave me a condescending smile. 'But some people with brain injuries will do that. It will lessen as he recovers. Your Chris is a survivor,' he said. 'And he is recovering. He's not having seizures, and his speech is not slurred. Those are good signs.'

'I'm glad,' I said. 'When Chris woke up and talked to me, he insisted on getting out of bed so he could catch the person who shot him.'

'Yes, yes. He may be agitated at first, but you and the nurse persuaded him to rest.'

'And then he fell asleep,' I said. 'He's sleeping now.'

'Again, that's good. He needs that sleep.' He patted my hand. 'I know this is frightening, but trust me, your Chris is recovering.'

'How long will he be in the hospital?' I asked.

'I'm not sure,' Dr Hallen said. 'He'll need rehab, and we have an excellent program here. He may need psychological counseling. Injuries such as this can cause depression in some cases. So let's not talk about getting him out, but getting him as healthy as possible. I have more good news for you. Chris is being moved to the step-down ICU now, while we've been talking. That's a sign of how well he's been doing.'

I smiled. 'That is good news.'

'Anything else?' he asked.

'Uh . . .' I struggled to summon the words. I had so many questions. Is Chris in pain? When will he eat solid food? Start walking? Start rehab? My exhausted brain didn't respond fast enough.

Busy Dr Hallen patted my hand and said, 'It's been good talking to you. Gotta run.'

When I headed back to the ICU, I was met by Nurse Stacey. 'Good news, Angela.' Her eyes were alight. 'Chris is on his way to the step-down ICU. Give the nurses there an hour to settle him in, and then you can see him. This is good for you and your honey.'

I tried a smile. 'Thank you,' I said. 'You've been wonderful.'

'My pleasure. Don't be a stranger. You and Chris come back and see us when he's up and walking. And that will be soon.'

While I waited to see Chris in his new room, I went down to the cafeteria for a bowl of vegetable soup, which tasted like veggies in lukewarm dishwater. I finished about half the bowl and ate all the crackers, then took a bottle of water back to my sleep room in the hospital to wait another half hour.

I called Jace and asked if he wanted me to finish searching Wendy's apartment.

'No need,' he said. 'I checked in with Nitpicker and they are almost finished. She has to vacuum for hairs and fibers and that's about it.'

'Find anything?'

'Everything but the flowered rolling bag. I suspect Wendy threw that out. The lab will tell us just how successful this search was.'

'Do you think Wendy killed Chloe?' I asked.

'Yes,' Jace said. 'And it has something to do with money. Maybe Chloe didn't want to give Wendy her share of the money from the threesome. I'm sure money's at the root of this. Wendy could easily have gone back to St. Louis during the six or seven days she was in Chicago to kill Chloe. It's not that far away.'

'It's about a four- to five-hour drive,' I said. 'Wendy could have rented a car in Chicago, drove to St. Louis, and then back to Chicago.'

'I'm getting a warrant to check her credit card accounts,' Jace said. 'We'll get her.'

He sounded so confident, I believed him.

At last, I could see Chris. His step-down ICU room was quite pleasant, for a hospital room. The walls were painted a cool blue, and the floor and built-in cabinets were light-colored wood. I could sit in a comfortable blue recliner. The room had a window, with a view of the winter woods.

I could stay with Chris for half an hour at a time now. I settled back in the chair, holding Chris's hand and watching him sleep.

I drifted off to sleep, knowing that things were going to get better.

TWENTY-EIGHT

'Well, well, aren't you lovebirds cute.'
I woke up to the mocking voice of Detective Ray Greiman. Fuzzy-headed after my nap, I wondered if this was some weird dream. Greiman was standing at the foot of Chris's hospital bed wearing black leather gloves and his black Hugo Boss cashmere coat. Cashmere! For a cop.

He had to be dirty to wear a $2,000 coat.

Behind him stood two uniforms, Pete and Mike. Pete looked smug and gleeful. My old friend Mike looked rumpled and unhappy. This was no dream.

Chris slept peacefully. For once, I was grateful he wasn't awake. I must have fallen asleep holding his hand.

'I'm gonna need that hand you're holding, darlin'.' Greiman used the same mocking tone. I wanted to slug him, but I knew if I let him get under my skin I'd have more problems.

'I'm not your darling.' My voice was frosty. 'Use those words again, and I'll sue you six ways from Sunday.'

'Please move your hand, Ms' – he gave the word a derisive buzz – 'Angela Richman. Officer Christopher Ferretti is under arrest for theft and corruption.'

I felt like I'd been whacked in the head. 'He's what?'

'He's under arrest for theft of evidence.'

'What are you talking about?' This couldn't be true.

Greiman was just warming up. Now he talked with an arrogant flourish, savoring each sentence. 'Approximately twenty thousand multicolored M-30 fentanyl pills are missing from the Chouteau Forest Police evidence room,' he said. 'Yes, that's right. Twenty thousand.'

He paused, waiting for me to react. I refused to give him the satisfaction.

'As you know, fentanyl is fifty times stronger than heroin and a hundred times stronger than morphine,' he said. 'It's one of the deadliest drug threats in Missouri.'

'Is there a point to this, Ray?' I asked.

'Yes. That missing fentanyl stash is important evidence against a major drug dealer. Now that these drugs are no longer in the evidence room, the man could go free. Imagine, a dangerous drug dealer set loose on our streets. Think of the damage he could do.' Again, he was overacting and enjoying this way too much.

'What's this got to do with Chris?' My voice was trembling.

'Officer Pete Clayton searched Officer Ferretti's patrol car after the shooting, and found fentanyl hidden under the spare tire in the car trunk.'

'The spare tire? Give me a break,' I said. 'Chris wouldn't be that stupid. Or that obvious.'

'I'm in charge of the investigation into Officer Ferretti's shooting, and Officer Clayton is assisting. We believe that Ferretti didn't intend to keep the contraband there long. Ferretti was working with a drug dealer, helping distribute this dangerous drug in the Forest. Their deal went sideways, and the dealer tried to kill Chris.'

'Which drug dealer?' I asked. 'And why would this dealer leave the drugs in Chris's car?'

'The dealer heard another police car approaching – that was Officer Pete Clayton's vehicle – and took off.'

'Wait a minute. I thought Mike found Chris.'

'He did,' Greiman said. 'But apparently two cops were too much for the dealer.'

'Did Officer Clayton see this dealer? Or get a license plate number?'

'Unfortunately, no,' Greiman said. 'He stopped to render aid to a fallen officer. That was his first priority.'

'I thought Mike was doing that?'

'Someone needed to stay with Ferretti while Mike called for help.'

'What about tire tracks?' I asked.

'Those were trampled at the scene.'

'So you have nothing,' I said.

'I have fingerprints and DNA from a corrupt police officer who stashed illegal drugs in a department vehicle.'

'And when did you search Chris's car?' I asked.

'Two days ago,' Greiman said.

'And I'm supposed to take this accusation on the word of your acolyte, Pete?'

'What did you call me?' Pete looked angry.

Mike rolled his eyes.

'An acolyte,' I said. 'It means a devoted follower. If that word is too hard for you, how about toady? Or ass-kisser? Or—'

Greiman interrupted me. 'In view of the fact that you are upset by the injuries to your boyfriend, I'll ask Pete not to file a complaint against you for verbal abuse.'

Pete stood there smirking. 'Yeah, but only if Detective Greiman says it's OK.'

'We're very sympathetic, Angela.' Greiman's voice was silky. 'After all, Officer Ferretti is going to spend the rest of his life in prison, and I'm not sure how long that life will be. Cops aren't popular in prison. Maybe you could bake him a cake with a file in it.'

'No!' I was shaking with fear and anger.

'What's the matter?' Greiman said. 'Oh, I know. You can't cook. You'll have to find another way to sneak in that file.'

I gripped the chair arms to keep from slugging him.

'Now, if you'll excuse me, Ms Richman, I need to get over to that side of the bed and continue.'

I stood up and moved into the far corner. I imagined myself lunging at Greiman, my fingers wrapped around his throat, and squeezing. Then I saw myself in jail, with Chris alone in the hospital. I tried to take calming breaths.

Breathe in . . . I watched Greiman take out his metal handcuffs and hold them up so I could see them.

Breathe out . . . I watched Greiman snap the cuffs around Chris's left wrist. Now my unconscious lover was handcuffed to the hospital bed. I fought for control.

'What are you doing?' I said. 'Chris isn't even awake. He can't escape.'

'But you could help him get away,' Greiman said.

'Right. I'm going to throw a two-hundred-pound man over my shoulder.'

'You're capable of anything, Richman,' he said. 'Just to be on the safe side, I'm posting an officer outside this door. Mike will take the first shift.'

Greiman turned toward the door, but not before he said, 'And as soon as your honey wakes up, I'll read him his rights and he will be arrested and charged. Have a nice day. Come along, Officer Clayton.'

'And I'm not an anklet.' Pete was defiant. He walked two paces behind Ray.

The two of them stalked out the door.

'No, Pete,' I said, as he was leaving the room, 'you are definitely not an anklet.'

'You are, however, an idiot,' Mike said, after Greiman and Pete were down the hall.

'Don't make me laugh, Mike,' I said.

The red-faced old cop patted my shoulder. 'Aw, Angela, I'm so sorry,' he said. 'I don't for a minute believe Chris had anything to do with drugs. Never in a million years. I'll talk with Jace, and the two of us will find out what the hell is going on here.'

'I hate Ray Greiman,' I said. 'He's lazy and dishonest.'

'And the worst detective on the force,' Mike said.

'How does Greiman survive?'

'The chief protects him. Greiman occasionally gets a slap on the wrist, but that's about it. He has a real knack for skating by, and only a place as backward as the Forest would let him stay on the force. I hate it that he uses his badge to take advantage of gullible young women. I heard he brought a hooker to that fancy dinner with the chief, and they sat at the chief's table.'

'She wasn't a hooker, Mike. Chris and I were there, too. She was a nice young woman who was in over her head. She didn't know how to dress for a formal event and Greiman didn't give her any guidance. When it was clear that her skimpy outfit was embarrassing, he virtually abandoned her.'

'Typical,' Mike said.

'What's the story on Pete Clayton?' I asked. 'The anklet.'

Mike gave a derisive snort. 'That boy's dumber than a box of rocks. He got the job because his family knew someone important in the Forest.'

'Typical,' I said.

'Pete has no special skills for the job. He thought he could walk right in and be promoted to detective. He hates doing the scut work, like guarding doors and directing traffic. And in a department this small, we all have to do that. Naturally, Pete gravitated to a malcontent like Greiman, who told Pete how mistreated they both were. Pete follows him around like a puppy dog, and does whatever Greiman tells him.'

'Do you think the two of them could have cooked up the story that Chris was meeting with a drug dealer?'

'It's possible,' Mike said.

'For what reason? What do they have against Chris?' I asked.

'Greiman is jealous of Chris.'

'Why? Greiman is a detective,' I said. 'Chris is a patrolman.'

'Chris is respected. Greiman isn't. And Chris has you.'

'Me?' My voice was a surprised screech. 'Greiman hates me.'

'He's never going to be president of the Angela Richman fan club, but you and Chris have something he wants – class. Greiman was laughed at for bringing a woman who dressed like a hooker to that dinner. I heard you and Chris looked like a million bucks. As for Pete, that lame brain does what Greiman tells him.'

'So how did those drugs get in Chris's patrol car?'

'If they were ever in the car,' Mike said. 'I think they were planted. That's what Jace and I are going to do. Find out what's going on.'

'May I get you some coffee?' I asked. 'The nurses let me use their lounge. Their coffee's better than what's served in the cafeteria.'

'Don't mind if I do,' Mike said. 'I take mine black.'

'Watch Chris and I'll be right back.'

I hurried down the hall, unlocked the nurses' lounge, and saw the coffee pot was almost empty. I dumped the tarry dregs in the sink, and brewed a fresh pot. Ten minutes later, I returned with two large coffees in foam cups and two packets of Oreo cookies from a machine.

'Ah, thank you.' Mike inhaled his brew. 'Fresh coffee. Just what I needed.' When it cooled he sipped it and said, 'Not bad, not bad at all.'

Mike loved gossip, so I wasn't surprised when he asked, 'When did you cross Greiman?'

I sat across from Mike in a visitor's chair. 'Ray and I clashed almost from the beginning. I was a new death investigator when we were called to a suicide. A woman from one of the moneyed Forest families was going through a bad divorce. She was found dead in her Bentley, with the garage door shut.'

'Carbon monoxide poisoning?' Mike said.

'Yes. Because the woman was divorcing, Greiman said her death was a suicide. He couldn't imagine that a woman could live without a man. But the victim's sister and the housekeeper insisted the dead woman would never commit suicide. I believed them. Greiman didn't care. His shift was almost over and he wasn't getting overtime, so he wanted to wrap up the case as a suicide and go. I refused to move as fast as he wanted, and examined the body thoroughly. During the examination, I noticed that the victim, who'd died in her car, was wearing clean white socks. How did she get from her house, across a dirty courtyard and into a garage, with clean socks?' I took a long drink of my cooling coffee.

'Someone carried her body to that car and made it look like a suicide,' Mike said.

'Yep. My relationship with Ray went downhill from there. He doesn't like me any more than I like him. He's complained that I have "a stick up my ass."' I crunched a cookie.

'That means you're professional,' Mike said.

'I admit that Greiman, with that thick black hair and those expensive clothes, is handsome in a superficial way.'

'Doesn't do much for me,' Mike said, dipping an Oreo in his coffee. 'He's got mean eyes.'

Mike ate his cookie while I said, 'For some reason, the chief seems to like Greiman and respect his opinion.'

'Well, the chief is not real bright and he's bone lazy,' Mike said. 'Greiman knows when to laugh at the chief's jokes. He tells him he's right, even when he isn't. Greiman will bend inconvenient rules for the chief. He'll also lie for him.'

'That makes sense,' I said.

I finished my coffee and said, 'So what do I do next, Mike? How do I get those stupid handcuffs off Chris?'

'You're going to need your friends, Angela. Call your lawyer friend,' Mike said. 'All he has to do is whisper the word lawsuit to Buttkiss and those cuffs will pop right off. And call Katie. She's another smart cookie.

'Speaking of cookies,' Mike said. 'Thanks for the coffee and Oreos. Now I'm going to sit outside the door. Call me if you need anything. And don't you worry. We'll figure this out.'

TWENTY-NINE

Katie was spitting mad. She was working late at the office when I called her at six o'clock, and told her Greiman had handcuffed Chris to his hospital bed. Since the ME's office was at the back of the hospital, she ran straight to Chris's room.

Jace was heading home after a long day, but when he heard about Chris, he turned his car around and drove to SOS.

A few minutes after Jace joined us, Monty arrived.

I had commandeered (OK, swiped) chairs from various empty rooms, and found five cups of coffee. The four of us held a meeting in Chris's room near the door, so Mike could hear us. The veteran patrol officer was an important ally.

Katie looked frazzled, and kept twisting a lock of her brown hair. Monty was his usual smooth, well-dressed self. Jace was worried, but I wasn't sure why. Thankfully, Chris slept through the excitement.

Rather than keep repeating the story of why Chris had been handcuffed, I told the story once to the assembled group. Katie was the first to respond.

'Greiman!' she said. 'I should have known. That man suffered a craniorectal inversion.'

'What's that?' Jace said.

I jumped in to explain this medical term. 'It means Greiman has his head stuck up his—'

'Anus,' Katie finished, using the technical term.

I laughed and Katie took a bow.

'An affliction that plagues many on the Forest force,' Jace said.

Mike stuck his head around the door frame and added, 'And not just the force.'

'OK,' I said. 'How do we get those cuffs off Chris? And before he wakes, I hope?'

Monty said, 'Angela, since you're acting for Chris, will you hire me as his lawyer?'

'You're hired,' I said.

'Good. I suspected you'd say that. I came prepared.' He opened his briefcase and handed me a contract. I signed it.

'It says you want a five-hundred-dollar retainer,' I said. 'Will you take something as old-fashioned as a check?'

'Works for me,' he said. 'I'll show the contract and the check to the chief, if he asks. Later, I'll tear up the check.'

'Don't you dare,' I said.

'We'll discuss that another time,' he said. 'Now, if you'll excuse me a minute, I'm going to call Chief Butkus.'

'And scare the crap out of him,' Mike said.

While Monty was in the family waiting room threatening the chief, Katie said, 'I finished the autopsy on Chloe Westbrook. As you suspected, she'd been hit on the head and knocked unconscious, then strangled with her purse strap.'

'Was she hit with the pottery vase?' I asked. 'The killer hit her hard enough to break that heavy vase.' I took a long drink of coffee. I needed the caffeine to stay awake.

'I found tiny bits of red-glazed pottery in her hair, so yes. She was out cold when she died, so she didn't suffer.'

'That's what I told her sister, Zoe,' I said. 'Glad it was true.'

'Best I can figure out, Chloe was killed two to three days after the murder of Selwyn Skipton,' Katie said.

'When Wendy was supposed to be in Chicago,' I said.

I turned to my detective friend. 'What did the lab find at Chloe's apartment, Jace?'

'Not much. The fingerprints Nitpicker found on the broken vase belonged to Chloe.'

'Oh.' I couldn't hide my disappointment.

'There was a partial print on the purse strap that belonged to Wendy. And two of Wendy's blonde hairs.'

'Is that enough to get Wendy for Chloe's murder?'

'Probably not,' Jace said. 'An attorney could argue that the hairs were transferred to Chloe as the result of her sex work with Wendy. Same thing if Chloe brought that purse to the threesome.'

'Do you think Wendy killed Chloe?' I asked.

'Absolutely. And I think the fight was over money. But we have nothing to prove it.'

'Anything useful from Wendy's apartment?'

'Too early.' Jace looked weary, with dark bags under his eyes. His blue no-iron shirt was wilted and his blue striped tie had a grease spot on it.

He took a drink of coffee, and his cell phone rang.

Jace gulped the coffee and answered his phone.

'If she wants to, I don't see any problem with that,' he said. 'When are you going there next? Half an hour? Works for me.'

He ended the call and said, 'That was Nitpicker. Zoe wants permission to visit her sister's pet parrot, Buddy. Since the bird will eventually be hers, I don't see a problem with that.'

Monty was back, with a big smile on his face. 'The chief caved,' he said. 'I mean, he graciously agreed that an unconscious man does not need to be handcuffed to a hospital bed. He insists on keeping a police officer stationed at the door.'

'Fine with me,' I said. 'Just so those cuffs are off.'

'Mike is going to get a phone call ordering him to remove the cuffs,' Monty said.

'I'm ready.' Mike held up his cell phone.

It rang, right on cue. Mike stood in the room and talked extra loud, so we could hear. 'Hello? Chief Butkus. Yes, I'm right by Officer Ferretti's door. You want the cuffs off? Yes, sir. I'll do that right now.'

Mike hung up and said, 'You heard that, right? Come watch the grand opening.'

Mike marched over to Chris's bed, and unlocked the cuffs with his key. Chris didn't move.

Katie saw my worried face and whispered, 'Chris is OK, Angela. He's still tired and he needs sleep to heal.'

Mike tossed the cuffs in the red biohazard waste container.

'You're not going to give those cuffs back to Greiman?' I asked.

'Chief didn't tell me what to do with them,' Mike said. 'Hospitals are crawling with germs, and I wouldn't want to endanger the force's finest detective.' He winked and shut the top of the biohazard container. 'Now Greiman's out thirty bucks. He should be out of a job.'

I enjoyed that bit of petty revenge, and lifted my coffee cup to salute him. Monty and Katie joined me.

'OK, OK,' Mike said. 'Now that the cuffs are off, we have to prove that Chris is innocent, or once he's awake, they'll get slapped right back on.'

'I'll take notes.' I opened my iPad. 'First question, what was Chris doing at the shooting site?'

'Nobody knows,' Mike said. 'He wasn't in his normal zone.'

'Is that bad?' I asked.

'Not necessarily,' Mike said. 'Officers are often out of their regular zones. He could have been looking for a clean bathroom or food.'

'Wasn't he shot on a country road?' I asked.

'Uh, yes,' Mike said. 'So scratch those two. He could have been following up a contact, or returning to the station. There could be lots of good reasons.'

'How was Chris found?' Monty asked.

'What do you mean?' I asked.

'I mean who found him and why? There has to be a reason,' Monty said. 'Did a passing citizen call it in? Was the dispatcher alerted when he didn't respond to his radio? Was the radio emergency button pressed on his hand-held? Was the "officer down" sensor on his radio triggered?'

'What's that?' I asked. 'I seem to be particularly thickheaded today.'

Mike stepped in to answer. 'You aren't thickheaded. You've got a lot on your mind. The "officer down" sensor detects whether a radio has been static for a certain amount of time, or if it's been tilted beyond a certain angle. If the officer doesn't respond, it will automatically transmit a call for help. From what I've heard, none of those had anything to do with who found Chris.

'As you know, I found him,' Mike said. 'I had to be out there to interview a suspect. I called the ambulance. Then Pete stopped by to help. He was more trouble than he was worth, getting in my way.'

'I know Chris called me on his cell phone after he was shot,' I said. 'He didn't mention anyone being with him. He talked to me and then I think he fainted.' I started to tear up at the memory, and bit the inside of my mouth to keep from crying. Katie patted my hand.

'If Chris passed out, that would give whoever shot him time to rub stuff on his skin to transfer his DNA,' Katie said.

'The shooter could pull out a couple of Chris's hairs,' Mike said, 'and put his fingerprints on the bag of drugs. That would be easy with an unconscious man.'

'Why did Chris stop at that spot?' Monty said. 'Did he see something? Did he get a call or a text that sent him there? Was it an ambush?'

'Where's his cell phone?' I asked. 'And I was the last person to speak to Chris. Why didn't the great detective interview me?'

'We're talking about Greiman,' Mike said. 'We all know he's careless. He won't interview you. But we do need Chris's cell phone.'

'Are Chris's things in the room?' Katie asked.

I jumped up, opened the narrow closet and found a clear plastic bag with Chris's name on it. My heart stopped when I saw his bloodstained shoes.

'There's no uniform,' I said.

'They probably cut it off him when he was prepped for surgery,' Katie said.

'His duty belt isn't in here either,' I said. 'That had his weapon.'

'What else was on his belt?' Monty was taking notes now.

I closed my eyes and tried to picture the belt. 'Chris is right-handed, so his magazine pouch and pepper spray are toward the front of the belt on his weak side, his left. He has two sets of handcuffs, carried flat against his lower back. He has . . .' I stopped. I couldn't remember anything else.

'A backup flashlight?' Mike asked.

'Yes,' I said.

'How about an expandable baton?' Mike asked.

'Yes.' Now I could see his belt clearly. 'He also had his portable radio, and a cell phone pouch.'

I held up the bag. 'None of those are here,' I said.

'We can see that,' Mike said.

'Sorry, I didn't mean to be Captain Obvious,' I said.

'Is there a receipt in the bag?' Monty asked.

I removed the shoes. 'Nothing.'

'Check inside the shoes,' Monty said.

I reached into the right shoe, and held up a piece of paper. 'Yes. This says the belt and attached items listed here are being kept in the hospital security office. Two people have signed the receipt. The list seems to include everything including Chris's weapon and his cell phone and charger.'

'We need that cell phone,' Monty said. 'I'll get it in the morning.'

'What about Chris's duty bag?' Mike asked.

'He usually stashes that in the trunk,' I said, 'along with his weather gear, and a first aid kit.'

I was feeling better now. If the hospital had Chris's weapon and cell phone, we had a better chance of finding out what was going on.

'Was Chris found outside his car?' I asked.

'Yes,' Mike said. 'I found Chris on the passenger side of his car.'

'Did Chris return fire?' Monty asked.

'No,' Mike said.

'So why do you think Pete stopped by to help you with Chris?' I asked.

'I don't know,' Mike said. 'That's not his assigned zone, either, but no one asked how Pete happened to come across Chris. When an officer is down, it can be really confusing.'

'What happened to Chris's patrol car after the shooting?' I asked.

'It was towed to the police garage,' Jace said. 'It's a crime scene.'

'Worked by Greiman and Pete.' I tried to focus on something positive.

'Mike and Jace, who do you think shot Chris?' I asked.

'First, Chris wasn't involved with drugs or drug deals,' Jace said. 'I want to make that clear.'

'That's what I said to Angela,' Mike added. 'No how, no way.'

'Do you think the shooter could be Ray Greiman?' I asked.

'I'm no fan of Greiman,' Mike said, 'but I don't think he'd shoot another cop.'

'What about Pete?' I asked.

'Possible.' Mike shrugged. 'The kid is lazy and entitled. I've heard him complaining that he doesn't make enough money and he wants a new car. I could see him getting cozy with a dealer for easy money.'

'If he shot Chris, do you think Pete used his duty weapon?' I asked.

'Well, as you saw today, Pete's a dim bulb,' Mike said, 'so it's possible he used his own gun to shoot Chris. But no projectiles or casings were found at the scene.'

'Well, Greiman is investigating,' I said. 'He's lazy.'

'Yes, he is,' Jace said. 'Except Greiman took over the investigation. I was assigned the case first. I looked for projectiles and casings but didn't find anything. There were weeds all over the place – I'm talking giant ragweed six feet tall, pokeweed, and other tall plants with thick, hairy stems. Plus, poison oak. Poison ivy was wrapped around all those plants. I wanted to go back there when I was wearing protection so I could do a better search, but I didn't get the chance.'

'How come you know so much about weeds, city boy?' I asked.

'Because I wandered into a patch of poison ivy on another case. That stuff itches like fire. I about scratched my legs off. Took weeks to get rid of the rash. After that, I made it my business to study the local weeds – poison sumac, poison oak and poison ivy.'

'Leaves of three, let them be,' Mike said. 'I found that out the hard way as a rookie.'

I changed the subject, before everyone jumped in with a poison weed story. 'Greiman said the drugs were stolen from the evidence room. How did they get out?' I asked.

'I've got an idea about that,' Mike said. 'Let me do some checking first.'

Jace's phone rang. It was Nitpicker. 'Whoa, whoa,' Jace said. 'Slow down a minute. I can't understand a word you're saying. OK, I'll put my phone on speaker so everyone can hear.'

He pressed the speaker icon and we heard Nitpicker say, 'Jace, Angela, you've got to come to Chloe's apartment and see this. I mean, hear it. I think we can nail Wendy for Chloe's murder.'

'It's almost eight o'clock,' Jace said. 'Can it wait until morning?'

'No!' Nitpicker said. 'Get over here. Now.'

THIRTY

Jace raced down the hospital halls so fast, Monty and I had trouble keeping up with him. We shrugged into our coats and ran past people in wheelchairs, a man carrying flowers, and two women helping a frail dark-haired woman walk down the hall.

'Hey,' shouted one of the helpers. 'Slow down! You're going to hurt someone.'

We didn't slow down, and thankfully, we didn't hurt anyone. When Monty and I made it out the front door, we really poured on the speed to run to his car. The winter night was pitch dark and cold. The brisk air woke me up.

'I'll drive, Angela,' Monty said.

'Fine with me.'

Katie had agreed to stay behind and watch Chris. Monty knew where Chloe's apartment was located. We followed Jace there. Jace didn't put on his lights and siren, but he drove ten miles over the speed limit. Monty followed in his wake.

I settled back in the leather seats in Monty's Mercedes. They were much more comfortable than any hospital chair, and the car smelled like leather and sandalwood cologne. I enjoyed being surrounded by quiet luxury.

'Thanks for bailing out Chris,' I said.

'Any time, Angela. I'm here for both of you,' Monty said. 'I think Chris has been set up. When we find out who did it, there will be hell to pay.'

And nobody knew how to raise hell better than Monty. I was glad he was on our side.

The drive to the Peacock Apartments took less than ten minutes, thanks to Jace's speeding. Monty's car pulled into a visitor spot next to Jace's unmarked car. The detective, who'd looked so tired when we first met in Chris's room, had a second wind. He hurried into the apartments, and flashed his badge at the receptionist. Monty and I caught up with him in the elevator.

The slow elevator gave me a chance to catch my breath. 'You really took off when you got the news from Nitpicker,' I said.

'You didn't see today's *Forest Gazette*, did you?' Jace asked. 'Look up the editorial.'

I opened my iPad and called up the paper. The editorial's headline asked: *Are Our Young Women Safe in the Forest?*

'Nothing like spreading fear,' I said.

'The chief's been getting calls all day,' Jace said, 'and every time he gets one, he chews me out again.'

I read through the editorial, which said a 'promising Chouteau Forest University student' was 'brutally murdered.' No mention of Chloe's side hustle as a sugar baby.

The article said, 'Kudos to Chief Butkus, who caught the killer of prominent citizen Selwyn Skipton.'

'Hah!' I said. 'Butkus took credit for your arrest of Wendy. And Selwyn is once more a "prominent citizen" instead of a "dirty daddy."'

'I'm used to the chief stealing the credit,' Jace said. 'He does that to everyone. Keep reading.'

The elevator clanked and groaned. I hoped it wouldn't get stuck.

I concentrated on the article. 'No one is safe when an innocent young woman is murdered in her luxury apartment. The police must protect our wives and daughters – and all the citizens of Chouteau Forest – so that peace and prosperity can be restored to our community.'

'I can see why the chief went ballistic,' I said. 'The editorial uses "luxury apartment," "wives and daughters," and "prosperity." This is code for "someone is killing rich women in the Forest."'

'You got it,' Jace said. 'And the longer it takes to solve this murder, the more the pressure on me mounts.'

With a clunk and a shudder, the elevator landed at Chloe's floor. We tiptoed past Alice's door, but the nosy neighbor stuck her head out of her doorway. Alice was wearing a dress with tumorous blue roses. 'Oh, Detective,' she said, her voice syrupy sweet. 'That parrot is making a racket again.'

'I'm on my way there right now,' Jace said.

'Oh, good,' Alice said. 'I'd hate to have to complain to the chief of police.'

'Stand in line,' I said.

'What did you say?' Alice was gearing up for combat.

'Ms Richman said, "Everything will be fine,"' Jace said.
Monty raised an eyebrow. 'I'll explain later,' I whispered to him.
Jace knocked on the apartment door and Nitpicker answered. Behind her was Zoe. Chloe's twin was wearing a pink sweater and jeans, and looking younger and prettier, despite the air of sadness surrounding her.

Nitpicker looked festive in jeans and a turquoise sweater that matched her new hair color. She was dancing around the stylish red, black and gray apartment. 'We have a witness!' she said.

'Where?' Jace asked.

'Right in front of you.' She waved her hands at the cage. 'Ta-da! It's Buddy.'

Jace was red with fury. 'A parrot. Your witness is a blasted parrot! You've got to be kidding.'

He turned on his heel and started toward the door. Monty stopped him. 'Hold on, Jace. That's not as crazy as it seems. Parrots have been used in other cases.'

'Name one,' Jace said.

'I can name several,' Monty said. 'A woman in Michigan was convicted of her husband's murder, thanks in part to her parrot. Police first thought someone had murdered the husband and tried to kill the wife. She survived being shot in the head. But the parrot repeated the husband's last words. The parrot supposedly said, "Don't fucking shoot!" in the husband's voice. Turns out the woman murdered her husband and then tried to kill herself. The details of the shooting were remarkably vivid, as reported by the parrot. And it was an African grey.'

'Just like Buddy,' I said.

'Another parrot witnessed the rape and murder of a woman in Argentina,' Monty said. 'The parrot repeated the whole terrible crime, and gave the police a vital clue.'

'OK,' Jace said, 'Maybe it's worth listening to.'

Monty was wound up now, and he kept talking. 'Then there's the parrot in New Orleans that had to go into witness protection.'

'You're joking,' Jace said.

'I kid you not,' Monty said.

'The bird belonged to a crime boss who was suspected of child abuse, among other crimes. Late at night, the bird would sometimes cry like a child, then sound like it was moaning in pain, and then make a noise like *whack*, or *thwack!* as if someone was being hit.

The bird had to be hidden because it knew too much and wouldn't shut up.

'There's more . . .'

'That's enough,' Jace said. 'It's late and I'm tired. Let's get on with it.' He plopped down on the couch. I sat next to him. Zoe took the chair closest to the cage, and Monty took the other chair.

Nitpicker, looking a bit like a tropical bird herself, jumped in. 'I've been taking care of Buddy. He's been depressed. I've tried to play with him, but Buddy hasn't been eating much, he's pulling out his feathers, and he mostly sits in the corner of his cage. My aunt Selma told me birds get depressed like people, and Buddy has been showing the symptoms. He won't talk, either.

'So when Zoe asked to see the bird, I hoped her visit would help. The change was amazing. As soon as Zoe walked in here tonight, Buddy started talking. He said, "Chloe-Zoe, Chloe-Zoe, Buddy loves Chloe-Zoe. Give us a kiss. Give us a kiss. Kiss Buddy, Zoe."'

Zoe continued, 'When I opened the cage door, Buddy sat on my wrist and said, "Buddy's a good boy. Buddy's a pretty boy" just like he used to.' She looked happier than I'd ever seen her.

She reached into the cage, and Buddy hopped on her wrist.

Buddy interrupted Zoe by whistling and chirping. Then the parrot barked like a dog, meowed like a cat, and said, 'Buddy's smart. He's a smart boy.'

Zoe smiled. 'Now that's how Buddy sounds when he's happy.'

Buddy nuzzled her neck.

'But this time, Buddy said something new,' Zoe said. 'Something I've never heard him say before. Let's see if he'll do it again.'

She petted Buddy's head with her index finger. Buddy paced back and forth on Zoe's arm, fluffed his wings and said in a high, frightened female voice, 'Don't kill me. Don't kill me. Please don't kill me. I don't have your money, but I'll get it. I promise.'

I froze. Buddy's words were clear.

The next voice from the parrot was also a woman's, and it was low and angry. 'I want it now, bitch. Now! I screwed that disgusting old man and you promised me. Twelve. Thousand. Five. Hundred. Dollars. I want my share.' The parrot enunciated each money number as if it was a separate sentence.

Now Buddy was back to the higher-pitched woman's voice. It sounded whiny. 'It's not my fault he wouldn't pay the whole twenty-five thousand. I gave you half of what I got.'

'That's not good enough,' said the second voice. 'I want my money. I need it.'

The first voice sounded terrified. 'Put down that vase, Wendy. Please! Don't hurt me! Don't!' The parrot screamed four times and then made a gurgling noise.

Zoe was crying. 'I think Buddy witnessed my sister's death,' she said. 'Her parrot gave us the details.' Buddy nuzzled her neck again, as if to comfort her.

'Sure sounds like it,' Nitpicker said.

Zoe's sobs were louder. Nitpicker patted her back. I got Zoe a glass of water from the kitchen and a box of tissues. It must have been horrible for Zoe to hear her sister's death reenacted. I guided her back to her chair. Zoe sipped the water and wept quietly while we talked. Buddy sat on her shoulder, looking alert and bright-eyed.

'So what do we do?' Jace said. 'Take the cage into the DA's office?'

'No, parrots can't testify in court,' Monty said. 'For one thing, they can't be sworn in. Also, they can't be cross-examined.'

'Then what was the point of this exercise?' Jace sounded angry. No, fed up.

'Buddy gave you the details of why Chloe was killed,' Monty said. 'He mentioned Wendy's name and that Chloe was hit with a vase. We can tell Wendy that we have a witness. When we tell her the details, I think she'll cave.'

A weary Jace had the last word. 'We don't have anything unless we can prove that Wendy was in St. Louis on the day of the murder.'

THIRTY-ONE

Back in Monty's car, the lawyer asked, 'When was the last time you ate, Angela?'
'I don't remember. I may have had lunch.'
'If you don't remember, you haven't eaten.' He turned his car toward I-55.
'Where are we going?'
'To that diner by the highway, to get you a square meal.'
'No. I need to get back to Chris.'
'Katie is with Chris. She can take better care of him than you can. Besides, I think the diner's special today is chicken and dumplings with cornbread, and Katie says that's your favorite meal.'
'But—'
'No arguments,' he said. 'I'm hungry too, and there's nothing more dangerous than a hungry lawyer.'
Half an hour later, we were in my favorite highway diner, with red leather booths and waitresses who called me 'hon.' A steaming plate of chicken with cloud-fluffy dumplings was in front of me, along with a skillet of homemade cornbread and honey butter.
'Can I get you some coffee, hon?' Brenda the waitress said. She was a pretty, plump woman with neat, permed hair.
'I'll have orange juice and a glass of water,' I said. I was too jangly from all the coffee I'd already drunk today.
While Monty slathered his burger and fries with ketchup, I told him about nosy Alice, the neighbor who complained about Chloe's noisy bird.
'Nosy neighbors can be good witnesses,' Monty said. 'Did she see anything useful?'
'No, there's never a snoop around when you need one.'
I buttered my cornbread and bit into it. Mm. Just the way I liked it. 'Were those stories about using parrots as witnesses true?'
'Sure.' Monty took a bite of his burger, and ketchup splurted out on his plate. 'There are all sorts of stories about animals appearing in court, especially in the fifteenth and sixteenth centuries. Many of those involved murderous pigs who were tried and convicted.'

'I know that pigs can eat people,' I said. 'I've read news stories where they've killed farmers.'

'That's usually how the pigs wound up in court,' Monty said. 'A French sow attacked and killed a child. The killer was put on trial, and there were lawyers for the defense and prosecution. The sow was found guilty and sentenced to be executed. For some reason, the sow was dressed in men's clothes and hanged. There are lots more of these stories.'

Monty mopped up the excess ketchup with a couple of fries.

'Let's go back to the parrot,' I said. 'Any chance that talking birds will be allowed to testify in court? They're very smart.'

'Too many problems. How do we know that Buddy actually heard Chloe being murdered?' Monty asked.

'Because of what he said. And his words match the facts.' I speared a tender piece of chicken breast.

'But what if we don't know the facts?' Monty asked. 'Or what if Buddy is imitating something he heard on TV? People could be convicted on the word of a parrot that watched *CSI*.'

'But Buddy said the name Wendy.'

'He did. How do we know Buddy didn't just drop that name in there because he heard Chloe say it on the phone?'

'OK, I get it,' I said. 'But I wish we knew what animals were saying to us, don't you?'

'Some of them, like cats and dogs.' Monty finished his last bite of burger and said, 'However, I'd just as soon not know what this cow was saying on the way to the slaughterhouse.'

After he said that, I was glad I'd finished my chicken and dumplings. Brenda took my empty plate. I buttered the last of the cornbread, and ate it. We turned down dessert. Monty called for the check and refused to split it with me.

It was almost nine o'clock by the time Monty parked in the SOS lot. 'I'll go in with you to get Katie and bring her home,' he said.

Home. I wished with all my heart that I was going home with Chris. I missed him so much.

Monty's phone rang. 'It's Katie,' he said, and put the phone on speaker.

'Where are you?' Katie sounded worried.

Fear stabbed me. 'Right here in the hospital parking lot,' Monty said.

'What's wrong with Chris?' I asked.

'Calm down, Angela,' she said. 'He's fine. He had a bad dream and he wants to talk to you.'

My heart froze. 'I'll be right up.'

I didn't wait for Monty to get out and lock his car. Once again, I was running through the hospital, this time toward Chris's room. It was after visiting hours, so there was less chance I'd mow down a patient.

The hospital elevator was too slow, so I ran up the steps, and arrived at Chris's room out of breath.

A new police guard was sitting at Chris's door, Ted, the baby-faced uniform with a buzz cut. Ted let me into the room.

'How's Chris?' I ran past Katie to the bed, and saw he was sleeping. I kissed his forehead, but he gave no sign he was awake. The swelling from the surgery was going down, and his hair was growing back. He almost looked like my Chris again. If only he would wake up.

Katie was at my side. 'Let him rest,' she said, her voice low. 'Let's take a walk down the hall to the family conference room.'

I didn't question why she wanted to leave the room. I followed her down the hall. 'We'll be back in a few minutes, Ted,' she said. 'May we bring you some coffee or a snack?'

Ted held up a Thermos and said, 'I'm good. Thanks.'

Once Katie and I were in the family conference room, I reached up and pulled the plug on an annoying TV newscast. The room, with its bland furniture and anonymous artwork, seemed steeped in the sorrow and anxiety it had overseen.

I sat on the rock-hard couch and asked, 'What's going on, Katie?'

'Ted seems to be a good guy,' she said, 'but I'm not sure who his friends are in the cop shop, so I'm playing it safe.'

I nodded, waiting for her to get to Chris.

'Chris slept almost the whole time you were gone,' she said. 'About quarter till nine he started thrashing around and saying, "No, no! Don't shoot!"'

'That's what he always says, Katie.'

'But this time, he shouted, "Don't shoot, Pete!" He's not saying "eat" or "feet" like you thought. He's saying "Pete."'

'So Pete shot him,' I said. Anger flared up in me. 'Next time I see that creep I'll rip his face off.'

'That would be remarkably stupid,' Katie said. 'We need to catch Pete and send him to prison.'

'Greiman's mixed up in this, too,' I said. 'I'm sure of it.'

'Let's get some evidence first,' Katie said. 'I texted Mike and told him what Chris said. Mike is on duty here tomorrow morning at eight. We're meeting in Chris's room with Jace and Monty to discuss our next steps.'

I felt better. 'You said Chris was asking for me?'

'Yes, he was awake for a few minutes. I asked him if he remembered what he'd been dreaming about and he said no. Then he asked, "Where's Angela?" I said you were working. He said, "Tell Angela that I love her, and there's something I want to ask her." I told him, "Ask her yourself." Chris tried to stay awake, but he drifted back to sleep.'

I felt a flash of disappointment. 'Oh. I missed him.'

'Chris will be awake longer soon,' Katie said. 'His thrashing around set off the alarms and a nurse came in to check his vitals. He's fine, Angela, and right now you should be glad he's out of it. As soon as he's awake full time, that idiot Greiman will be back and slap the cuffs on Chris again.'

'Unless we can find out who tried to kill Chris,' I said.

'That's what tomorrow's meeting is about,' Katie said.

'Oh, and I talked to the nurse,' she said. 'I got permission for you to spend the night in his room, if you want to sleep in the recliner.'

'Yes, yes, I do.'

We started back. Even in the unflattering neon lights, Katie looked rested and well, and she'd been here at the hospital since seven this morning.

Monty was waiting for us, back in Chris's room. Katie helped me make the recliner into a place to sleep. With a couple of pillows and two thin hospital blankets she'd warmed for me, the recliner was as comfortable as sleep gets at SOS.

Katie tucked me in, lowered the room lights, and then left with Monty.

I held Chris's hand and listened to him breathe, all the while wondering what he wanted to ask me. Was he going to ask me to marry him again?

I hoped so. Because this time, I knew the answer.

I would definitely say yes.

THIRTY-TWO

I woke up at six the next morning when a cleaner came into Chris's room, and rattled the trash can.

The cleaner, a big, dark-skinned woman whose name tag said 'Rosa,' apologized. 'Sorry, miss, I didn't mean to wake you.' She seemed to mean it.

'No problem, Rosa. I have an early morning meeting. I need to be up now. Thank you for waking me.'

'First time I've heard that one,' Rosa said with a laugh, and continued mopping the floor.

I dug a twenty out of my purse and said, 'And thank you for keeping Chris's room clean. I know how dangerous hospital infections can be.'

Rosa leaned against her mop, pocketed the money and smiled. 'Two impossible things in one day,' she said. 'I'd better buy me a lottery ticket. I'll take good care of your man, don't you worry.'

Chris was still sleeping. I kissed him good morning. Outside, Ted was snoring in his chair. So much for security.

I tiptoed past the sleeping guard and went to my sleep room to get dressed. I was on call today, so I wore my DI suit and rolled my DI case to my car, just in case. It was only seven fifteen – enough time for me to zip over to Supreme Bean for coffee and muffins. I made it back to Chris's room with ten minutes to spare.

Rosa the cleaner was gone and Mike was guarding the door.

'Bless you, my child,' he said, helping me carry the coffee and muffins into Chris's room. We set the breakfast on a closet shelf. Then I helped Mike move in a table we found in an empty room down the hall. Mike put the coffees out on the table, and I set the bag of goodies next to them, and pulled a pile of paper napkins out of the bag.

'Breakfast is served,' I said.

Mike and I arranged three chairs around the table, then he helped himself to a chocolate chip muffin and coffee. He stood near his chair by the door and said, 'I got here at seven for my shift, and the kid, Ted, was sound asleep. All the noise in these halls, and Ted was snoring. I could have led a brass band down the hall, and he'd have slept through it. I had to shake him awake. Our crack security claimed he'd just "closed his eyes for a few minutes."'

'Is Ted friends with Greiman?' I asked.

'Can't tell,' Mike said. 'I do know the kid is cagey and smart. Maybe too smart to align himself openly with any one faction. But I'd be careful around him, just the same.'

'I plan to.'

Katie and Monty arrived, with Jace right behind them. After helping themselves to coffee and muffins (Katie took the sensible bran, Monty had blueberry and Jace settled on cranberry), the meeting started. Katie handed Jace a packet of medical syringes. The syringe needles had different colored tips: red, blue, green and orange.

'Something you're not telling us?' Mike said.

'What are those?' I asked.

'Needles,' Jace said. 'My wife is a crafter, and has all sorts of uses for these medical needles. She sells things on eBay and makes Christmas money.' Jace sounded proud of his wife's skill.

'I think I've found something.' Mike looked excited to be delivering this news. 'I found out that—'

My work cell phone rang, and so did Jace's.

'I have to take this,' I said. 'I'm on call.'

Jace and I got the same message. He told the group, 'There's a suicide at the old Levin mansion. Grace Levin shot herself. Do you know her, Angela?'

'My mother did,' I said. 'Her husband died a few years ago. They were both very rich and very kind. They don't belong to the society circuit. Grace started an annual scholarship for needy students at Chouteau Forest University, and every Christmas she gives new toys to the children in shelters. There's more, but those are the ones I know about. I don't know why she'd kill herself.'

'Well, I'm the lead on the case.'

'I'm glad I won't have to work with Greiman,' I said, 'but I'm really sorry Grace is dead.'

Jace stood up and said, 'Sorry, Mike, we have to run. Let's meet again here the same time tomorrow.'

'I'll bring the coffee and muffins,' Katie said.

Jace was out the door while I was still buttoning my coat. I saw he left the needle packet behind on the table and stuck it in my purse.

Mike looked disappointed, but he knew we both had to take off.

'I'll stay with Chris,' Katie said. 'Right now it's a slow morning – until you finish the death investigation on Mrs Levin.'

I left, too, wondering what Mike's news was. Well, I'd find out tomorrow. I raced to my car and set off for the Levin home.

The Tudor-style place, built in the Twenties, was pretty, but with only four bedrooms, rather modest for a Forest mansion. Surrounded by two acres of oak trees, it had a swimming pool and guesthouse.

I parked in the circle by the front door, and hauled my DI case out of the car trunk. Demetrius, the new uniform, was guarding the door. He kept the logbook. Demetrius handed me a pair of booties and said, 'Sammy Berger caught the case. He's talking to Jace in the foyer.'

Sammy was the uniform I'd worked with the night Janie Duvalle's vintage Corvair slid off the bridge and killed her. The night Chris proposed to me. The last night we were together.

The foyer was square and dark with a blue oriental rug. Jace was sitting on a built-in bench with blue cushions. Sammy stopped talking to Jace as soon as he saw me.

'Hey, Angela,' he said. 'It's a little warmer today than the last time I saw you.'

'By about thirty degrees,' I said. Sammy was tall, with thick black hair, broad shoulders, and a kind smile. The sort of man you'd want to bring home to Mother.

'Hey, I'm sorry to hear about Chris,' he said. 'Tell him we're all pulling for him.'

'I will, Sammy. Thanks.'

Jace interrupted. 'So what do we have here?'

Sammy opened his notebook and read from his notes. 'Grace Levin's grandson, Aiden, called nine-one-one at seven forty-six this morning and reported that his grandmother had committed suicide. He says Mrs Levin is eighty-one, and she shot herself in the head while watching television sometime last night.'

'An eighty-one-year-old woman shot herself?' Jace said. 'That's unusual. Older women rarely shoot themselves.'

Sammy checked his notes again. 'Aiden says his grandmother was depressed. The housekeeper, Nellie Waters, who's worked for Mrs Levin for twenty-five years, says the grandmother was definitely not depressed and religious, besides. The housekeeper says Mrs Levin is Catholic and she considered suicide a mortal sin.

'Personally, I think there's something off about the scene and the kid,' Sammy said, 'but that's your department, Detective.'

'Where are the housekeeper and the grandson?' Jace asked.

'I kept them separate. The housekeeper is in the breakfast room and the grandson in the guesthouse. I put two uniforms on the grandson – one at the guesthouse door and another inside, in case he tries to mess with any evidence.'

'Good,' Jace said. 'They can stay that way while we check out the scene.'

'Also,' Sammy continued, 'Nitpicker says she's on her way and she'll be a little late, and Todd the videographer has already started in the family room.'

'Thanks, Sammy.'

We followed Sammy through the formally furnished living and dining room to a family room at the back of the house. Todd nodded at us, and continued to video the room.

The family room looked cozy, with a beige rug, overstuffed furniture, and a fireplace with a fifty-five-inch TV over it. The gas fireplace was turned off.

The dead woman was stretched out in a brown corduroy recliner facing the TV. At the woman's right side was an end table with a brass lamp, a cup of tea, a TV remote and a framed photo of a tall, gray-haired man smiling at a white-haired woman. Her hair was in an elegant chignon and she wore a lace cocktail dress. He wore a tux. They were holding hands tenderly.

The frame said, 'Happy Fiftieth Anniversary,' and the couple did look happy. This was Grace Levin before the gun blasted her face, I thought.

The weapon was on the floor by the left side of the chair. Also on the left side was what looked like a bullet hole in the carpet.

The decedent wore a plain gold wedding band and an old-fashioned gold watch.

The gunshot wound was on the left side of her head, just above her ear. Blood and brain matter stained the chair and her blue bathrobe. Her white hair was drenched in blood. The damage to her head was horrific. The gunshot wound had peeled back part of her scalp and her left eye had slid down and stared crazily off to the side.

I started to feel dizzy when Jace brought me around by calmly discussing the decedent.

'Sammy is right,' he said. 'There is something screwy about this scene, Angela. The weapon has been dropped by her left hand, but I think the victim was right-handed.'

'So she'd have to reach around her head to shoot herself,' I said. 'What's the weapon's make and model?'

Jace squatted down and peered at the revolver, but left it in place, so it could be processed. 'A Rohm RG-14,' he said. 'A cheap handgun. What the old-timers on the force used to call a "suicide special." Unlikely a woman like Mrs Levin would own one of these.

'And look at the end table by her chair. It's arranged for the comfort of a right-handed person. A leftie would have to reach across herself to get the remote or her tea.'

'Awkward,' I said.

'Plus, her watch is on her left wrist,' Jace said. 'Most people wear their watch on their less dominant side.'

'Is that a bullet hole fired into the carpet?' I asked.

'Yes,' he said.

'Is it a test shot? I know some suicides fire a shot to make sure the weapon is working.'

'Maybe,' Jace said. 'If this was a murder, the killer also could have wrapped Grace's hand around it and fired the gun a second time to make sure the victim had gunshot residue on her hand.'

I looked at the photo of the happy couple to remember what the real Grace Levin looked like. Then I forced myself to look closer at the woman's shattered head. 'I don't see any powder burns on her skin, Jace. That weapon was fired some distance away. A suicide would hold the weapon closer to her head.'

'This is starting to look more and more like a murder,' he said.

Jace stayed with me while I did the death investigation. After photographing the body and its relationship to the fatal weapon, I started at Grace's battered head, noting the gunshot wound, measuring and documenting the blood and spatter. Once I settled into my routine, I no longer felt queasy. I had a job to do, and Grace had a story to tell.

I put a paper bag on her damaged head. It felt disrespectful, but her skull was shattered and I didn't want to lose any tissue or evidence.

Aside from the blood and tissue from the gunshot wound, Grace appeared healthy. Her right forearm had two large (three- and five-inch) bruises. She could have injured herself, but I wasn't sure. The skin on someone her age was thin and bruised easily.

I photographed and noted her jewelry: a yellow metal ring and a yellow metal Bulova watch with a yellow metal band. Then I bagged her hands in brown paper and sealed them with evidence tape.

Grace was wearing a long, sleeveless, blue, cotton nightgown and a blue terrycloth bathrobe, as well as blue terrycloth slippers. She'd been dressed for bed at the time of her death.

I wished she'd died peacefully in her sleep.

THIRTY-THREE

Nitpicker finally arrived, rushing into the room with apologies. She stopped when she saw the decedent, with the bags over her head and hands. Nitpicker knew this was a bad one.

'That poor woman. Who did this to her?' she asked.

'Grace Levin was shot in the head,' I said, 'and I had to put it in a bag because her skull was shattered. Her grandson says she shot herself. She was eighty-one.'

'Awful,' Nitpicker said. 'And odd. Men are more likely to shoot themselves in the head than women. Most men who kill themselves with weapons are middle-aged whites.'

'Women don't like to mess up their faces by shooting themselves,' Jace said.

'I don't think that's true,' Nitpicker said. 'And it's sexist. People kill themselves with what they have handy, and more men own guns than women. At least they used to. That's starting to change, and we're seeing more female gun suicides, but older women are still rare. What weapon was used?' she asked.

Jace pointed to the gun on the floor and said, 'A Saturday night special. A Rohm RG-14.'

Nitpicker studied the handgun by the recliner. 'Ugly little thing,' she said. 'That's the same make and model that John Hinckley Jr used to shoot President Reagan.'

'Before you start work,' I said, 'Jace is going to help me turn the decedent so I can check the back of her body.'

I spread a clean, white sheet on the carpet, and Jace helped me move the body to the sheet on the floor. The decedent's back contained blood and brain matter from the shooting. I measured and photographed them. There were no other wounds. I zipped Mrs Levin into a body bag and called the morgue van.

Meanwhile, Nitpicker went to work, photographing the revolver by the chair from several angles, before picking it up by the checkered part of the grip in her gloved hands. She photographed and diagramed the revolver's cylinder, showing the position of each of the four remaining bullets. Then she unloaded the firearm, and packed each bullet separately.

I asked her questions for my Firearm Fatalities form. I'd already noted the manufacturer and type of weapon, as well as the distance from the body.

"'Is there any blood, body tissue, etcetera, found on the external surface of the firearm?'" I asked her, quoting from the form.

'No,' Nitpicker said.

'What about inside the muzzle?'

'Nothing, again,' Nitpicker said. 'And we know that back spatter can usually be found inside the barrel when the muzzle is less than three inches away.'

'Another reason why this probably wasn't suicide,' I said.

The form wanted to know if there was any gun cleaning equipment sitting out at the scene (no). The other questions, including the gun's ownership and the Suicide Indicator Questions, would have to be answered later.

'If we're lucky,' Nitpicker said, 'there are prints on this weapon and the ammunition. I don't want to smear the gun prints, so I'll get my portable super-glue fuming kit in my car, and super glue the revolver here.'

Nitpicker came back with her home-made kit: a clear plastic storage bin about the size of a carry-on suitcase, an electric cup warmer, a small metal container about the size of a tea strainer, an old coffee mug, and of course, a plastic vial of super glue.

'Has the kitchen been processed, Jace?' she asked.

'It's clear,' he said.

'Good. Let's set this contraption up in the kitchen where I can open a window,' she said. 'Super glue fumes are dangerous.'

Jace and I removed the salt and pepper shakers and placemats from the table, and spread clean kitchen towels over the surface to protect it.

Nitpicker took the lid off the storage bin, and plugged in the cup warmer. The bin had a small notch at the top for the cupholder's electric cord. Then she filled the metal container with super glue and put it on the cup warmer. Next, she filled the coffee mug with water and put it all inside the bin.

'Why do you need the water?' I asked.

'Super-glue fuming requires humidity,' she said. 'As soon as the glue warms, I'll put the weapon in.'

Sammy informed me that the morgue van had arrived. The paperwork was signed and I watched Mrs Levin leave her home for the last time, hoping she was at peace. By the time I returned to the kitchen, Nitpicker had completed the super-glue fuming process.

'We have fingerprints,' she said. 'I'm guessing they'll be Mrs Levin's. I'm hoping we'll get the killer's prints off the ammunition. Amateurs often forget to wear gloves when they load their weapons.'

'We'll leave you fuming in the kitchen,' Jace said. Nitpicker groaned at the corny pun.

'I'd like to talk to the housekeeper first,' he said.

Nellie Waters was weeping in the sun-drenched breakfast room. She seemed to be in her late forties, slender and brown-haired. Her brown eyes were red from crying. She dried her eyes on her apron when she saw us.

Jace introduced us and she said, 'I'm sorry.'

I wasn't sure why she was apologizing.

'For what?' Jace asked.

'For crying.' The housekeeper was sniffling now, but the tears were gone. 'I loved that dear woman. I can't believe Mrs Levin would kill herself, especially not with a gun. She hated guns. Wouldn't allow them in her house.'

I opened the Suicidal Intent Questionnaire for Investigators on my iPad and said, 'That's what we're trying to establish, Ms Waters. If Mrs Levin really committed suicide.'

'Ask away,' she said. 'And call me Nellie.'

'Was Mrs Levin in a gloomy, depressed mood?'

'No,' Nellie said. 'She was a cheerful woman who had many friends. She had days where she felt a little down, but she'd busy herself with a project and bounce back.'

'Did she have trouble sleeping?'

'No.'

'Did she lose interest in her life, sex, previously valued activities, or personal hygiene?'

'No to all of that,' Nellie said. 'Mrs Levin was a widow, and she did not have a boyfriend. After her husband died, she wasn't interested in other men. She had a better social life than I do. She played bridge twice a month, went to a monthly book club meeting, had a weekly yoga session and went mall-walking every Tuesday. She was active in her church's women's club and looking forward to a cruise to the Caribbean in January with two old friends.' Nellie smiled. 'Mrs Levin was remarkably energetic.'

'That answers my next question,' I said. 'Was her thinking slowing? Was she agitated? Feeling guilty? Did anything upset her?'

'She was fine,' Nellie said, 'except her grandson Aiden was troubling her.'

'Why?' I asked. 'What's wrong with Aiden?'

'Everything, if you ask me, though Mrs Levin loved him. Aiden has had behavior problems since he was a little boy. He set fire to the Christmas tree when he was six. His parents got him counseling, but it didn't work. He's always been obnoxious.' Nellie was twisting her apron as she talked.

'Is Aiden her only grandchild?' Jace asked.

'Yes, he's the only child of Barbara, Mrs Levin's daughter, who is married to a lawyer. They live in Atlanta. When Aiden turned twenty-two and graduated from college with a useless degree in English Lit, his parents insisted that he get a job. Aiden thought he was too good to deliver pizzas or work at an entry-level job. He expected to be hired by a major university as a full professor. Naturally, that didn't happen. His parents kicked him out two years later when he continued to refuse to work, and soft-hearted Mrs Levin took him in. She let her grandson live rent-free in the guesthouse. He's been here for the last two years.

'Aiden uses drugs and runs with a wild crowd. Mrs Levin gave Aiden a new car and an allowance of a thousand dollars a month, but that wasn't enough for him. He wanted more. He was constantly asking his grandmother for money. I think she was getting tired of it. She mentioned last week that perhaps her daughter and son-in-law were right, and Aiden should work.'

'Did Aiden know this?' Jace asked.

'I don't know,' Nellie said.

'Who inherits Mrs Levin's money?' Jace asked.

'Her daughter Barbara and her grandson Aiden.'

She stopped, as though exhausted by recounting this history.

Jace and I kept silent for a moment, and then I said, 'I have just a few more questions.'

'Go ahead,' she said.

'Did Mrs Levin talk about death or suicide?'

'Death, occasionally,' Nellie said. 'She was eighty-one, after all, and her friends were starting to "drop off the twig," as she liked to say. Mrs Levin rarely mentioned suicide, except when a friend's daughter killed herself. Then she said, "That poor child. She must have been in terrible pain."'

'Has she had any recent visits to her doctor?' I asked.

'Yes, and the doctor said she was in good health. Mrs Levin was proud of that. "Old age isn't for sissies," she told me. "I have to work to stay healthy."'

'Is this the anniversary of her husband's death, or someone else she was close to?' I asked.

Nellie thought for a moment, and then said, 'No, her husband died in March and her sister in August. Those are the people she was closest to.'

'Any other friend or family member die of a self-induced injury or medication overdose?' I asked.

'No.' Nellie seemed to be tiring.

'Two more questions,' I said. 'When did you last see Mrs Levin?'

'Yesterday,' Nellie said. 'I cleaned the downstairs and then went grocery shopping. I fixed her favorite dinner of roast pork, green beans, and mashed potatoes, with chocolate ice cream for dessert.'

'Did her grandson eat with her?' Jace asked.

'No, not unless he wants money.' That sentence had a bitter edge. 'He almost never comes to see his grandmother unless he wants something. After dinner, Mrs Levin went upstairs to shower and change into her robe and pajamas. I cleaned up the dinner dishes and then fixed her a cup of tea. When I left at six thirty, she was sitting in her recliner, watching *Columbo*. That's the last time I saw her.' Nellie burst out crying. Jace awkwardly patted her shoulder and I ran to the kitchen to get her a glass of water.

When I handed it to her, I said, 'May I make you a cup of coffee or tea?'

Nellie was sniffling now. 'I'd like to go home, please, if I could. It's been a long day.' She left, looking tired and defeated.

'On to the grandson,' Jace said.

Outside, it was warm, almost springlike. The snow was melting. We followed the flagstone path to the pool and the guesthouse, a miniature version of the mansion. Robert, the other new uniform, was guarding the guesthouse door. Jace knocked and Eddie, a second uniform, answered the door. He had his big hands on Aiden's shoulders. Mrs Levin's grandson was bare-chested and barefoot, wearing only pajama bottoms. Aiden might not work, but he definitely worked out. The man had six-pack abs. He regarded me with a lazy smile tinged with contempt.

'Aiden Quest?' Jace asked.

'That's me. What can I do for you?'

'Put some clothes on,' Jace said. 'We'll wait in the living room.'

Eddie went with Aiden while he dressed.

The guesthouse seemed to have a large living room, a bedroom and a galley kitchen. The living room had the same overstuffed furniture as the family room in the big house, and at first glance, appeared tidy. On closer look, I saw the signs of hard partying: a cigarette burn on the coffee table, a brown stain on the beige carpet, and a picture on the wall whose frame had been carelessly mended.

Aiden came out of the bedroom about ten minutes later, wearing jeans, a tight T-shirt, and boat shoes. I studied his face, but saw no sign of sorrow. His entitled sneer spoiled his conventionally handsome face. Aiden slouched in an overstuffed chair and Jace and I sat across from him on the couch. Eddie stood behind Aiden's chair.

'We understand you found your grandmother's body,' Jace said.

'Yeah, poor old Granny Grace,' he said. 'Who'da thought she'd off herself?'

'Was your grandmother depressed?' Jace said.

'Oh, yeah, really down.'

'What were the signs of depression?' I asked.

'Well, she was old, real old. She was eighty-one and wrinkly.'

'Those are not signs of depression,' Jace said. 'Those are signs of age.'

'Well, they'd depress me,' Aiden said.

'But this isn't about you, is it, Aiden? Your grandmother was shot in the head.'

'Yeah, I know that. I found the body.'

Hm. He said 'the body,' not 'my grandmother.'

'What time?' Jace asked. 'What time did you find her?'

'About seven forty-five this morning.'

'Why did you go see her at that hour?'

'Are you joking? She's my grandmother. I go see her all the time.'

'That's not what I heard,' Jace said. 'I heard you only saw her when you wanted something.'

Anger flashed across Aiden's face like lightning in a summer storm. Then he smiled. 'The housekeeper told you that,' he said.

'Nellie doesn't like me, and she's a snoop. She got all bent out of shape because my friends were chillin' here and she told Granny I was using drugs.'

'And were you?'

Aiden shrugged. 'Just a little coke. No big deal.'

'Where did your grandmother get a weapon?' Jace asked.

Aiden's eyes shifted. 'She kept a gun for protection.'

'Where?'

'Uh, upstairs in the nightstand by her bed.'

'I didn't ask where she kept her weapon,' Jace said. 'I asked where she got it.'

'My grandfather got it for her. For protection.'

'He did, huh?' Jace said. 'Seems kind of dangerous, when most of the neighbors hire a security service.'

Aiden didn't say anything, but he shifted in his chair.

'And why would your grandmother walk downstairs with a weapon when she could have killed herself in her bed?'

Aiden shrugged.

'Is that a reason?' Jace asked.

'I don't know why she'd do that.'

'Is your grandmother left- or right-handed?' Jace asked.

'I don't know,' he said.

'That's obvious.' Jace stood up. 'Let's go, Angela.'

He turned to Aiden. 'And you, don't leave town.'

'Gee, just like in the movies.' Aiden tried to make a joke, but the smile slid off his face.

THIRTY-FOUR

Jace left Officer Eddie Taylor with Aiden, to make sure Grace Levin's grandson didn't run. Neither were happy with that arrangement.

As we walked back to our cars, Jace asked, 'Want to get some coffee?'

'First, let me call Katie to make sure Chris is OK.'

Katie answered her cell phone. 'I'm just about to start Mrs Levin's autopsy,' she said. 'Monty is with Chris. I just checked and they're both fine.'

I was free to grab coffee and a quick lunch. I met Jace a few minutes later at Supreme Bean. I loved how that shop smelled – strong coffee and baked goods. If that scent could be bottled, I'd wear it as perfume.

We both ordered strong Colombian coffee and salads with grilled salmon.

After we were settled at a corner table with our coffee and food, I asked, 'What do you think of Aiden? Did he kill his grandmother?'

'I'd love to arrest that arrogant little twit, but I don't have enough evidence.'

Jace harpooned a hunk of salmon as if he was stabbing Aiden. 'I'm hoping Nitpicker finds his prints on the ammunition.'

'Aiden didn't seem to care about his grandmother at all,' I said. 'He wasn't even upset about finding her body.'

I took a long drink of coffee and felt the caffeine revive me. I asked Jace, 'What about Mrs Levin's daughter? Do we have to inform her of her mother's death?'

'No, Nellie called her,' Jace said. 'The daughter and her husband are flying in tonight.'

'I'm glad we're relieved of that duty,' I said. 'And I'm sure Nellie broke the news better than the creepy grandson.'

'Ugh,' Jace said. 'Don't mention him again. You'll ruin my appetite.' He took another big bite of his rapidly disappearing salad.

'Here's another appetite killer,' I said. 'I checked online for the flights to Chicago. There's one almost every hour, especially if you consider Midway Airport.'

'Midway,' Jace said. 'I should have thought of that airport. Midway is much smaller than O'Hare, and closer to downtown. Wendy could have flown out of there. But I checked her credit card bills, Angela. The only charges were for a round-trip flight from St. Louis to Chicago.'

'Wendy doesn't have a sister, does she?' I asked.

'Nope,' Jace said. 'She's an only child. Too bad she doesn't have a twin.'

'But she does!' I said. 'I mean, she could pass for Chloe's twin.'

'Was Chloe's driver's license in her purse when you processed it?' he asked.

'I'm not sure.' I pulled out my iPad and checked my report of Chloe's death investigation. 'No driver's license and one credit card, a Visa. Don't you think she'd have more than one credit card? I'll ask her sister.'

I had Zoe's cell phone number in the report. I called it and held my breath while the phone rang. Zoe answered. I put the phone on speaker, so Jace could hear, and then asked, 'Do you know how many credit cards your sister had?'

'Two,' Zoe said. 'A Visa card and an American Express.'

'Good,' I said. 'Can we get a warrant to check the charges on Chloe's Amex card?'

'You don't need one,' Zoe said. 'I've picked up my sister's mail. I have her latest American Express bill right here.'

'Terrific. Are there any charges for out-of-town trips?' I asked.

'Hang on just a minute while I go through the bill.'

I heard Zoe tear open the envelope and then she read the charges. 'There's not a lot here on the Amex,' Zoe said. 'She mostly used her Visa. Here we go. I see a charge for gas. A restaurant meal. More gas. Her cell phone service . . . Wait a minute. This is weird. Here's a charge for a round-trip ticket from Chicago Midway Airport to St. Louis, and it says Chloe made the trip both ways in one day. She didn't take a trip to Chicago.'

Jace sat bolt upright in his chair, hanging on every word. Zoe sounded excited, as if she was on the trail of something. 'Here are some Uber charges for forty-five dollars each,' she said. 'My sister didn't go to Chicago, and she never used Uber. She liked Lyft.'

'What are the dates?' I asked.

'No, no,' Zoe said. 'This can't be right. This is the day she died.' Zoe burst into tears. 'Who would do this?'

'I have a good idea, Zoe,' I said. 'Stay right there. Detective Budewitz and I will be right over. Are you at your dorm room?'

'Yes,' she said, through her tears.

'That poor young woman,' Jace said. 'Chicago Midway Airport video is government property. All I have to do is ask for the video. And there might be cameras at the TSA checkpoints. I'll get on that now.' He started typing furiously on his phone.

'What about Uber?' I asked.

'We'll need Wendy's cell phone records,' he said. 'If she ordered that ride on her smart phone, we've got her. Maybe Uber's records will show the cell phone source of the order. Uber might surrender the records voluntarily. If not, I'll have to start the process with a subpoena duces tecum for a deposition where they bring the records. I hope I don't have to go that route, but I'm prepared to go to the mat for this information.'

Jace typed some more while I finished my coffee and then cleared away our dishes. I picked up a cup of hot tea to-go and a chocolate chip cookie for Zoe. I figured she'd need some comfort. Seeing that bill must have torn open fresh wounds.

At last, we were ready to go. I followed Jace's car to Zoe's dorm. At the dorm, her door was unlocked. We knocked and found her curled up on her bed, weeping, her blonde hair spilling over her pillow. The drab room was so neat it looked like she was expecting an inspection.

Chloe sat up, thanked us for the tea and the cookie, and sipped the tea while she talked. She gave us Chloe's Amex bill in an envelope.

'Looking at that bill hit me hard,' she said. 'Wendy did that, didn't she? She made my sister pay for her murder.'

'It looks that way, yes,' Jace said. 'I know it was difficult to open that bill, but when you found those charges on Chloe's account, you gave us the information to help us arrest Wendy.'

'Good,' Zoe said. 'I hope she rots in jail.'

'Is your sister's Amex account closed?' Jace asked.

'Yes, I closed all her accounts. How long will it take before you have what you need to arrest Wendy for my sister's murder?'

'If we're lucky, a day or two,' Jace said. 'And Wendy can't get away. She's stuck in jail awaiting trial for the murder of Selwyn Skipton.'

'You'll let me know, won't you?' Zoe said.

'Of course,' Jace said.

We left her in the dorm. On the way to the car, my cell phone rang. It was Monty and he sounded happy.

'Angela,' he said. 'Chris is up. He's awake. Can you come now?'

'Yes, I'm on my way,' I said.

'It's Chris, Jace. He's awake. Do you need me for anything else?'

'You go on, Angela. You're free. Go see him.'

I raced to the hospital and hoped I'd make it before Chris fell back to sleep. Mike was guarding the door to Chris's room and gave me a thumbs-up as I ran inside. And there was Chris, sitting up in his bed, and looking remarkably alert.

He held out his arms, with the IV lines trailing from them, and said, 'Angela, come here.'

I gingerly allowed him to enfold me. As he put his arms around me, I felt like I'd come home.

I covered his face with kisses while he held me tight. Finally, we disengaged, though I sat by his bed and held his hand, as if he might float away – or me. I hadn't felt this happy in a long time.

'What are you grinning at?' he asked.

'You,' I said. 'I love you.'

'I love you, too, Angela.' We kissed again. When I looked up, Monty was gone.

Then Chris said, 'Monty filled me in on what's been going on. Greiman arrested me while I was out.'

I felt a huge burden slide off me. I wasn't sure how I was going to tell Chris he was under arrest.

'Greiman,' I said. 'Don't worry. We'll get him.'

Chris held my hand and looked at me seriously. 'Angela, you know I didn't have anything to do with drugs,' he said.

'Of course not,' I said. 'I never doubted you for a second. Neither did Monty, Katie, Jace or Mike. We're all working to beat this.'

He smiled, though thanks to his still swollen face, it was slightly lopsided, and scratched his chin.

'What do you think of the fur on my face?' he asked.

I studied him for a minute. His face looked thin and drawn, but if the beard was shaped properly, it could look stylish.

'It's a new look,' I said. 'A barber could make something of it. I like it.'

'Me, too,' he said.

We held hands, just happy to be with each other. Then I said, 'Chris, do you remember anything from the day you were shot?'

'Not really,' he said. 'Monty asked me that, too. I remember I had to meet Pete Clayton, but I don't remember where or why.'

'How did Pete get in touch with you? Did he call or radio?'

'I don't remember that, either,' he said.

'You know you were found on Jasmine Trail,' I said.

'Jasmine? That's way out in the country, and out of my usual patrol area.'

'Right,' I said.

'I have no idea why I was out there, Angela,' he said.

'You called me as the ambulance was approaching,' I said. 'You tried to tell me that Pete had shot you, but I couldn't quite understand what you were saying. You also wanted to ask me something. Do you remember what it was?'

You wanted to marry me, I thought.

'No,' Chris said. 'I don't remember a thing.' He fell asleep, and I sat there, holding his hand, and wondering if we were engaged. What if he'd changed his mind?

THIRTY-FIVE

I woke up at two o'clock in the morning, my hand cramping from holding Chris's for so long. He was snoring, and for once, I was happy to hear him imitating a buzz saw. I quietly pried my hand out of his grasp, stood up and stretched. I needed some sleep, and not in the hospital recliner.

I tiptoed out of Chris's room, past the uniform on guard. I didn't know his name, but he was asleep anyway. The hall was deserted as I made my way to my sleep room, and it gave the hospital a ghostly air. In my room, I put my phone on to charge, set my alarm for seven o'clock, undressed and promptly fell asleep.

I was sleep-dazed and groggy when my alarm went off at seven, but fully awake by the time I'd showered and dressed. For the first time since Chris's accident, I woke with a sense of optimism. I could feel a kind of crackling energy. Arrests would be made. Good things were converging, and they would all happen today.

I was in Chris's room by seven forty-five, and waved at Mike. The uniform was on guard outside the door.

Katie had beat me to Chris's room. She looked fresh and rested this morning.

Chris was awake, too. I nodded at Katie, and kissed Chris good morning.

'You look alert and well,' I said. Now Chris clearly seemed on the mend. Another reason to hope for good things today.

'I feel good,' he said. 'If I have another good day, the hospital will start physical therapy and then I'll be out of here.'

And on the way to jail, I thought.

'And where did you get the good news about PT starting?' I asked.

'Dr Hallen stopped by at six this morning and told me. I'm looking forward to eating real food, too. What did you do yesterday?'

I told him about Mrs Grace Levin's shooting death, and why Jace and I didn't think it was suicide.

Katie and I moved the purloined table close to Chris's bed, so he could hear us. Jace arrived next, and while we waited for Monty,

Katie told us about Mrs Levin's autopsy. Mike stuck his head around the door, so he could hear.

'The victim didn't commit suicide,' Katie said. 'Mrs Levin was right-handed, and there's no way she could have shot herself in the head with the gun held at that angle. Also, she had no physical reason to be depressed. She was in excellent health for her age.'

'So the killer took her life and her remaining years,' Jace said.

'At least a decade,' Katie said. 'Maybe more.'

'That grandson has a lot to answer for,' Jace said. 'I'm waiting to hear if Nitpicker got any prints when she fumed the ammunition.'

'What's the time of death?' I asked.

'Between ten and eleven at night,' Katie said.

Monty came tearing into the room, briefcase in hand, blaming an accident on Gravois for his lateness as he sat in the last chair. Mike looked both ways down the hall and then joined us. He didn't sit down, in case he had to hurry back to his post by the door.

We helped ourselves to the coffee and muffins Katie had brought while Mike told us the news he'd wanted to give us yesterday.

'Do you know Doughnut Dan?' he asked.

Katie and I looked blank. We knew many of the characters at the cop shop, but Doughnut Dan was a new one.

'He's the lazy cop who's on duty in the evidence room,' Jace said.

'Lazy.' Chris snorted. 'Dan's a pet rock in a police uniform.' I was cheered to hear Chris cracking jokes again.

Mike went back to talking. 'Dan was working the day the fentanyl evidence went missing. He got his nickname because Dan almost always has a box of doughnuts on his desk. Cops who want a favor know to bring him more doughnuts.'

'This sounds promising,' Monty said.

'There's more,' Mike said. 'I found out the evidence room camera went out for half an hour about the time the theft supposedly occurred. The log showed that Chris was the last person to sign into the evidence room, but the cop car tracker showed Chris was actually on patrol in downtown Chouteau Forest.'

'So Chris didn't sign in,' I said. 'He's innocent.'

'We already knew that,' Mike said.

'Just to play devil's advocate,' Monty said, 'maybe Chris left his car downtown and hiked over to the cop shop.'

'And who was driving Chris's car at the time?' Mike said. 'The car was moving around downtown.'

'I stand corrected,' Monty said.

'Damn right,' Mike said. 'Now, if I can finish my story, Jace discovered that Doughnut Dan has a daughter in college and her tuition for her upcoming senior year had just been paid. Twenty thousand dollars.'

'So someone gave him a sudden bonus,' Monty said.

'I have another bonus,' Jace said. I swear he had canary feathers around his mouth.

'Well?' Patience was not one of my virtues.

'Rumor has it that Pete Clayton has a gambling problem,' Jace said. 'Two weeks ago, I was coming out to the police lot, and heard Pete and Greiman arguing. I stepped behind a patrol car to listen. Pete was telling Greiman he needed five hundred dollars to pay his rent. Greiman asked Pete what happened to the five hundred he'd given him last week. Pete said he'd lost it. Greiman said, "Lost it how? The money fell out of your wallet?" Pete didn't say anything. Finally Greiman said, "You went gambling again, didn't you? At the casinos in St. Louis?" Once again, Pete said nothing.

'Greiman was furious. He said, "I'm not giving you a damned thing. I might as well set fire to my money if you're going to throw it away at a casino. Get out of here, you stupid asshole."'

I was outraged. 'You didn't tell us this earlier, Jace? It's the key to everything.'

Jace defended himself. In fact, he had an edge in his voice. 'Half the force hits Greiman up for money, Angela. He's single and doesn't have any kids. Everyone thinks he's loaded. He lends other cops money and then they owe him favors. It's one way he survives so many scrapes.'

'OK,' Monty said. He took control. 'So we're guessing this Doughnut Dan and Pete conspired with the drug dealer to get the fentanyl out of the evidence room. Pete then put the blame on Chris.'

'Why go after Chris?' I asked.

Monty glared at me for interrupting.

'That's easy,' Chris said. 'Greiman can't stand me, and Pete's his puppy dog. He does what he's told. I was an easy target.'

Monty resumed outlining his theory. 'As I was saying, Pete somehow contacted Chris, lured him out to that lonely road, and then shot Chris in the head and figured he'd killed him.'

'And I ruined his plans by refusing to die,' Chris said. He gave us a big, lopsided grin. 'I knew this thick skull of mine would come in handy.'

'So what do we do next?' Katie said.

'We need to prove a connection between Doughnut Dan and Pete,' Jace said.

'What if I get Chris's duty belt from hospital security?' Monty said. 'If Chris's phone is still in the belt, it might have a lead.'

'Didn't Greiman take the belt with my weapon and phone when he arrested me?' Chris asked.

'I don't think so,' Monty said.

'That man is so careless.' Chris shook his head.

'This time, Greiman's carelessness may work in our favor,' Monty said. 'When we finish here, I'll track down Chris's belt.'

'Once we can establish a connection between Pete and Doughnut Dan,' Jace said, 'we can subpoena bank records, and trace the money back to the dealer. Then we'll be following paper trails.'

My optimistic mood came crashing down. There would be no good news for Chris today, or for many days to come.

Jace's cell phone rang. 'It's Nitpicker,' he said. 'I have to take this.'

I suspected Jace was still annoyed at me because he didn't put his phone on speaker. Instead, he went to the other side of the room. I could hear his noncommittal responses. 'Uh-huh . . . OK . . . Yeah, thanks.'

Jace came back to the table and said, 'Finally, we have good news. Aiden's fingerprints are all over that ammo. I'm going to make an arrest.'

'Do you want me to go with you?' I asked.

'No, Angela, you stay here and help Monty. I'll need you to photograph and document the contents of the duty belt.'

Yep, Jace was definitely mad at me.

Katie left for work and Mike went back to his post. Monty opened his briefcase, rummaged for a paper, and told Chris, 'Now that you're awake and lucid, sign this and I'll get your duty belt.'

'I thought Angela already hired you,' Chris said.

'She did, but she's not your official fiancée, so I need you to sign.'

Chris didn't flicker an eyelid when Monty mentioned the word 'fiancée.' Chris's marriage proposal had been wiped from his memory. But not mine.

'Now I'll reclaim your duty belt,' Monty said.

'I thought you were going to do that the other day,' I said.

'Got distracted,' Monty said. 'Angela, let's get the receipt and go.'

The receipt was still in Chris's bloodstained shoe. I felt sick when I saw his blood. I'd have to bring in a pair of Chris's shoes and throw these out.

Monty took off for the hospital security office on the first floor so fast I struggled to keep up with him. As we hurried there, I said to Monty, 'I think Jace is angry with me because I yelled at him for not telling us about the fight between Greiman and Pete.'

'You shouldn't have done that, Angela,' he said. 'Cops gossip like an old-fashioned ladies' sewing circle. A good cop like Jace wouldn't want to get caught up in silly time-wasters. Most of what he hears goes in one ear and out the other. And don't forget, the chief has him under incredible pressure. Jace is no whiner, but I know the pressure is getting to him.'

I'd been chastised, and rightly so. 'I'll apologize when I see him again,' I said.

The security department's front office was a cluttered beige closet of a room. A security officer named Kelsea, a short, sturdy woman in a khaki police uniform, stood behind a high counter. On the counter was a bank of computer monitors divided into multiple boxes so the officer could watch the hospital's halls, doors and parking lot.

Monty presented the receipt and the paper signed by Chris. Officer Kelsea took the paperwork into a back room. We waited five minutes before she came out with two cardboard boxes. She showed Monty Chris's weapon, with a trigger guard attached, in one box. 'We don't allow weapons in this hospital,' Officer Kelsea said. 'Please remove it from the premises. Then we'll give you the officer's duty belt.'

'Wait here, Angela,' Monty said.

On camera, we watched the lawyer hurry down the hall to the main parking lot, where he opened his car trunk and stashed the weapon in the box inside. When he returned, Kelsea handed Monty the duty belt box and we returned to Chris's room.

We opened the box on Chris's hospital bed. His black leather belt and its many holders were splashed with his blood. My stomach twisted.

Chris didn't seem upset at all. 'I can see this will need some cleaning,' he said.

I photographed the belt with my point-and-shoot camera.

Chris inventoried the contents and I photographed and listed them: magazine pouch and pepper spray. Two sets of handcuffs. Backup flashlight. Expandable baton. Extra rounds. Portable radio, and finally, a cell phone pouch.

The pouch was empty. My heart sank. Another dead end.

'Wait a minute,' Chris said. 'Did we check that pouch back there on the belt? That's where I keep my extra nitrile gloves.'

I photographed the pouch, including the blood smear on the Velcro flap. I opened it, and inside was Chris's cell phone, smeared with more blood. 'Does it still have a charge?' he asked.

I gloved up and then pressed a button. 'Yes. It's at twenty-eight percent.' We looked at the phone's menu. There was an outgoing call to me.

'Wait!' Chris said. 'There's a text from Pete.'

I held my breath while Monty called up the text. 'It says, "Meet me."'

'That's it?' I couldn't hide my disappointment.

'It was sent roughly two hours before you were shot, Chris,' Monty said. 'It could mean anything, including "meet me for lunch."'

'So it's useless,' Chris said.

'Pretty much,' Monty said.

We sat in glum silence for a long moment before Chris said, 'Was any brass found at the scene?'

'What?' I said.

'Brass. If I was shot by Pete there would be brass casings at the scene. We could compare the casings with the brass Pete left at the police firing range and see if they match.'

'Jace was going to check, but the scene was covered with poison ivy,' I said. 'You can still get it in the winter.'

'It started warming up yesterday,' Monty said. 'The snow is melting. Do you have a couple of Tyvek suits in your DI case, Angela?'

'Yes.'

'Then let's suit up and go look for those casings in the poison ivy patch. I own a good metal detector.'

Before I knew it, Monty and I were slogging through crime scene weeds. We were clad in white protective suits, hoping to find the brass left behind by the attempt on Chris's life. The dead, woody vegetation was crusted with patches of melting snow.

Three hours later, we had a plastic bucket filled with our finds, including a badly rusted cone-top beer can (a hybrid of a flattop can and a bottle), a 1967 quarter, a carburetor, a Toyota hubcap, and a fork. It was growing dark and I was chilled to the bone when I passed the metal detector near a clump of poison oak draped in swags of poison ivy, and the machine sounded.

I gingerly poked around in the poisonous weeds until I saw the sweet glimmer of brass. Two casings.

I screamed like I'd discovered the mother lode.

THIRTY-SIX

After we recovered the brass, everything seemed to move quickly. I followed Monty to his office, and showered there with strong soap to get rid of any poison oak or ivy. He lent me an old sweat suit of Katie's. Then he brought me a cup of coffee and I settled down to call Mike with the good news.

'Get that brass over to me,' he said. 'I'm off work at five today. I'll stop by the police firing range and get the brass analyzed. The range master is an old buddy. He'll do it and keep quiet. We can trust him.'

'How's Chris?' I asked.

'He's napping.'

'Who's on guard tonight?' I asked.

'Ben,' he said. 'He's a good guy. Now don't worry so much, OK? We'll take care of Chris.'

Next, I called Jace to tell him we found the brass, and apologize for my jerky behavior. To my relief, Jace forgave me. He was thrilled by my news. He'd had a banner day and was anxious to talk about it.

'While you were in the field,' he said.

'For real,' I added. 'In the weeds.'

'I had the pleasure of arresting Aiden for the murder of his grandmother.'

'Did his parents give you any trouble?' I asked. 'Aren't they lawyers?'

'Not the right kind. His dad's a tax attorney,' Jace said, 'and his mom's a real estate lawyer. Neither one knows much about criminal law. Aiden's parents cautioned the kid not to say a word, and then said they'd get him a local lawyer.'

'You must be happy you wrapped up that investigation so fast,' I said.

'I am.' I heard the relief in Jace's voice.

'And I must have been living right,' he said. 'I heard back from Midway Airport. They emailed me the video for the day Wendy flew to St. Louis. I knew the time of Wendy's flight, so I didn't have to slog through too much grainy video. We have her on tape leaving for St. Louis and coming back the same day. Uber gave us the info we needed, too. Wendy ordered the rides to and from the airport on her phone, and paid for them with Chloe's credit card. I finally had enough to arrest Wendy for the murder of Chloe Westbrook. And she's already in jail for killing Selwyn.'

'Congratulations,' I said. 'You can take a well-deserved rest.'

'And get the chief off my back,' Jace said.

'It's four o'clock,' I said. 'I'm taking the brass to Mike at SOS before he leaves.'

Mike was looking a little rumpled at the end of the day, but he was happy to take the evidence bag with the brass. 'Now we'll get the sucker,' he said.

'I hope so.'

'Oh, by the way, Greiman came here today and read your honey his rights, reminding him that he's under arrest and as soon as Chris is well enough he can finish his rehab in the county jail.'

'How did Chris take it?'

'He didn't say a word. Monty had coached him well.' Mike patted my shoulder. 'Now you hang in there, Angela. We'll have this straightened out real soon.' The veteran cop was a wise friend.

Chris was awake, but looked exhausted and pale. I kissed him and asked, 'How was your day?'

'Good and bad,' he said.

'Tell me the bad part first,' I said. 'Let's get it over with.'

'Greiman came blustering in here like he was some big deal lawman and arrested me for theft of evidence and a bunch of other stuff. He says I'm on suspension without pay.'

'I bet he enjoyed that,' I said.

'He did. Monty had prepared me for the worst and told me not to react, and I didn't.'

'Must have driven Greiman crazy,' I said.

I kissed Chris and held his hand, then said, 'I have some good news for you. Monty and I went looking for brass in the weeds at your crime scene, and we found two shell casings. Mike is going to take them to the range master and compare them to Pete's brass.'

Chris brightened immediately.

'Now tell me your good news,' I said.

'I sat up in that chair for twenty minutes this afternoon,' he said.

He pointed to the recliner. Chris, my strong, fearless Chris, seemed so proud of this feat, it hurt my heart.

'That's real progress,' I said.

'It is, but I feel like I've climbed Mount Everest.' He yawned. 'I'm so tired.'

Katie, Monty and Jace came through Chris's door in a noisy gaggle.

'Angela,' Katie said. 'Come to dinner with us at Gringo Daze. We have a lot to celebrate.'

'But what about Chris?'

'Monty is going to call his office manager, Jinny Gender, to stay with Chris.'

'Oh, no, you don't,' Chris said. 'I appreciate the offer, I really do, but let Jinny enjoy her evening. I've had a big day and I'm really tired. I'm just going to sleep.'

'But—'

'Go have fun with your friends, Angela. I can't do much right now, but I insist you go out. Mike says Ben is on duty tonight and I know him. He's a good guy. He'll keep an eye on me.'

'I don't know.' I was still worried. Pete could come back and try to finish him off. If Ben was like the rest of the so-called police guards, he'd either be flirting with nurses or sleeping. Chris wasn't strong enough yet to fight off an attack.

'Go ahead, Angela. Please? I'll feel better if you go out and enjoy yourself.'

Katie put her arm around my shoulders and guided me out the door. 'Come on,' she said. 'You need a break.'

I followed the convoy of cars to Gringo Daze, the Forest's Mexican restaurant. The owner showed us to a table in a back room, near the Spanish-tiled fountain. Monty ordered pitchers of sangria for our table. We toasted one another and ate guacamole and corn chips before our entrees arrived. I ordered a chicken burrito.

I tried to enjoy myself at dinner, I really did, but I couldn't. I was too distracted. I had a feeling that Chris was in danger, and no matter how many times I told myself he would be OK, I didn't believe it.

I poked at my burrito like it was roadkill on a plate. I couldn't eat. I had to see Chris.

I couldn't sit in the noisy restaurant any longer. I said I had a headache and excused myself. Katie gave me the stink eye. She knew I was lying, but I didn't care. I left some money and grabbed my coat. When I got to my car, I reached into my purse for my keys and found the packet of medical syringes for Jace's wife. I'd give them to Jace tomorrow.

I drove straight to the hospital and parked. Once inside, I ran to Chris's floor. Ben wasn't in his chair by Chris's door. He was down the hall by the soda machine, giggling with a redheaded nurse. He didn't notice when I entered Chris's room.

Inside, I saw Pete, standing over Chris's bed. Chris was sound asleep. Pete had a needle in his hand and was mumbling to himself, 'He's not going to testify against me.'

Pete held a syringe filled with a clear fluid. The muscular cop wore jeans and a plaid shirt with the sleeves rolled up to his elbows.

'Pete! What are you doing?' I said. I ran to the foot of Chris's bed.

'I'm making sure Chris doesn't testify against me,' he said.

I knew it. Pete was seriously unhinged, and help was nowhere nearby. I prayed Chris stayed asleep while I tried to talk Pete down. 'Chris isn't going to testify. He can't remember what happened.'

'You're lying,' he said.

'No, I'm not. What's in that syringe?'

'Poison,' he said. 'Ant poison.'

'Are you nuts?'

He turned to me with flaming eyes. The answer to that question was yes. As I stepped closer, I realized Pete was also high. I had to stop him.

'Drop it, Pete.' I moved a bit closer.

'Angela, I can't go to jail,' Pete said.

I looked around wildly for a weapon. The table and extra chairs from this morning were gone. There was no way I could whack him with the recliner. Then I remembered the syringes for Jace's craft-loving wife. I pulled out the biggest one, with the red plastic tip guard. I knew Pete wasn't very bright. He thought I'd called him an anklet. My idea just might work.

'Drop the syringe, Pete,' I said, taking a step closer. 'Or I'll stick you with this. See the red plastic tip on the needle? It's a warning.'

Pete eyed the syringe.

I kept talking. 'This needle is filled with air, Pete. If I stick you in the radial artery, which runs right up your arm, you'll die. There's a big bubble in this syringe. Now, if I inject your artery with a massive air bubble – what the docs call an air embolism – your heart will stop. No blood flow. You'll die of a massive heart attack. Right here in the hospital. No one can save you.'

I scooted another step closer.

'If you kill Chris, he'll die quickly, but you'll die in stages. Piece by piece. Until you feel like an elephant is sitting on your chest. And then, boom! You're dead.'

Another step closer.

'And I'll get away scot-free. When I stick this needle in your artery, it will leave a little hole that will be overlooked in your autopsy. Especially since the assistant medical examiner is a friend. So back away, Pete. Or you're going to die. Your chest will explode. Last chance to save yourself.'

'No, I can't.' He was ready to plunge the needle into Chris's arm.

I heard a loud *zonyx!* and Chris released a mighty snore.

Pete was so startled, he stumbled forward. That was the distraction I needed. I ran over, and plunged my syringe in Pete's forearm. 'You're a dead man,' I said. 'I hit the artery. Can you feel the bubble travelling to your heart, Pete?'

He looked terrified.

'Feel the pain in your arm, jaw and neck?'

Pete was milk white.

'That's the bubble traveling up the artery.'

Pete was dripping sweat now.

'Ah, I see you have the cold sweats. Won't be long now. You're having trouble breathing, aren't you?'

His breathing was labored. I suspected he was having a panic attack.

'Shortness of breath is the next symptom, Pete.'

He clutched his chest.

'And after that comes nausea or vomiting.'

Pete threw up in the waste basket next to the bed. Then he screamed – an oddly high, girlish shriek for a big man. 'What did you do?'

'You didn't listen, Pete. Now you're going to die. You have maybe two minutes before your heart explodes. Anyone you want to say goodbye to? Your mother? Your girlfriend? Time's running out.'

'Help!' Pete hollered. 'I've been murdered.'

THIRTY-SEVEN

'What the hell is going on in here?' I could barely hear Katie over Pete's frantic screeching. My friend was standing in the doorway, a furious guardian angel holding a leftover burrito in a take-out box.

Behind Katie was Ben the cop, saying, 'Yeah, that's what I want to know.'

'Save it, stud,' Katie said. 'If you'd stayed at your post instead of skirt-chasing, you'd know what was going on.' She slammed the burrito box on Ben's empty chair.

The hunky cop looked like he'd been slapped. Ben was used to charming women to get what he wanted. They never talked to him like that.

Pete was still howling by Chris's bed, afraid to move. The big lunkhead looked terrified. Katie came close to examine his wound. Pete held out his forearm with the needle stuck in it. The skin around the needle was swelling, and thick red blood was seeping out.

'Pete tried to kill Chris with a syringe filled with poison,' I said. 'That's the syringe on the floor. To save Chris, I jabbed Pete with a syringe full of air.' I held up the pack of syringes for Jace's wife. 'I used one of the needles you gave Jace. I hit the artery and released a giant air bubble.'

Katie caught on instantly. 'Oh, those needles.'

She examined Pete's arm, which was starting to turn purple. 'Looks like you hit the radial artery, Angela,' she said.

Pete's eyes widened with fear. 'Do I need surgery?'

Katie looked solemn. 'I'd better prep you for immediate surgery. You have a serious problem. I'm afraid you are "*tamquam muta et mallei percutientes lapides sacculi*."'

Pete leaned against the bedframe, his chest moving up and down. He had trouble breathing. 'Is that going to kill me?'

'It just might,' Katie said. 'There's no cure, I'm afraid.'

'What does "*tamquam muta*" whatever" mean?' Pete's voice quavered.

Katie's eyes narrowed. 'That's Latin for "you're dumb as a bag of hammers," Pete. Angela stuck you with an empty needle. You'll get some bleeding and a little bruising but you won't die. You're going to live, and spend a long time in prison.'

She turned to Ben. 'If you want to save your career, pal, you'd better call the chief. You can ask Angela what happened and then interview that bozo Pete by the bed.'

Katie texted Monty, who'd been waiting in his car in the parking lot. He was going to drive Katie home after she delivered my burrito.

Instead, Monty rushed up the stairs, ready to do his lawyerly best. Somehow, Monty's suit was still unwrinkled.

The chief showed up soon after, looking grim. Then there was chaos – shouts, denials and demands.

Pete refused to let Katie wash his wound. 'I don't trust you,' he said with a snarl. 'I demand to go to the emergency room.'

The chief sent him there under guard. Ben walked Pete to the ER. The doctor simply washed the wound. The chief had also requested a drug test, and Pete tested positive for fentanyl. He was higher than a kite.

When I was finally able to leave, Katie and Monty walked me to my car. 'You know it's unlikely you'd kill someone with an air bubble in a needle that size,' Katie said.

'Yep. But many people who aren't familiar with medicine believe you can.'

It took weeks to sort out what happened. The investigators found out that Pete had more than thirty thousand dollars in gambling debts at the St. Louis casinos. Doughnut Dan, the evidence room cop, was desperate to pay his daughter's tuition. Pete and Doughnut Dan agreed to help the drug dealer by getting rid of the fentanyl in the evidence room. The dealer gave each of them $50,000.

Then Pete hatched the loony plot to frame Chris. He figured if he killed Chris and the drugs were found in the dead officer's patrol car, Chris would take the rap for Pete's crime. Good thing I'd found the brass with Monty's metal detector. It confirmed the details of this part of the story. The brass was from Pete's gun.

Chris remembered that Pete shot him. That's what he'd been trying to tell me.

Pete's plan went south when Chris survived. Pete wasn't thinking too straight by then. He'd kept some fentanyl for himself, and it left him addled. He sneaked into Chris's room while Ben was trying to get the nurse's phone number. Pete tried to kill Chris with a needle filled with ant poison, and I walked in at the right time.

Monty explained this next part to me umpteen times, but I never quite understood how the feds figured in Pete's investigation. I did know that Pete was hit with a long list of state, local and federal charges for felonies and misdemeanors. Law enforcement didn't throw the book at Pete, they hit him with a whole law library.

Here were some of the charges:

Two counts of first-degree attempted murder, possession of a firearm during the commission of a felony, aggravated battery, attempted murder of a law enforcement officer. Plus conspiracy charges, including theft of a controlled substance, and forgery of official records. I think Pete was also charged with malfeasance in office.

Pete finally did something smart: he pleaded guilty and took a life sentence. He may get out in fifty or sixty years. If he survives. Like he said, they don't like cops in prison.

As for Chris, he managed to sleep through the melee in his room. I stayed with him all night. Even though Pete was arrested, I was afraid to leave Chris alone. Greiman might come back. I didn't trust anyone at the CFPD except Mike. As soon as the chief caught on to what was happening, the charges against Chris were dropped.

When Chris woke up at seven the next morning, Katie, Monty, Mike and I were all in his room.

'What's going on?' Chris looked surprised at the crowd.

'You're free,' Monty said.

'I am? How?'

I told him about Pete and the battle over the needle. 'I slept through that? I can't believe it.'

'Angela saved you,' Monty said.

'You helped save yourself, Chris,' I said. 'You let out a loud snort and that gave me the distraction I needed to stab Pete with a needle.'

Chris was indignant. 'I don't snore.'

'You do,' I said. 'And I'm glad. Snoring saved your life.'

Now Chris smiled. A genuine smile. He looked relieved.

'Oh, and Greiman did you a big favor, Chris,' Monty said.

'How?'

'Because Mr Big Shot Detective swaggered in and arrested you while you were in a coma, Chouteau County has to pick up most of your medical bills.'

'That's a relief,' Chris said. 'Why didn't I have the county sheriff's department guarding me? Isn't that the usual procedure?'

'Because Greiman didn't want to let his prize out of his sight,' Monty said. 'Greiman talked the chief into agreeing with him. So the Chouteau Forest PD also has to pick up the overtime for guarding you.'

Chris thought that was hilarious. I enjoyed listening to him laugh.

When the dust settled after Pete's arrest and Chris was reinstated to the force, Monty turned around and sued the CFPD for false arrest, among other things.

The next day after the second murder attempt, I was alone with Chris in his room. He was going to eat his first solid food. It wasn't a very inspiring meal or a healthy one. He had a tray of dry turkey with mashed potatoes and gravy, a white roll with butter, carrots, applesauce, milk and a small can of orange juice that he opened with a metal ring. Chris wolfed down the meal as if he was served a five-star dinner.

After the attendant took his tray, Chris said, 'Angela, I want to ask you something. I'll only ask once and if the answer is no, I'll never do it again.'

My heart was beating fast as he took my hand and said, 'I love you. I've loved you since our first date. Will you marry me?'

'Yes,' I said. 'Oh, yes.'

'Even though I'm not fully recovered and may never be?'

'I don't care. I'm taking you "as is,"' I said. 'I love you. Forever.'

He slipped the metal ring from his juice can on my ring finger and said, 'I'll replace this ring with a better one later.'

We laughed and kissed and I said, 'Scoot over,' and climbed into bed with Chris. It felt good to be close to him again, and feel his warmth. We sat side by side in the narrow bed, talking. Chris put his arm around me, and we kissed.

'I thought you'd forgotten that you'd asked me to marry you,' I said.

'Never,' he said. 'I didn't want to marry you when I thought I was going to prison.'

'But—'

He kissed me again. 'I know you would have said yes. That's

how you are. But I didn't want to drag you into my legal problems.'

'I want to share your problems,' I said.

I held up my left hand to show off my ring. 'If I knew I was getting engaged today,' I said, 'I would have had a manicure.'

THIRTY-EIGHT

Chris spent the next four months in the hospital, recovering from his surgery and then going through intensive rehab. He had to relearn basic skills, including how to walk. Once he mastered those, he had to build his strength and improve his coordination. Rehab was a tough slog for him, but for the most part he stayed cheerful.

Katie and I brought him meals and snacks, and he soon was his regular weight.

Katie was so thrilled that Chris and I were engaged, it was almost like having my mother here. I wore my orange-juice-can ring every day.

Three weeks later, Chris asked me to be at the hospital at two o'clock. I was on call that day, and prayed that everyone stayed alive in the Forest. Thankfully, they did.

At one thirty, I stopped by Supreme Bean and picked up two coffees and two chocolate chip cookies. Chris was just back from his afternoon exercise session and seemed sleepy, but the coffee woke him up.

I was sitting by Chris's bed, sipping my coffee, when an elegant man with a black leather case knocked on the door jamb. Chris invited him in. The tall, thin man wore a gray pinstriped suit. His thick, gorgeous hair was like polished silver. 'I'm John August,' he said, 'and I've brought a selection of engagement rings to look at.'

I shut the door to Chris's room, and Mr August opened the black leather case on the hospital bed to reveal a dazzling array of wedding ring sets on black velvet.

'Oh.' I wasn't expecting this. The rings glittered and glowed, even in the harsh hospital lights.

'Congratulations on your engagement, Ms Richman,' August said. 'Officer Ferretti asked me to bring an assortment of rings for you.'

'Choose the ring you like, Angela,' Chris said.

Each ring seemed prettier than the last. I tried on various

styles, and finally settled on a sapphire and diamond ring. I'm going to sound like a gushing bride here, but let me have my moment.

The pear-shaped diamond was flanked by two blue princess-cut sapphires. The wedding band was white platinum that fit into the engagement ring.

'I like this one,' I said.

'Excellent choice,' August said. 'Sapphires are the symbol of faithfulness and everlasting love, and diamonds stand for love, strength, and eternal beauty. A very romantic selection.'

John August put the ring set in a blue velvet ring box, and presented it to me. He bowed and congratulated us again. I walked him to the room door.

After he left, I shut the door. Chris removed my juice-can ring and asked me to marry him. Again.

'Yes,' I said.

He slipped the engagement ring on my finger.

'It's perfect,' I said.

'Like you,' he said. With a straight face, too.

Chris started to throw away my juice-can ring, but I stopped him. 'Oh, no. I'm keeping my original engagement ring.'

I joined him in his bed and we kissed and cuddled until he fell asleep. I slept comfortably on his shoulder, happy that the small pleasures of my world were returning. I was awakened by the rattle of the dinner carts in the hall.

I got up, combed my hair, and showed off my engagement ring to everyone I passed, like I was twenty years old.

I knew Donegan, my lost husband, would understand my joy. I was lucky enough to have the love of both men.

Chris was in the hospital for another month and a half after our engagement. When he was ready to go home, he moved in with me. I rented a hospital bed so he could sleep in my living room, and drove him to his doctors' appointments and physical therapy sessions. He still tired easily, had balance problems, and walked with a cane, but he was making a good recovery. A better recovery than I thought he would.

By that time, it was April, and we were in the middle of a lovely Missouri spring. The white dogwood bloomed first, followed by pink clouds of cherry blossoms. My mother's flower garden returned to life. Chris and I went for short walks in the sunshine, and enjoyed the sweet smell of spring grass.

In June, Chris was well enough to climb the stairs to my bedroom, and soon we were able to truly celebrate our love.

I reminded Chris that I'd had the winning auction bid on a trip for two to Fort Lauderdale, Florida, and we could stay at a condo on the beach. Chris's surgeon gave him permission to fly, and we wasted no time.

A week later, we stepped out of the airport into the breathtaking Florida humidity. I wondered if I'd made a mistake. But by the time we'd settled into our beachside condo, I knew we were in the right place. The ocean breezes were cooling and the warm, salty air felt healing. The sunsets painted the skies flamingo pink and purple.

The condo was a small, three-story building on the beach, painted white and turquoise. We had the condo on the top floor, and we were grateful it had an elevator. The condo was simply furnished with wicker furniture and cushions in tropical colors. Its best feature was a balcony overlooking the ocean. I felt right at home there.

One night, as we were walking hand-in-hand along the beach, Chris said, 'Let's get married.'

'Where?'

'Here. On the beach. I've checked it out online. We can apply for our marriage license tomorrow. And there's no need for a permit to get married on this strip of beach.'

I looked at the moonlight shimmering on the restless ocean and said, 'This is perfect.'

'You're sure you don't want a big wedding?'

'No. I would like to have some of our friends here. Can we call Katie and Monty and see if they can get away?'

'Yes,' he said. 'Let's do it.' We sealed our promise with a kiss in the moonlight.

The next morning, we went to the county courthouse to get our license, for the absurd price of $93.50. That fifty cents cracked me up.

'There's a three-day waiting period for Florida residents,' the clerk told us, 'but you don't have a waiting period because you don't live here.'

Next, I called Katie and said, 'How'd you like to wear a ridiculous chiffon dress?'

'I wouldn't,' she said.

'You'll have to if you're going to be my maid of honor.'

'Not even for you will I wear a bridesmaid dress,' she said. 'Besides, who's officiating?'

'What?'

'Who's tying the knot?'

'Oh.'

She laughed. 'You didn't think about that, did you? Just so happens I'm an ordained minister, and ministers in my church can perform weddings in Florida.'

'What church?' Katie wasn't the churchly type.

'The Universal Life Church. I was ordained by mail for a dollar.'

'I see you spared no expense, Reverend.' My friend was full of surprises. Who would have guessed she was a mail-order minister.

'Why don't you ask Jace's wife, Rita to be your maid of honor?' Katie said.

'Good idea. We'll fly them down.'

Another set of calls confirmed that Rita would be delighted to be my maid of honor, and she and Jace agreed to fly down the day after tomorrow. Jace was in the room with her, and when she asked him about attending our wedding, Rita got his instant and enthusiastic approval.

'What's your wedding theme?' Rita asked. 'Do you want me to wear a special dress?'

'No, just wear whatever you like,' I said. 'This wedding is very casual.'

'I'm glad you want me to get a new dress, Angela,' she said.

I laughed.

'We'd like you to come as our guests,' I said.

'Absolutely not,' Rita said. 'We'll get our own tickets and hotel. Jace has been working such long hours, Angela. He needs a getaway. We both do. Our boy can stay with Grandma and Grandpa.'

Katie and Monty flew in early the next morning, and caught a cab to our condo. I was thrilled to see them. We welcomed them into our temporary home, and all four of us sat on the balcony overlooking the ocean, sipping cool drinks.

Katie wore jeans and a crisp white blouse. Monty wore a Hawaiian shirt with an eye-watering design of blue and red parrots, and carried a briefcase.

'A briefcase?' Chris said. 'On vacation?'

'I bring glad tidings, Chris,' Monty said. 'The Chouteau Forest

Police Department wants to settle your case. If you agree, we'll sign the paperwork today.'

'What are they offering?' Chris asked.

'Your old job back, if you want it.'

Chris shrugged. He wasn't sure he wanted to return to the force.

'And a settlement of two point five million dollars.'

Now Chris was staggered. His eyebrows jumped straight up and the color drained from his face. I could hardly breathe. I grabbed his hand.

'For real?' he said.

'Yep, even when I take my cut, you'll have about two million.'

'That's . . . that's fantastic,' Chris said.

'You'll have to sign a nondisclosure agreement.' Monty was grinning from ear-to-ear. I was trying to catch my breath.

'Bring out your pen,' Chris said, 'and show me where to sign.'

The signing was over quickly, and Monty left to FedEx the document to his office manager, Jinny Gender, taking Chris with him.

Katie insisted that we go shopping for a wedding dress. We agreed to meet the men late in the afternoon for drinks and food.

I found my wedding dress in a boutique on Las Olas, the Fort Lauderdale shopping district. The dress was strapless and pale pink, like the inside of a sea shell, with a full, swingy skirt that stopped at my knees. I bought new strappy sandals, and stopped at the florist to order a bouquet – pink peonies – and a flower crown for my hair. I wouldn't wear a veil.

'OK,' Katie said, 'you have something new and blue – your sapphires in your ring – but nothing borrowed or old.'

I was touched she remembered the custom that brides wear something old, something new, something borrowed and something blue for good luck. 'I'll wear my mother's earrings for something old,' I said.

'Would you like to borrow my evening purse?' Katie asked. 'I brought it just in case.'

'Of course,' I said. I was so glad my friend was with me.

We stashed my wedding finery at our condo, and then met Monty and Chris at an oyster bar by the water. The men were several drinks ahead of us, and we had to work hard to catch up.

The rest of the afternoon and evening was spent eating oysters and homemade potato chips, drinking, laughing and swapping stories. The soft, salty breeze felt comforting. I couldn't remember the last time I'd felt so relaxed.

At one o'clock in the morning, the staff was putting the chairs up on the empty tables and mopping the floor.

'I think it's time to go,' Monty said, and gave a small belch. He asked for the bill and called for an Uber, and we staggered out to wait for the car.

'We'll drop you off first, Angela,' Monty said, his words only slightly slurred.

'And Chris,' I added.

'Oh, no, you're getting married properly,' Monty said. 'You can't see the groom until the wedding at six o'clock. I'm Chris's best man.'

'You are definitely the best,' Chris said. He was definitely three sheets to the wind.

'OK,' I said, 'but you and Katie have to keep Chris sober until the wedding.'

'Right.' Monty saluted me. 'Then he's all yours.'

'Wait!' I said. 'What about his clothes?'

'Already have them at our place. He'll be fine.'

The Uber arrived, and soon was at our condo. 'I'll come by at four thirty tomorrow to help you dress and take you to the wedding,' Katie said.

Monty walked me to the condo door. 'Congratulations, Angela,' he said. 'You and Chris deserve your good luck. I hope you enjoy it for a long, long time.'

'We wouldn't have it without you and Katie,' I said, and ducked inside before I got too sentimental.

THIRTY-NINE

I was glad that Chris didn't spend the night at our condo. I woke up at ten the next morning, feeling extremely unbridal. In fact, I had a towering hangover.

A couple of aspirins, a lot of black coffee, and a greasy breakfast at a beach restaurant revived me. I prayed I'd stop burping before the ceremony.

I took a short stroll by the ocean. I never tired of watching the water's ever-changing colors – turquoise shading to purple and then gray. Sun-pennies sparkled on the water. The sky was a cloudless china blue.

I went home, sat on the balcony and listened to the soothing sounds of the ocean. I was falling in love with Florida.

Maybe it was the hangover, but I started feeling uneasy. My mind was crawling with 'what ifs': what if Chris had a relapse? What if I had another stroke? What if he went back to work and got shot again? What if . . .

The prewedding jitters vanished when Jace and Rita arrived at noon. Wearing shorts, flip-flops and summery tops, they were ready to enjoy their vacation. Rita was slim with brown eyes and an easy smile.

Jace and Rita were fascinated by the ocean, and we sat on the balcony for a while, watching the waves roll in and enjoying the warm breeze. Jace looked relaxed, and his signs of stress seemed to vanish by the minute.

'This is the life,' he said, reaching for Rita's hand.

We walked to lunch at a waterfront restaurant and ate mahi-mahi sandwiches. Jace and Rita ordered colorful drinks with paper umbrellas, and I stuck to club soda.

We swapped stories and gossip. I told Jace and Rita that the CFPD had settled with Chris, but didn't mention the amount. They promised not to tell anyone.

'I have some good gossip,' Jace said. Then he took a big bite of his fish sandwich, and we had to wait for him to quit chewing.

'Hey, no fair,' I said.

Rita playfully bopped him on the head.

When he finally swallowed his fish, he said, 'You'll be happy to know that the chief tore a strip off Greiman for being too eager to arrest Chris and refusing to use the sheriff's deputies to guard him.'

'It's about time,' I said.

'It gets better.' Jace's eyes sparkled with mischief. 'The amount Chouteau Forest spent on the deputies is coming out of Greiman's pay.'

'That is juicy gossip,' I said. 'I suppose the chief isn't going to demote him.'

'Wrong. The chief can't save Greiman this time. He committed an unforgiveable sin – he cost the Forest major money. The chief was told either Greiman goes or he goes.'

'Easy to guess what the chief chose,' I said.

'How is Greiman going to pay back the department?'

'It came out of the severance pay the chief arranged for his buddy. I think Greiman will walk away with a dollar ninety-eight.'

'Couldn't happen to a nicer guy,' I said.

'Tell Angela what *did* happen to a nice guy,' Rita said.

'Mike Harrigan has been promoted to detective,' Jace said. 'He got Greiman's old job.'

'That's wonderful. Mike's promotion is long overdue.'

'Mike's not a politician,' Jace said. 'He'll be a fair and honest detective.'

We ordered another round of drinks to toast Mike. The three of us laughed and talked and watched the yachts chug by until it was almost four o'clock.

'Time for me to get ready,' I said. 'We ordered an Uber for you at five thirty. I'll see you at the wedding.' They hugged me goodbye.

Once I was back at the condo, the doorbell rang. The florist arrived with my wedding flowers. I'd finished showering and drying my hair when Katie showed up to help me dress.

She wore a pale gray suit with a pink and turquoise scarf, the brightest colors I'd ever seen her wear.

'You look quite festive, Reverend Stern,' I said.

I put on light make-up – lipstick, foundation, and eyeliner – and my sandals. Then Katie helped me into the strapless dress and zipped it up.

I twirled around, and swished the full silk skirt.

'That is one hell of a dress,' she said.

I put on my mother's pearl-drop earrings. Katie pinned on the flower crown and handed me her silver purse for the something 'borrowed.' Inside was an embroidered handkerchief. I added lipstick, a comb and a credit card.

I gathered my peony bouquet. The fragrance reminded me that peonies were my mother's favorite flower. Between the flowers and Mom's earrings, I felt like she was with me.

'Ready?' Katie asked.

My pulse was pounding and my heart fluttering. We walked out to the waiting Uber and made the short drive to the beach. The sun was sinking, taking the day's heat with it. The ocean was a misty blue. Most of the beachgoers had left for home.

Katie and I met the wedding party under a palm tree. Rita wore a stylish light-blue lace dress and carried the pink bouquet I'd had delivered to her hotel. Jace wore a summer-weight beige suit with a blue and beige tie. Rita loved to coordinate his clothes and I knew she'd chosen his outfit to go with hers. They held hands and smiled at each other.

Then I saw Monty get out of a cab, followed by Chris. Chris had left his cane behind and walked without it. He was wearing a white linen suit and a pink boutonniere.

I ran over to him and said, 'You look so handsome.'

'And you look like a dream.' His voice was soft. Chris kissed me deeply and Monty said, 'Hey, you two, you have to be married to do that.'

We all walked closer to the water. Katie said, 'We are gathered here to celebrate the marriage of our friends, Christopher Ferretti and Angela Richman. Do we have the rings?'

'I have Angela's,' Monty said.

'I have Chris's,' Rita said.

'Then let's recite the vows,' Katie said. 'Repeat after me, Chris: I, Christopher Ferretti, take you, Angela Richman, to be my wedded wife.'

Wedded wife, I thought, dreamily. That means Chris is united to me for life.

Katie said, 'To have and to hold from this day forward.'

As Chris repeated those words, I thought of the Song of Solomon, 'My beloved is mine, and I am his . . .'

Katie said, 'For better, for worse, for richer, for poorer, in sickness and in health . . .' The crucial words that sent many a marriage on the rocks. Chris and I would weather the storms together.

Chris repeated the words and then Katie said, 'To love and to cherish, till death do us part.'

In other words, forever.

I looked into Chris's eyes as I recited my vows, and saw tears in them.

'Now, let's have the rings,' Katie said. 'Chris first.'

Monty handed Chris my ring, and Katie had Chris repeat these words as he slipped the ring on my finger: 'I give you this ring as a symbol of my everlasting love for you.'

Then I slipped on Chris's ring and said, 'This ring is a token of my love for you. I am yours, today and forever.'

'By the power vested in me, I now pronounce you man and wife,' Katie said. 'You may now kiss.'

We did. And I can say that married kisses are the sweetest.

EPILOGUE

After the wedding, Monty took us to a seafood restaurant on the Intracoastal Waterway, set in a yacht basin. We watched the proud ships while we ate seafood and drank champagne. The wedding party toasted us and gave silly speeches.

At the end of the meal, the staff brought out a two-tiered cake with pink butter-cream roses. The cake-cutting called for more champagne and then coffee.

We went home after midnight, and Chris carried me over the threshold.

Selwyn Skipton's wife wanted nothing to do with his building in downtown Chouteau Forest, or the room upstairs. She sold it to Maya Richards, the owner of the Forest chocolate shop, for an exorbitant price. Maya quickly paid off the loan by buying a new bed for Selwyn's apartment, and renting it out as a love nest with chocolate and champagne, for five hundred dollars a night. The whole Forest wanted to spend a night in what became known as the Dirty Daddy Suite.

With two counts of murder one, Wendy was eligible for the death penalty. She pleaded guilty and got life without parole, in exchange for giving the police the details.

Wendy said that Selwyn had a secret desire to have a threesome with twins, and he promised Chloe and her sister Zoe twenty-five thousand dollars. 'Zoe was such a prude, she wouldn't do it,' Wendy said, 'so Chloe asked me. We look pretty much alike and the old man didn't wear his glasses, so he couldn't tell the difference. I had a ton of credit card debt and I really needed that money. All of it. I was facing bankruptcy.

'I met up with Chloe. Selwyn wanted us to wear black lingerie. Good stuff and we got to keep it. Before he started, he paid Chloe twelve thousand five hundred dollars in cash. The sex wasn't much fun, but he didn't last long. We ate a nice dinner in the room and then had champagne and chocolate.

'He was feeling frisky and wanted to go again, so we crawled back into bed with the old dude. It was over quickly. Chloe wanted the rest of the money he'd promised. He refused. He said she was a slut and we didn't have a contract, so there was no way we could enforce it. He laughed and said it was Chloe's word against his and nobody would believe her. She was nothing but a prostitute. Then he laughed at both of us and called us cheap hookers and said we wouldn't get another dime.

'Now we were both angry. Chloe whacked him on his head with the champagne bottle and knocked him out. Selwyn's tie was in the pile of clothes by the bed. Chloe grabbed it and looped it around his scrawny neck. We each took an end and pulled until he was dead.

'It was Chloe's idea to give him the scarlet letter "A." She was so mad. She cut up this red sweater she'd bought on sale and stuck in her purse. We stapled the pieces to his chest. "He was an adulterer," Chloe said. "Men should wear the scarlet letter, too."

'When a person dies, it makes a mess, you know. We spent hours cleaning that place. I took the dirty sheets and pillowcases in my rolling shopping bag. She took the vacuum cleaner bag, the trash and his clothes – except for the tie. We remade the bed and put him back in it.

'Then Chloe turned the heat way up. She saw that on TV and said it would confuse the police about decomposition. It did, didn't it?'

'Chloe forgot about the flies,' Jace said. 'You can't fool Mother Nature. They told us when he died.'

Wendy shrugged and started talking again. 'Anyway, we threw away those rolling bags. I tried to get the rest of my money from Chloe. I knew she was rich. She refused. So I killed her.

'I knew you'd figured that out,' Wendy said. 'But I couldn't understand where you got the witness.'

'He was in the room,' Jace said.

'No one was in there.'

'The parrot was, and he heard every word. He repeated what happened when Chloe was murdered.'

'The parrot?' Wendy started laughing. 'I got the ultimate bird.'

* * *

Zoe inherited about a hundred thousand dollars from her sister. She moved into an apartment near campus, where she could keep Buddy. She graduated with honors.

Chris and I honeymooned in Fort Lauderdale. We both liked it there. Chris didn't want to go back to the CFPD force, and I wasn't sure I wanted to return to my job, either.

'What are we going to do?' he asked.

'Listen to the ocean,' I said. 'Take walks on the beach. Think about what we want to really do. Maybe we won't want to go back to work.

'Meanwhile,' I said, 'we'll have to live happily ever after.'